MASTER OF THE WATERWAYS...
GOD OF THE CREEKS

MASTER OF THE WATERWAYS

GOD OF THE CREEKS

MICHAEL ARNONE

LUMINARE PRESS

WWW.LUMINAREPRESS.COM

Luminare Press
442 Charnelton St.
Eugene, OR 97401
www.luminarepress.com

LCCN: 2021915431
ISBN: 978-1-64388-716-6

To Karen,
my wife.
Thank you for your
love, patience, and support
through twenty years
of authorship.

Acknowledgments

⸺⧽⧽⧽⸺

THIS JOURNEY STARTED IN 2001. AT FIFTY-NINE, I SUF-fered a heart attack that necessitated open heart surgery.

Four bypasses later, into recovery mode, for therapy, I took up my pen and started to dabble.

Twenty plus years later...you are holding the results.

With fatherly love, many thanks are tendered to my son Tony Arnone and my daughter Lisa Free, who in their loving and charitable way, decided to put their money where my mouth was. Besides massive encouragement and constant reassurance, they gifted me (Happy Birthday & Merry Christmas) funds to publish the novel.

To them I will always be deeply indebted in love and gratitude.

To my darling wife, Karen (KK), the deserving recipient of the novel's dedication, I extend to her a lifetime of appreciation for her steadfast patience, support, and love. She endured every struggle, kept up the encouragement and provided constructive comment and recommendations the reader can enjoy in the myriad of structure and storytelling decisions.

Many others helped too. For his expertise in the proper use of the Spanish language, special thanks must be paid to my good friend, Senor Humberto Delgadillo.

Recognized also are many others...friends, relatives, neighbors, etc., for their feedback after reading bits of the work throughout the years.

Thank you all, you know who you are.

And...Let's do it again, soon!

TABLE OF CONTENTS

"Let us acknowledge the Lord: Let us press on to acknowledge him. As surely as the sun rises, He will appear, He will come to us like the winter rains, like the spring rains that water the earth." Hosea 6:3

Prologue

⁂

CALIFORNIA NIGHTS MAKE FOR STRANGE BEDFELLOWS. April's dying rains should warm the springs of May. But in 1875, frigid northern winds chilled the drenched landscape, making the nights insufferably cold.

During that glacial May, Rancho Piedra Blanca suffered an arctic frost that scurried rancho hands to fire vineyard and orchard pots throughout the icy nights and into the small hours of the morning.

Animals suffered too, especially those obliged to share, with the *curandera,* their home in the shepherd's hut, high on the summit of San Simeon.

Josefina Espinoza, a native of Tulu, Mexico, as if conjured out of the spring mist, simply materialized at the hacienda's front door presenting her meager credentials. Tempered with skepticism, the rancho's patron, Joaquin de Leon, allowed her but a modest residency…a share of the shepherd's hut with longtime occupants—the donkeys, cows, and horrible pigs.

Oozing a devious gratitude, she played along, bowing to the don. Loathing his patronizing hospitality, she masked her ambitions, biding her time.

The May nights grew colder still.

Tired and hungry with the day's work done, the animals hurried to the hut's warm shelter to discover their entry barred. With no intention of letting them in again, *curandera* Josefina locked them out.

Uncertain what to do, the congenial beasts grew miserable. Night after night, the temperatures dropped, creating such painful discomfort, the donkeys, cows, and horrible pigs could bear it no longer.

At last, they chose the donkey, their most scholarly member, to present to the *curandera* an appeal for mercy.

Surely the donkey's logical reasoning and superior negotiating skills would win over the *curandera* and allow access to the warmth of the hut again.

With the gusty wind chafing ice-covered ears, the donkey poked his head into a breach in the hut's wall.

Braying his case with passion, answering his supplications too swiftly, the uncaring witch, brandishing an oak cane, struck him viciously across his ample forehead. The gash streamed blood into the donkey's eyes obscuring from his sight the *curandera's* merciless face that laughed at him in scorn.

"Be gone, pathetic beast. To return would bring you and your wretched friends the devil's curse. The hut is mine forevermore, never again to be shared with the likes of... donkeys, cows, and horrible pigs."

CHAPTER 1

Rosa and Manuel

—⦙⦙—

The smell from Rosa's kitchen tantalized Manuel's slumber, whetting in him so late in life a younger man's appetite. Albeit sleeping ruled him today for the first time in months, the old man hungered for his Rosa's chilies, tortillas, and pinto beans.

Oh! It wasn't just the chilies cooking…no! The heady bouquet painted cherished dreams of the old Mexican village where he and his bride kissed tenderly on the very bed where Rosa was conceived. Savoring this dream, he did not fight these stirrings, treasuring more each day the life he and Rosa had grown to love in the coastal town of Cambria.

Forty years had passed since Manuel, accepting the invitation of his childhood friend Jose, had swayed Rosa to leave Mexico City and her mother for the promising paradise of California and Rancho Piedra Blanca.

In his dream, he thanked Jose and congratulated himself for making such a wise decision.

The rising sun peeking majestically over San Simeon awakened him. His reverie faded watching Rosa on her way to the kitchen. For that blissful moment, she was his eighteen-year-old bride once again, handsome and coy, perfumed in lavender and aloes.

"Breakfast can wait a little longer," he thought. *"Rosa's chilies and frijoles will taste even better after this."*

"Rosa!"

She came to him, laughing to herself.

Relishing her tender passion and doting on her eggs and chorizo, he lingered a bit longer, kissing Rosa goodbye, a ritual performed every day at every parting.

"How many years now, Rosa?" he asked.

"Too many," she chided.

As he did every day, Manuel finished his coffee and, through the window of his truck, handed Rosa the empty cup.

"Gracias, senora, you have filled this hombre with your tempting chilies and satisfied his passionate desires."

Her face blushing into a giggle, she shouted, "Hurry back, senor…my chilies will be waiting."

With dust rising up behind the old flatbed and Rosa blowing kisses to him in the rearview mirror, Manuel drove away a contented man. He hummed happily along the three miles of gravel road taking him south to the northern acreage turnoff. There he would spend the morning irrigating alfalfa planted on the rancho's highest pasture.

By noon, the thirty-four acres drank in their share.

"Now, to change the creek's path to the lower fields…that takes a precise turning of the water tables, and yes, yes, the flow is just right."

Pleased with his perfection, a radiance of angelic contentment washed over his face. Basking in enormous power, with arms outstretched and eyes skyward to the heavens, he proclaimed in a thunderous voice, "I am Master of the Waterways and God of the Creeks."

Begging God's forgiveness and laughing at his irreverence, he rubbed his sore knees.

Marking noontime, Manuel drove his flatbed west to the seaside vineyard camp to share the midday meal with a gathering of ranch hands.

Torrents of rain flooding the winter's staging area forced hands to relocate for gatherings to the springtime camp that overlooked the coastline vineyards atop the rancho's Pacific plateau.

It was a very special day because Angelina's mother, Conchita, prepared the menu.

Everyone could expect a table of wonders if Conchita was the chef. Famous for incredible banquets prepared on the open stone hearth, Conchita served fare that would be simple, delicious, and filling. From rellenos to tamales and chili verde to menudo, the eating would be delicious and the laughter never-ending. As the women came to congratulate Angelina on her first pregnancy, the simple lunch turned into a fiesta.

Bribing his mother-in-law to invite the men too, Francisco, the father-to-be, promised Conchita he and his brothers would play music at the fiesta…and when she ordered it, paint the outside of her house.

With Martine on trumpet, Raphael on guitar, and Francisco on accordion, the Brambila brothers guaranteed Conchita that all who came to the fiesta would not only enjoy her delicious meal but happy musical entertainment as well.

"This is a very good thing," Conchita agreed. And so, the men were invited too.

When Manuel arrived, he found Pablo, the old shepherd, leaning on his ever-present staff, waiting for him at the edge of the campground. Without a sound, the old man greeted him with a hearty hug and handshake.

Manuel smiled. "It is good to see you, my friend."

No one knew Pablo's age. For as long as anyone could remember, he had worked on the rancho. In fact, in everyone's memory, there never was a time without Pablo. And in all that time, no one ever heard him speak.

No one really knew if he could.

Nodding at Manuel, Pablo merely smiled his kindly grin and pointed his staff at Conchita who came running toward the two men.

"Enough formality; the fiesta has already started."

Arm-in-arm, she, Manuel, and Pablo joined the others on the huge patio surrounding the stone hearth. Then the proud chef piled her many delicacies onto everyone's plate.

Laughing and roaring compliments to Conchita, "oohing" and "aahing" with every bite, the happy guests ate their fill.

Music played and ranch hands sang the old songs with gusto. It was a good time. No one would go back to the fields hungry.

Angelina, her mother, and all the attendees would always treasure the day's celebration.

Teasing Francisco and Angelina about how babies are made, everyone laughed reliving Chucho and Martha's naughty "hat" dance.

Manuel regretted his Rosa could not be there that day. But it was not possible. She had been called to the grand hacienda to prepare for Monsignor Carmona's annual overnight stay.

On the first Sunday in March, tradition called on the monsignor to travel to the rancho from Mission San Miguel for the "Blessing of the Foals," an annual celebration of the rancho's newborn animals.

"I will tell Rosa about the party," Manuel said, "and try not to leave anything out. And the food!" he shouted. "Aah, Conchita, your salsa and frijoles are worthy of the God of the Creeks!"

CHAPTER 2

The Patron, Emilio de Leon

The low morning clouds faded to vapors, and the afternoon westerlies bent the marshes into beautiful sculptures in the cattails and tall grasses growing thick and lush along the small creek.

In local parlance, the waterways of Monterey and San Luis Obispo counties were "stretched." Irrigation would not be a problem like last year.

The rains came almost daily. That was very good, especially so for Manuel, renowned to all as the rancho's "God of the Creeks."

He parked the flatbed on the promontory high above the rancho's grand hacienda. There he could see the entire estate and the massive stone hedge that encircled it.

The closest pond swelled in needed relief. Manuel raced to the switches to prevent a spillover into the fallow fields below. *My timing is just right.*

He looked back at the flatbed and noticed the truck bed slanted slightly. The right rear tire was low. *I must see Jose on the way home and have that poor excuse for a tire fixed, or else I will be walking home to Rosa.*

The misstep was slight, but he felt a twinge in his left knee. Favoring it, he used the stone hedge to regain his balance. Hobbling toward the picket fence a few steps away, he rested and assessed the damage.

Testing its strength, he flexed his left leg for a few moments and smiled. *The pain is almost gone!*

With blessed assurance, he headed once again toward the floodgates to relieve the pond and direct the water flow onto the newly planted fields to the west.

He took off his cap, admiring his craftsmanship. The early March winds swayed the nearby windbreak, fluttering his kerchief and ruffling his gray hair. Running his fingers through what remained, he looked instinctively to check the sun's position through the gathering clouds. *It is half-past one...dinner with Rosa is at six o'clock...that leaves me just enough time.*

"First, I will open the switch to the thirsty crops. Let me see. Hmmm, the fields need six acres plus runoff...OK! I will open the gates for three hours, take a short siesta to half-past four, dreaming of rellenos, see about the tire, then home to my Rosa."

Favoring his knee, he moved gingerly toward the water switches to discover a trail of pockmarks descending from the dirt road above. They continued down the middle of the six-foot tract that separated the white picket fence from the ancient stone hedge, and ended at a flattened overgrowth where three meandering creeks formed a shallow pond.

Following the trail to the fork in the creek, Manuel stopped to examine eyeglasses sticking curiously out of the mud.

Cleaning the mud, he wondered aloud, "What is this? Are these Alfredo's? Has the stable boy lost his way home again?"

But the spectacles did not resemble Alfredo's. They looked familiar, but Manuel could not place them.

"Where are the limbs for over the ears?"

Then he remembered the Patron wore, perched on his nose, those funny pince-nez eyeglasses that had no arms.

"But why would the Patron come here?"

The twinge in his leg started up again. He rubbed it vigorously, issuing a stern warning. "Listen, knee…your pain is of no use. My Rosa's magic will make you disappear like you never happened." Chuckling, he turned to the switches… then trembled to a stop.

There on the naked mud lay a felt hat and pearl-handled cane. A sudden tremor shook him when he noticed a man's foot, bare except for the argyle sock, thrusting ominously through the picket fence.

Dreading what he would see next, he closed his eyes and pulled back the brush. The sight of the old man's body turned his trembling to panic. His breath failed and his legs collapsed, landing him hard on the mud. His soul wanted to scream, but no sound came forth.

Under the Patron's bloodied body, pools of blood soaked into the black mud. Battered and destroyed, his head had been crushed.

Running frantically to his truck, Manuel crashed into the cornerstone of the stone hedge, forcing him to roll onto the soft earth before he struggled to his feet. His knee hurt much more now.

Praying someone could hear, he screamed. "I must get to a phone."

He climbed into his truck and drove fast to the west.

CHAPTER 3

Jose and Jaime

⌒◦⌒

Driving into a dying sun, he flicked the tears running down his cheeks onto the windshield. Fighting for composure and to clear his confusion he shook his head moaning, "No savvy! No savvy! This is not a time to question 'why.' I need to be strong!"

Three miles away across from Jose's garage, and in front of Andoleto's grocery store, stood the nearest phone booth. Out of habit, and to save time, Manuel turned his truck down a small embankment and onto the well-worn hardpan, cutting across a fallow field that led to Andoleto's and the phone.

With the village in sight, the ancient truck, leaking tires and all, chugged rumbling off the hardpan onto the gravel road.

Painfully, Manuel parked the tired flatbed next to a family home in village San Xavier. For a moment he rested his head on the steering wheel before resolutely opening the door. Speculating that *it was too early for the wine*, his old friend Jose Ortiz watched Manuel's truck approach the village, wondering why he was driving so fast.

Laughing from across the road, he shouted, "Manuel, are you drinking today? What's your hurry, man? I can see for a mile behind you, and the cops are not chasing you."

But the old man did not answer. Instead, he ran to the phone as fast as his sixty-eight-year-old legs allowed.

His pockets empty, Manuel had no change for the call. "Jose! *Andale! Andale!* I need change to call an ambulance." While all the shouting emptied Andoleto's of its shoppers, Jose hurried to the phone booth to help his childhood friend.

With nickels and dimes in hand, Jose asked, "Why do you need the ambulance? Are you hurt? Madeline can help you if you are."

"It's not for me…it's the Patron. I found him on the north field at the floodgates," Manuel sobbed. "I think he is dead. Now, please let me call for help."

Villagers young and old wept. Some, falling to their knees, prayed to the Blessed Mother. Waiting for the operator to connect Manuel's call to emergency services, Jose comforted his friend.

Calming Manuel down, the police dispatcher instructed him to wait at the phone booth for the ambulance to arrive. The police would be coming as well.

Since the Patron's body was five miles to the east, Manuel's directions were essential.

Tomas, the village drunk, earned a quarter. "Stay here at the phone booth, Tomas," Jose said.

"Come to my garage when the police arrive…or if they need to speak to Manuel again."

Then Jose directed his oldest son, Jaime, to Manuel's home to pick up Rosa and bring her back to the garage. "If she asks what happened, just say that Manuel hurt his knee again."

"But Jose," Manuel interrupted, "Rosa will not be in Cambria. She is working at the Patron's and will bus home at the end of the day."

Jaime drove off to Rancho Hacienda de Leon with instructions to say nothing to the Patron's family.

"Let the police tell them in their own time," his father said. "Wait to tell Rosa what's happened. Say nothing to her until she is in the car and on her way back here with you."

The two men walked slowly out of the crowd and across the road to Jose's home behind the garage.

"Are you hungry?"

Manuel shook his head sadly. "No. No, just sad and confused, Jose. The Patron...he was so bloody."

Sitting in Jose's favorite chair, he buried his face in his hands and wept at last.

"His head...oh, his head, Jose! His head was caved in. Who would do such a thing?"

Jose held out a paper cup filled with homemade tequila.

"You need a drink, amigo! Here!"

But Manuel shook his head. "No, no...I need to stay sober for the police. We will drink later...we will get drunk later...not now."

CHAPTER 4

Maria and Juanito

The children stepped off the school bus, but their father, once again, was not there to pick them up.

"Papa is late again," Maria said. She was twelve years old and an excellent reader.

Her little brother Juanito snapped the rubber band around his notebook, ran to the tree stump, and sat down complaining. "Why is he always late?"

They waited at the farmland crossroads, two miles from their home, making excuses for him, again. He was probably very busy working at the livery and forgot what time to pick them up. Or maybe, the car would not start again, and he needed to jump the battery.

Maria began reading her lessons, making good use of her time. Juanito, bored and sulking, piled up a large mound of rocks and began target practice on the trees growing in the orchard behind him. Except for the thud of pebbles crashing through the branches, the crossroads remained country quiet.

Since the bus departed, not another car passed. The blue skies turned dark gray, and a cold wind rustled the crops in the fields surrounding them. Rain fell, at first a light drizzle, then a heavy downpour.

Content to heave rock after rock at the oaks and almond trees, the first-grader shivered from the cold wind. With the downpour, Maria ran and dragged him into the dilapidated bus shelter. That morning Juanito had forgotten his coat in the back seat of his father's car. He shivered now, sorry he did not have it. To warm up, he nestled with his sister inside their mother's old navy peacoat, the one Maria wore every day, rain or shine. He tucked his freezing hands in the coat's inside pockets, touching the rosary beads his mother, Veronica, left for Maria when she died.

"Do not catch cold. Papa will be very angry with you for not remembering your jacket."

Over the lightning and thunder, the quiet country road lit up with flashing lights alternating red and blue. A police car, siren screeching, approached the intersection. As the blaring car passed, the children covered their ears, staying out of the rain in the leaky shelter. Surprised, Maria recognized her grandfather's old friend, Manuel, waving to her from the backseat of the police car.

She thought, *He looks so sad.*

A white ambulance trimmed in green-and-black block letters on its side followed, with its siren silent. The vehicle slowed for possible traffic at the crossroad signal lights blinking red to yellow, yellow to red. The children stared after it until the taillights disappeared into the darkness.

Praying to Saint Christopher that nothing would happen to their father, Maria hugged Juanito close. A brief moment passed when a smile bloomed on her face. With Rosa sitting in the coupe's front seat, her papa rumbled up to the bus stop.

"Andale…Andale! Get in the car."

Rosa made way, pulling the passenger seat forward and letting Maria and Juanito climb into the back of the two-door coupe.

She reached for Juanito and wiped his runny nose with her apron. "Poor *niño*, are you cold?" He nodded and fell back into Maria's warm peacoat.

"Maria! Put on his coat and button it up for him."

Long after the police car and ambulance had passed, the jalopy lumbered off the soft shoulder onto the road heading back to San Xavier. There the children would be left in their grandfather's care.

Once Maria and Juanito were safe with Jose, Jaime and Rosa planned to drive to the floodgates, next to the stone hedge in the fields to the east.

CHAPTER 5

Wally Phelps—
Set 'Em Up, Billy!

⊸⊸⊸

Awaiting police instructions, the ambulance stayed on the dirt road above the scene. "Park here to the left," Manuel said. From inside the police car, he watched the two officers and photographer move out onto the scene.

The taller officer told Manuel, "Stay put and keep the window down. I'll let you know if you are needed." After the questioning at Jose's garage, Manuel nodded, glad to be finally left alone.

The heavy clouds broke apart and the rain finally stopped, but walking the scene on the sodden earth risked destroying evidence not readily seen. The blinding glare on the horizon painted long shadows, darkening the stone hedge and making it difficult to see.

The unsettled conditions prompted the detectives to radio the officers, advising them to get all pictures possible and secure the area for the night. The investigation of the scene would be delayed until morning.

Crisscrossing beams in the dark, the officers pointed their flashlights on the battered Patron below and directed the photographer to an acceptable vantage point. The tall officer shouted: "Wally, pick your ground carefully. Stay on the hardpan. Don't screw it up for the 'dicks.'"

Remembering the muddy prints near and around the body, Wally proceeded cautiously, careful not to compromise any evidence the detectives might turn up the next day.

THE PHONE RANG, AND PHOTOGRAPHER WALLY PHELPS, nursing his fourth gin and tonic, was feeling no pain. Why not? It was his day off, and he loved the happy hour at The Good Knight Tavern & Inn.

Billy the bartender yelled, "Hey, Wally, it's the station."

Graflex in hand, arriving five minutes after leaving the bar, Wally hurried to the squad room where two officers waited for him.

Refusing him a coffee stop, the cops laughed as Wally struggled to sober up on the ride to San Xavier. But being a bit drunk turned out to be a blessing. For all his experience at hundreds of crime scenes, this one stamped an indelible gore on his psyche.

The infamous Patron, powerful and rich, lay dead and disfigured. His face was gone; any expression of death, missing. Pools of blood flowing under the body and into the creek welled up a sickness in Wally's throat. Wrenching his stomach in a sweat-pouring nausea, he moved warily toward the body and the largest rock sticking up out of the mud. Moaning over and over, "Man…I'm sick, really sick," and crouching far to his right, he fought to keep his teetering equilibrium .

With a green face, Wally egged himself on by fending off nausea with a simple prayer. "Lord, please help me!" Like a true professional, he finished his job, taking all the gruesome shots and even switching lenses to better capture the minute details of the bloody close-ups.

MICHAEL ARNONE

Manuel regretted he had ever come to the floodgates that day. The popping flashbulbs that lit up the gruesome death painted a tableau of horror.

Observed in crimson relief through the police car's rear window, the shoe, the cane, the hat, and the disfigured Patron, forced Manuel to cry aloud, "Where is my Rosa?"

With the last photo in the can, Wally staggered on the outcrops and hardpan back to the police car. Reaching for the back door handle, his tormented stomach finally erupted.

His disgusting discharge splattered his camera and equipment bag and christened the rear bumper. Nausea relieved, he salvaged a lens cloth and wipe his soured mouth.

Wally got into the back seat. Manuel, a witness to every lurid detail, turned away to avoid the vile stench.

Paying Manuel no mind, Wally sat back and closed his eyes. And when the last bit of nausea vanished, an expansive Cheshire grin, brighter than Kelly's neon sign, flashed on his milky white face.

He had won the bet made with the two officers! "I didn't fall, coppers…I didn't fall!

"You two flatfeet are buyin' the next four rounds! Set 'em up Billy!"

———◦◦◦◦———

FOLLOWING THE DETECTIVE'S ORDERS TO ENSURE THE scene's integrity, the officers, at last, motioned the ambulance attendants to come down to remove the body.

Careful to keep them off the soft ground, the shorter officer, using his flashlight, pointed out the hardpan trail for the ambulance attendants to follow.

Treading the flashlight-lit path, the two men gingerly made their way to the body.

Utilizing upper-body strength only, they lifted the battered body onto a stretcher. Without a slip, they retraced, exactly, each step back to the ambulance. Sighing with relief, they place the very dead Patron in the ambulance and closed the doors.

Congratulations should have been in order, but the driver waved his partner off with, "My back is out!"

CHAPTER 6

Chevy Coupe, Police Car, and Ambulance

After dropping off the children with their grandfather, Jaime needed to fill his gas tank.

Jose mustered less than a half-gallon of gas from his garage. That was enough for Jaime to reach the nearest pump five miles south at the rancho's utility yard. While Rosa and the children prayed to Saint Christopher for his safe return, Jaime raced the coupe out of San Xavier in a drenching downpour.

Lightening the tension, Jose joked. "I hope you can come to dinner next Sunday. You can even bring poor Manuel, God of the Creeks, with you!"

Ignoring Jose's attempt at humor, Rosa cried out, "Evil reaches out to all of us this day. Pray, everyone, for Jaime's safety."

Sipping chocolate shakes made by Gloria Andoleto herself, Maria and Juanito sat happily at Andoleto's famous ice-cream counter blowing kisses to Rosa.

"Listen, Rosa, do not tell Jaime about the shakes. He will kill me if he finds out I let you treat the kids to dessert before dinner!"

Rosa brightened, smiled, and then, with a poker face, seized her moment's good fortune. "For what it's worth, Jose, maybe a tune-up on the old truck? Maybe a new set of tires, and I am not talking retreads."

His balding forehead wrinkled, and from under his shirt Jose's paunchy belly broke into waves.

Rosa laughed. "You know, you could be Santa Claus if you had a longer beard."

"Rosa! It's too cold to live that far north. Besides, you know I was joking…no?"

Deadpan, she looked him in the eye and said, "No!"

With tenderness and love, Rosa pinched both his fat cheeks, making him laugh all over again.

Cautioning Jose, she warned, "Be sure to take care of *niño* and *niña*, or I will take them away from you." Smiling, letting down her motherly armor, she cupped his ears and kissed each side of his jolly face.

When Jaime returned, Rosa kissed the children, and told Jose, "After I see to Manuel, I will let you know about Sunday dinner. OK?"

In his goodbye wave, Jose spoke his affirmation, and Jaime and Rosa were gone.

Day was done, the rain stopped, and the night sky grew darker and darker.

Rosa yelled, forgetting who was driving, "Turn on your lights, you fool." Then, she quickly realized her mistake. "You are not Manuel. Sorry, Jaime. I am rattled, and my nerves are talking too loud."

"Do not worry, Rosa, and thanks for reminding me. No wonder the road turned so dark."

Uneasy, without another word all the way to the flood-gates, they worried how Manuel would be.

Reaching the turnoff to the gates, it was pitch-black. Despite balding tires and the muddy roads, the Chevy held the wet curves, pulling to a safe stop.

Rosa looked up to the sky, "I don't like this. It is so dark… not even one star shining." The darkness broke when beams of light flashed over the stone hedge.

Next to the stone hedge on the dirt road ahead, they saw, an ambulance and police car. Two men in the distant car were haloed by their flashing lights. Then the lights went out and all was blackness again.

Jaime switched on his high beams and lit up the dormant police car that came back to life. The taller officer aimed his flashlight in the high beam's direction, and shouted, "Do not advance…stay where they are."

In the next second the silhouetted ambulance, flashing lights on and off, started driving toward Rosa and Jaime. Passing the parked Chevy, the ambulance turned onto the eastbound gravel road and sped off.

The police car crept alongside and a disheartened Manuel, exhausted and weeping, got out next to the parked Chevy. Rosa embraced him very gently. Kissing his cheek, she whispered in his ear so only he could hear. "Come, my darling husband. Come home with me now to our safe home, I will make you well."

Jaime held open the Chevy door helping Rosa into the backseat. With affection and respect, he clasped Manuel's right hand, guiding his father's old friend into the front seat of the coupe.

With their lights flashing, the police car cleared the road ahead and escorted Jaime's Chevy and the tearful couple all the way to their Cambria home.

CHAPTER 7

The Old Stone Hedge and the Picket Fence

The picket fence stood proudly inside and exactly six feet away from the ancient stone hedge. The two boundary fences, one of wood and the other of stone, traveled in tandem, mimicking the other's every turn. Together, they fixed forever the boundaries of Piedra Blanca, and the rancho estate of Don Emilio Jose Vincenti Barrazo de Leon.

Paralleling its older counterpart precisely, the picket fence mirrored the stone hedge's every curve and jut, every dip and rise.

Built on a foundation of rock, when the primordial hedge rose up out of the creek, the pickets, resting on submerged footings, marched dutifully along in conforming ranks. If the wall of river rock climbed a hill or descended to the valley floor, the pickets followed obediently, side by side, in precision step.

From above the hacienda where the avocado grove crowned the hills, to the majestic oak trees guarding the rancho's main entry, to the newly planted vineyards thriving in the oceanside fields, the picket fence followed in concert, plodding the same course ancient architects determined for the stone hedge.

The origin of the stone hedge remained a conundrum. When asked how it came to be, Pablo, the old shepherd, shrugged, shaking his graying head.

The stony perimeter that encircled Rancho Piedra Blanca, a California land grant awarded in 1840 to Alphonse de Leon, was there, had always been, and that is all anyone who remembered could say.

Word of mouth spoke of the earliest Salinan Indians as its builders, but the speculative tales were silent on details. The "old stone hedge" was constructed on an eight-foot base, pyramided to a one-foot cap, and stood five feet tall.

The hedge featured larger boulders of smooth river rocks at its base with smaller ones graduating to the top. To accommodate wagon and horse traffic, the builders left openings every mile.

Any reason ancient builders surrounded their village burial grounds with the "stone hedge" finds its answers in myth and storytelling only.

Christened the "old stone hedge" by the Californios, the rock wall's origins remained a mystery. Unlike the hedge, everyone agreed that the picket fence spawned entirely from the Patron's imagination.

No one knew why he built it…or dared to ask. The accepted wisdom was: "He had a good reason."

Conjecture split between two camps. The first believed the fence was there to keep the ghosts of tribal enemies outside their burial grounds. The second insisted the Patron built it to prevent his mother, Annabella, from leaving the rancho.

Whatever the reason, Jorge Muñoz grinned happily when he and his cousins were chosen to do the construction. And why not…did not the Patron himself do the hiring?

There could be no mistake building the picket fence. If the Patron said to build it, Jorge would oblige.

With the Patron's demand that the fence be completed by Easter Sunday, seven and a half months away, the timetable was set.

Jorge allowed himself two weeks to report his necessary needs and wants back to the don.

He and his cousins utilized the next five days, calculating the time, manpower and supplies, lumber, nails, saws, hammers, and paint required to enclose the huge estate.

Finding suppliers who assured delivery took another eight days. They committed that all materials, especially the lumber, would be on hand when the job started and readily available till completion.

The morning came for Jorge to present his report to the Patron. He felt good about what he accomplished in such a short time. Relaxing confidently there at the bottom of the steps outside the Patron's office, he beat the reporting deadline by a day.

Jorge beamed, dressed in his only suit but without a tie. Feeling more presentable without muddy shoes, he congratulated his good sense for taking the time to spit-polish his ancient brown Oxfords.

Smiling, he extended the report to the Patron. Without accepting it, the Patron acknowledged Jorge. Aided by the pearl-handled cane gifted to his grandfather by General Mariano Guadalupe Vallejo, he climbed the five steps to his office door. His spotless white suit and contrasting black-string tie, as always, enjoyed the company of a large red rose in his lapel. As Don Emilio crossed the threshold and walked toward his oak desk, Jorge followed him up the steps but lingered in the doorway.

He hung his hat. Then, with ritual care, the Patron gently placed the historic cane in a felt-lined sleeve built into the ornate hat rack. He sat down, at last, and motioned to Jorge to bring him the folder.

Jorge strode in confidently and handed the don his report, stepping back to await the verdict.

Placing the folder neatly on his meticulous desk, the Patron reached to his right and switched on the sculptured floor lamp, an exact likeness of his horse Rojo Grande.

He then carefully took the spectacles out of his right lapel pocket. Spreading them, he gently placed them on the bridge of his nose.

Tipping the pince-nez forward a bit to sharpen his focus, he read the handwritten report slowly and carefully, his ever-present cigar close at hand, sending smoke up to the copperplate ceiling.

After ten minutes of study, Don Emilio, looking up at an anxious Jorge, removed his spectacles, put them back in his lapel pocket, and took a pull on his cigar.

"You did a very good job on this, Jorge."

"Gracias," he replied, as a smile of relief spread on his happy face. In the next moment, his smile vanished.

"But Jorge, the amount of lumber is incorrect."

Jorge felt panic rising, but he gathered himself, confident his numbers were good.

Assuring the Patron of the exactness of his measurements, he offered, "I was very careful, especially of that number, senor."

To prove his accuracy, he walked around the desk and handed the Patron a blueprint drawn in a high school drafting class by his nephew Alonzo. "Look, please, at these drawings. You will see how the lumber was calculated."

Spreading the draft on his desk, the Patron retrieved his glasses. And when he had carefully reviewed it, he looked up at Jorge and, in a congratulatory tone, spoke.

"Please commend Alonzo. The drawings are very good—very good, indeed. Jorge, you should be proud that he is getting such a useful education, but I see clearly why the lumber calculation is wrong.

"When you remeasure, I am sure it will match my estimate." And then he pointed to the error.

"You are building the picket fence on the wrong side of the 'old stone hedge.' It must be constructed within the hedge, exactly six feet from it. Your nephew must redraft the new fence line on the inside, not the outside of the old hedge. That will greatly reduce the lumber, and your new estimates will match mine."

Jorge did not know whether to laugh or cry. Instead, he whimpered, nodding in vague agreement. In all previous discussions, the outside position for the fence had been taken for granted. Even a simple builder like Jorge knew that the picket fence, or any new fence, should match property lines. But to question the Patron for his reason was unwise.

Two days later Alonzo completed the redrafting, moving the fence line to the inside of the hedge, and the revised measurements agreed with the Patron's.

Still, even with this large reduction, the prodigious length of the fence required all available lumber in three neighboring counties.

Driving prices higher, the demand created a severe lumber shortage, forcing housing developers to postpone post-World War II building projects. For six months, angry builders halted construction starts until the massive fence was completed.

MICHAEL ARNONE

It was no surprise the white picket-fence fiasco, known to all as the Patron's Folly, wrought Don Emilio powerful enemies. No person could say for what purpose the Patron required it. Nevertheless, the fence construction ended ahead of schedule.

Completed on Good Friday at three o'clock in the afternoon, Jorge drove in the last nail as the church bells tolled the death of Christ.

CHAPTER 8

Holy Water and Burning Incense

━━━∽つ◊◯◊つ∽━━━

Promising a hopeful respite to the rancho's gloom, the rain and wind died, dawning a brilliant winter's day.

Shrouds draping window storefronts and lampposts refused to stir. And the lifeless flags, drooping half-staff in Plaza de Leon, lingered impervious to any stirring of the elements.

With funeral bands inscribed with "Emilio," the women prayed to the Blessed Mother, and the men shared what was known and speculated what was not.

No work would be done this day. All would attend the Patron's funeral.

Followed by horse and donkey riders, cars fluttering mourning kerchiefs merged from every village. Like worker ants funneling compliant lines, the mourners inched the dirt roads toward the great hacienda.

The size of the tiny village church necessitated funeral services be held in the Plaza Grande's garden that offered an exquisite open-fan design and colossal fountain centerpiece that accentuated the Hacienda de Leon entry.

For private family viewing, the Patron lay in its magnificent rotunda in a never-to-be-opened gold-leafed casket.

For the public service, the casket would be moved to the Rose Garden and be positioned at the base of the famous mural created years before by Diego Rivera, depicting the Patron as the people's great benefactor. Frequent guests at Piedra Blanca, Rivera and his wife, Frida Kahlo, were commissioned eighteen years before his death to create a memorial to the Patron's legacy.

A renowned artist and man of profound socialist ideals, Rivera graciously accepted the commission. Illness prevented completion of the mural, however. Two years later, he and Frida returned to Piedra Blanca from their home in Mexico City to complete the unfinished work.

It was Frida's decision that dictated the mural's setting and theme. She convinced the Patron it would be a mistake to insist that Diego represent the Patron as victorious General Antonio Lopez de Santa Anna at the Battle Chapultepec. She reasoned he would be best glorified in the likeness of the People's Grand Benefactor, Mexico's President Benito Juarez.

Frida prevailed. Ultimately, the rancho's favorite art treasure, the mural portrayed the Patron mounted on his rearing stallion, Rojo Grande, riding the rancho's rolling hills amid faithful vaqueros in a pastoral setting.

Like the tines of a giant fork, mourners traveled three dusty roads from respective villages, merging at the entry gate. From there, they joined in the processional walk to Hacienda de Leon, a half-mile way.

Cars dangling black kerchiefs of mourning parked all along the roadside. Horse and donkey riders tethered their animals to the picket fence, inside the "old stone hedge." To avoid embarrassing footfalls, riders made their way very carefully through the gathering herd to join hundreds of other mourners in the shade of the entry oaks.

Waving to Conchita, Jose and Jaime signaled their location with Maria and Juanito. With high hopes, pregnant Angelina waited at the entry gate for Francisco's return from the picket fence where he tied their donkey next to the yellow mare.

"Pray your son-in-law returns with boots unsoiled," Jose advised Conchita.

In his first appearance since the day of the gruesome discovery, Manuel maneuvered his flatbed into a vacant spot beside the stone hedge. Once again, hurrying to open Rosa's door, Manuel, always the gentleman, banged his bad knee on the stone hedge wall.

"Slow down, *viejo*," Rosa cautioned. "There is no need to rush. I know you will always be *mi esposo,* and I will always be yours. But I need you with two good knees. Besides, the Patron is not going anywhere."

He flexed and stretched, rubbing the sore spot. "I am all right!

"Don't worry so much." He scowled and motioned to Jose to save them a place.

Maria and Juanito ran to meet Rosa. Gathering them up like a hen with her chicks, she kissed and hugged them. Producing for each a pack of spearmint gum, she tempered their enthusiasm with the warning "no chewing during the service."

Happy to see Manuel looking so much better, Jose hugged him and shook his hand for a long time.

Manuel had been through so much, and Rosa's decision to keep him home until today was loving and wise.

Together the friends walked slowly to the shady area under the expansive oaks saved for the group by Jaime. Assuring everyone any trace of foul-smelling evidence was completely removed from his boots, Francisco sheepishly returned.

At the entry gate with staff in hand stood the old shepherd Pablo, ready to lead his beloved people on the processional walk.

Today, to everyone's surprise, he was dressed in a black suit, white shirt, and tie, with leather shoes and socks. No one ever remembered him wearing anything but baggy white linen pants, a shirt, leather sandals, and a broad-brimmed hat.

"Is that the shepherd?"

Manuel could not imagine Pablo all dressed up. But there he was, cleanly shaven, hair trimmed and combed.

Jose nodded. "Today...we are his herd of sheep."

Rosa put her finger to his lips. "Leave the old man alone, Jose. He is trying to do his part with the only thing he knows. Today we are his flock, and he is our shepherd."

Although the crowd grew and grew, with mourners constantly arriving, the atmosphere was subdued with little or no conversation.

To Rosa, the solemnity and quiet seemed right. "There will be plenty of time for talking at the reception."

At noon, with the ringing of the Angelus, the procession would start at the main entry and end at the Plaza Grande altar where Monsignor Carmona would celebrate the funeral Mass. Sadly, today he presided at a funeral instead of the happy Blessing of the Foals.

From the surrounding villages, seventeen parish priests—Franciscans, Carmelites, and Jesuits—came to assist the monsignor in the service.

Out of twenty-three altar boys in attendance, Julio and Philippe from Blessed Santa Maria parish were chosen to serve at the funeral Mass. They would accompany Monsignor Carmona from the hacienda's main gate to the elevated altar in the Plaza Grande.

The other altar boys were to walk at the side of their assigned priest, carrying incense for the censer and holy water for sanctification. To meet the mourners at eleven-thirty sharp, Monsignor Carmona led a serpentine line of priests and altar boys from the Plaza Grande altar to the hacienda's main entry gate a half-mile away.

At the twelfth chime, the monsignor signaled the keeper to unshackle the gate. Following the long line of priests and altar boys, the mourners commenced their processional walk to Plaza Grande.

Sprinkled in holy water and immersed in wafting incense, the congregation moved as one.

Reaching back into the past, the incense and clanging censers reawakened in Pablo the treasured days he and his brother Vincenti served as altar boys at Santa Teresa de Avila in Mexico City. His fondest recollections were Fridays during Easter season, when he kept the incense burning for the priest at each Station of the Cross.

He smiled as the aroma engulfed him and boyhood memories came flooding back. After serving as an altar boy at Easter services long ago, he prayed the black suit he wore today would permeate with pungent smoke in the same way his surplice and cassock always had.

Pablo remembered Vincenti's rage when his cassock was drenched carrying the splashing holy water bowl, and he laughed to himself how the children teased his brother unmercifully for peeing his pants.

As only old age can really know, the smile faded, tears welled up, and he cried out in a pain. "Vincenti, Vincenti, what happened to those days?"

Careful he was not seen weeping, keeping his eyes straight ahead, he wanted no one to mistake that his tears were intended for the dead Patron.

CHAPTER 9

I Am Pablo Cabrera Barrazo de Leon

On the outskirts of Mexico City, in a tiny village lean-to, the wet nurse caring for the newborn boy died. She was dead for a night and a day before her cold body and the starving child were discovered. Padre Humberto administered the last rites and arranged the funeral Mass, and until the child's parents could be found, brought the baby to his home at the rectory of Santa Teresa de Avila.

Six months passed with many inquiries made, but no one knew who his parents were, and no one ever returned to claim him.

Some said his mother had died in childbirth; others thought his father was a soldier. His lineage remained a mystery, and the only hint to his identity was a white knitted blanket embroidered with the name "Pablo."

A quiet, gentle child, Pablo shared the simple life of the rectory. He remained ever close to Padre Humberto and Juanita, the rectory's cook and housekeeper who nurtured him.

Long past her childbearing years and praising God for her many grandchildren, Juanita vowed no child would ever be left an orphan in her village, especially little Pablo.

With the meekness of a saint and the persistence of a barker, Juanita struck a bargain for a never-ending supply of food to feed her newest ward. The village midwife traded her well-honed practice of birthing babies for a constant supply of mother's milk.

For three years, Juanita's midwifery produced a steady stream of mothers who gladly took turns feeding little "Pablito."

Never an orphan, Pablo was blessed by the many mothers sharing their milk of life. It was no surprise "mama" was his first word. As he grew, and mothers no longer took him to their breasts, he became sad and lonely. And the next few years were problematic for the good padre and his cook.

Not that Pablo didn't feel loved, for he never tired of following Padre Humberto into the sacristy, or helping Juanita prepare the masa, or playing with the children of his nursing mothers. Surrounded by a community loving and kind, little Pablo, the orphaned *niño*, longed for the blessings of his blood parents.

Turning to Juanita and the good padre, he often asked who they could be. The cook would hold him close and, with her caresses, soothe his tears.

The priest provided no answer, yet his words comforted Pablo with a wisdom that burned in his soul. He could still hear the old padre…

"How good of God to bless you, Pablo, as you bless Him. Be gracious to Him for He bestows His grace on you. Have faith. Go before Him every day, joyously singing His praises. Cherish His blessings and in His glory, He will bathe your pain and suffering, freeing you to claim His promises. Oh, my son, if you are faithful to live your life in this way, your soul will be cured, and all loneliness will be gone."

At five years old, Pablo entered the revered convent school, where he delighted in learning and making new friends. A new boy joined the class and changed Pablo's life forever. Pablo and Vincenti, his new classmate, were inseparable. Vincenti's wealthy family embraced Pablo, the poor village orphan, and their friendship grew ever closer.

With Padre Humberto's permission, Pablo accepted the many invitations to Vincenti's home, the great Rancho de Leon of rolling hills and green pastures.

Those were exciting times when he and Vincenti, on their ponies, followed the vaqueros herding the cattle that fed the mighty Mexican Army.

But it was the bulls that brought the rancho its wealth and fame. The bulls of the Rancho de Leon were respected and feared, and Pablo wanted to learn everything about them.

The gigantic black-and-red Cabrera fighting bulls, which every Sunday charged and challenged the great matadors in the Plaza del Toro, brought wealth and fame to the rancho.

Gracious and generous, Vincenti's parents loved Pablo, and he accompanied the de Leon family everywhere, for they took Pablo to their hearts.

Over the next ten years, Pablo became Vincenti's brother and a second son to Don Joaquin and Delores de Leon. As the final step before formal adoption, with Padre Humberto and Juanita's blessing, the de Leon family sponsored Pablo as he entered secondary school.

Two years later, when the final adoption documents were drawn and no one could provide Pablo's actual date of birth, his new parents decided that he and Vincenti would share a common birthday: March 6, 1863. Don Joaquin and Delores always said that the two boys were inseparable.

A new life began for him on August 21, 1880. Pablo proudly took his place in the de Leon family. The pain of abandonment was gone. His prayers for parents and a much-loved brother were answered.

Thanking God for this miraculous blessing, the village orphan who never knew his parents would forever be known to the world as Pablo Cabrera Barrazo de Leon.

⸺◦◦◦⸺

Dozing in the Plaza Grande garden until the funeral ended, the old shepherd drifted in pleasurable reflection.

Many there who had noticed the sleeping old man were there to mourn the Patron's death. But many more like Pablo did not mourn at all. Those poor souls, unfortunate to have suffered at the hands of the dead Patron, were much relieved and happy his life had ended.

Troubled by commotion all around him, Pablo opened his eyes. Struggling for his daydreams to linger on, he reluctantly abandoned his precious reverie.

As the old pleasantness faded, a long-surrendered hopefulness filled his heart and energized his soul. Unwittingly, he began speaking aloud the echo sounding in his head.

Pablo had spoken! People within earshot were astonished, and Rosa, who greatly loved the old man, trembled at the sound of his voice.

"Shepherd, what is that you say?"

Hesitant at first, his confidence grew. With a face shimmering like an angel's, he expanded his chest and stood tall, holding his staff above his head. Smiling lovingly at Rosa, in a voice silent too long, he shouted for all to hear. "I am Pablo Cabrera Barrazo de Leon!"

Rosa shouted, waving across the courtyard to Manuel who chatted with the monsignor, "Manuel...Manuel! Andale...andale!" Her roar startled the quiet throng, and they turned toward the commotion. Manuel set down his punch glass, excused himself to the priest, and with bad knees and all, ran wondering what had happened. As he passed Jose, he grabbed his arm, howling, "Come with me, now!"

"What is wrong?"

Never before had anyone ever heard Pablo utter anything. Always a fixture at the dances, picnics, fiestas, and family celebrations, at no time had anyone ever heard from him a single sound, let alone a word.

Now, as if he just remembered his long-lost identity, he repeated his name, over and over.

"I am Pablo Cabrera Barrazo de Leon! I am Pablo Cabrera Barrazo de Leon!"

Claiming to be a de Leon shocked everyone. No one could understand—no one, that is, except the dead Patron's mother and rancho mistress, Annabella.

CHAPTER 10

The Storyteller and His Faithful Listeners

---∞∞∞---

When the reception ended, Manuel and Rosa drove Pablo home. The old flatbed lumbered over dirt roads to the shepherd's hut, a dark, single-room affair, overshadowed with primeval oak where he lived alone on the lonely hilltop of San Simeon.

While Rosa helped the old man out of the truck, Manuel raced ahead to open the hut's front door.

"Senor Pablo, can you direct me to your lamp?"

Pablo pointed to the right of the door where a lantern hung on a nail. The kerosene lamp came to life, and Manuel entered, placing it on a table in the center of the tiny room. Rosa guided the old man to the chair beside the table.

A narrow cot a yard away filled one side. On the shelf above, three dusty books lay next to an old-fashioned inkwell, pens, and a box of envelopes.

Patting Pablo on his shoulder, Rosa said: "It is late…I am sure you are very tired. In the morning, we will return to look in on you."

Unable to resist, Rosa confessed: "It is so strange to hear you speak. We loved you for many years without your voice. Now, what you say comes from so deep a place, we shiver with every word."

Smiling, he looked up into Rosa's brown eyes.

"Manuel and Rosa, my dearest friends, how does an old man repay wonderful people like the two of you for a lifetime of love and kindness?" He stood drawing them close, embracing them at the same time. "Your nearness brings me such joy and comfort."

Tears filled everyone's eyes.

"Perhaps you will stay a bit longer to brighten the life of a lonely old man…I would appreciate it if you can."

"Well, perhaps a bit longer, if it does not tire you," Rosa offered.

Searching for interest in his listener's eyes, Pablo confessed, "There are only two people alive who know the story of the de Leon family and my life. And I can think of no others I would choose to share it with than you—Manuel, my kind and noble friend…and you, Rosa, the woman whose love for years has nurtured all our souls.

"After all my years of silence, I find this day an eager excitement in me to share how I came to be the last surviving de Leon. Let this old shepherd tell you the story of Rancho Piedra Blanca and my life. Entry by entry, day by day, by the grace of God, I have written it all down, exactly so, as it happened. Please sit."

He turned to the bookshelf above and took down a leather binding filled with hundreds of handwritten pages. To indulge the old man, Rosa's look of compassion persuaded Manuel to stay.

How could they know this would be the first of many nights' sleep that would be traded for schooling in the history of the de Leons and Rancho Piedra Blanca?

Deciding on the best place to start, Pablo sat thumbing through the neatly arranged stacks of handwritten pages covering the table. Making the right selection, he reached to collect his battered tobacco tin and pipe, hand-carved from the burl of his favorite cypress tree.

They watched as he skillfully filled the bowl and tamped the tobacco tight. Manuel found the matchbox, lit the crusted oval, and Pablo drew the flame, filling the hut with the sweet aroma of blossoming pine. Finding just the right page, his old eyes sparkled, signaling the beginning.

Tempting curiosity, he asked, "Have you heard the stories of Josefina Espinoza?"

"Of course," Rosa said. "The old village *curandera*, who vanished one day long ago."

"Do you know you are sitting in her first home in Piedra Blanca? This same hut shared with the farm animals…the very donkeys, cows, and horrible pigs legend claims caused her never to be seen again?"

"There are many tales of her ending, senor," Manuel suggested. "But they are nothing but fanciful tales the villagers turn to when their children do not behave. I remember Jose chasing his young Jaime, screaming after him, 'I will feed you to the pigs!' You see, he poured a quart of paint on his sister Madeline's head."

"There are times when the old stories ring true," Pablo said. "Keep that in mind as I tell my tale. And when I finish, what you may once consider fable is, in fact, the truth. For you see, learning about the *curandera* is the key to the de Leon legacy."

Side by side, on Pablo's bed, the couple's interest warmed as the memories Pablo shared hovered above their heads like a cloud of smoke.

CHAPTER 11

Alphonse de Leon and Piedra Blanca

⎯⎯⎯◦⎯⎯⎯

A s if taking an oath, Pablo placed his hand on the pages of the opened journal and began.

"I started recording every day in this journal over sixty years ago when brother Vincenti and I rode, for the very first time, the long trail from Rancho de Leon in Mexico City to central California and Rancho Piedra Blanca.

"On the day we left, Mama Dolores de Leon handed me this journal, and I pledged to her that I would be faithful to write down all our adventures. And to this day, I have been true to the task. From the first to the last patron, from Alphonse de Leon's founding to Don Emilio's recent death, I have logged the history of this rancho and the pioneer de Leon family. You will see…it is an exciting story, filled with adventure and discovery. And you will also come to feel the joy and also the painful tragedy the family suffered along the way."

⎯⎯⎯◦⎯⎯⎯

"THE STORY BEGINS WITH A SEA VOYAGE IN FEBRUARY 1840, when Juan Bautista Alvarado, the governor of Alta, California, sailed from Monterey to meet President Anastasio Bustamante in Mexico City. With him, he brought his long-anticipated plan that forever changed the history of California and the fortunes of family de Leon—land grants to be given to loyalists who fought for Mexico's independence from Spain.

"Like so many other notable Mexican families in both California and Mexico, the de Leons for years petitioned that loyal Mexicans be honored with a California land grant. And Bustamante approved Alvarado's plan. The loyal Mexicans were invited to attend a gala celebration on the first day of April 1840 at the Presidential Palace in Mexico City. There the land grant patents would be awarded.

"The dalliances of handsome and resourceful Alphonse de Leon, the head of our family, were legend throughout Mexico City. In 1831, after thirteen years of humiliation, his wife, Lorena, left him. In Mexico however, divorcing a man like Alphonse proved difficult. She quietly went to live with her aging parents in Vera Cruz, awaiting the church to officially sanction the divorce.

"The union of Lorena and grandfather Alphonse, patriarch and founder of Mexico City's Rancho de Leon, produced one child, their son Joaquin. When his parents separated, Joaquin, still a young boy, remained in his father's custody. Soon to become Alphonse's next consort, Florencia Esquivel Armando entered into the household as Joaquin's live-in tutor and guardian.

"As the orchestra played at the president's awards ceremony, loyalist men with families at their side waited in the long reception line to receive their patent and to thank the governor and president personally. That night, some nine years after his parents separated, standing beside his father Alphonse was their twenty-one-year-old son and heir, Joaquin."

Rosa interrupted. "But Senor Pablo, how did it come to pass that Piedra Blanca was the rancho awarded to Alphonse de Leon?"

Pablo laughed at the question and the extraordinary circumstance that blessed family de Leon with the coveted Piedra Blanca. "Alphonse, the lady's man, also gambled heavily. Originally granted to the de Leons was a rancho in the area of Santa Margarita, a hilly area with no water.

"When the gala ended, many of the men retired with their cigars and tequila to the president's study above the ballroom. One thing led to another, and a poker game ensued.

"The players included President Bustamante, General Santa Anna, and other rich dignitaries also land grants recipients. The evening wore on and not well for Alphonse.

"With pockets empty and a straight flush in his hand, he wagered the home of the famous Cabrera bulls, his Mexico City rancho, against Santa Anna's coveted Central California grant located north of Mission San Miguel, in coastal mountains of San Simeon.

But when the poker game ended, Santa Anna held no claim to Piedra Blanca or to Rancho de Leon. Alphonse emerged the winner, and the legacy of Rancho Piedra Blanca began."

"But Senor, what became of the original land grant in Santa Margarita?"

"It was a generous time for Mexico and, as it turned out, for Alphonse as well. When Mexico's independence was won, Mexico confiscated all the lands the Spanish monarchy had gifted to the California missions.

"The property the missions were allowed to retain restricted possession to church buildings, priest's quarters, and adjacent gardens only. All other recovered lands were made available for the land grant awards. In the end, Mexico awarded to the Californios, Mexicans living in California and loyal native Mexican citizens, over seven hundred patents.

"And if the president, with a stroke of his pen, could award loyal Mexicans the ranchos of California, Alphonse could afford to be generous too.

"Exercising shrewd judgment and cunning instinct, Alphonse surrendered his claim to Rancho Santa Margarita, gifting it to the humbled general of the Mexican Army. His generosity allowed Santa Anna to save face and Alphonse retained a powerful ally.

"Eager to see a rancho he won with a straight flush, four months later Alphonse embarked on a six-month journey by horseback from Mexico City to his new California home north of San Luis Obispo. It was the first of four passages he and Fredrico Montoya, his majordomo, would navigate back and forth.

"Over the ensuing years, Alphonse sailed in and out of many ports, from Santa Barbara, San Francisco, and Monterey to Mexico, then French and Dutch freighters, from Zihuatanejo and Acapulco back to California on Russian and German merchant vessels.

"My father Joaquin retained charge of the Mexico City businesses in Alphonse's absences, managing all the de Leon holdings, including the Rancho de Leon and the Cabrera bull enterprise.

"With each succeeding journey, on horseback or ship, grandfather Alphonse developed important liaisons along the way. From tiny San Diego villages to the docks at the City of Angels and the ranchos along the El Camino Real, vital pacts and trade agreements were created.

"Always sealed with a handshake, those agreements made with his friends and associates ensured safe passage, encouraged commerce, and improved relations with the dons, friars and local Indian tribes.

"Four months into their initial journey, as a steady but light rain fell, Alphonse and Fredrico reached the City of Angels at last.

"After a welcome bath and a good night's rest in the fancy Royale Hotel on Olvera Street, horses were exchanged and supplies replenished."

"'Senor Pablo, did they leave Los Angeles immediately?'" Manuel wondered.

"They planned to reach Santa Barbara in three weeks. So they rode out the next day, to provide them ample time to meet along the trail north with the dons of many ranchos."

CHAPTER 12

Vaquero and Bear

With a mischievous smile on his lips, Pablo turned to his audience. "Perhaps you might know the story of the 'Brave Vaquero and the Bear'?"

Manuel searched his memory while Rosa shook her head. "I do not think I know that one, senor."

"Allow me then, the joy of telling you what next happened to Alphonse and Fredrico, our stalwart travelers. It happened as they approached the outskirts of Santa Barbara, anxious to meet with Don Jose de la Guerra Noriega of Rancho San Julian. Sorry to delay their travels, Montoya signaled de Leon his need to relieve himself. Fredrico hastily dismounted, tying his horse and pack mule to a leafless buckeye tree. He fairly trotted into the tree line, like a man holding a ball between his knees.

"A distant pond glistened in the morning sun. The idea to water the horses crossed Alphonse's mind. Instead, he decided to enjoy the lush forest and clear waters all around him while waiting for Montoya to finish his business. Difficult to negotiate, the muddied ground saturated by December rains hampered Montoya in his search for the right spot.

"Stomach grumbling, avoiding in his path the thornier manzanita branches that poked at him, nevertheless he stumbled onward.

"In his mind, he reviewed his breakfast and came away with the conclusion the chilies were the culprit.

"Cramps at their worst, surrendering the search for the perfect spot, he unbuckled his pants, squatting in the mud. Relief began, but the interruption was immediate.

"Discovering the indisposed Montoya, a giant grizzly breached the underbrush. At the spectacle of the man, the huge bear stopped his advance and sank a bit into the mud. Holding his breath, Montoya did not move. The giant grizzly, more startled than Montoya, raised up to its full height and cautiously took a few steps closer to inspected the squatter.

"Montoya confessed afterwards that the bear was much taller than his horse, and the first sight of him stopped his business completely.

"Greeting Montoya with growls more curious than menacing, the bear stood his ground trying to decide who Montoya was and why he smelled so bad.

"By then, the horses picked up the bear's scent and began to bay wildly, with the pack mule bucking in the air.

"Alphonse shouted, knowing something was wrong. 'Amigo, are you all right? You are scaring the horses with your stink.'

"But the answer returned was a deafening growl.

"Business unfinished, with pantaloons around his ankles and holding his arms above his head, Montoya rose up slowly. Standing no more than twenty feet away, he roared back at the bear as loudly as he could.

"Off his horse and running toward the commotion, Alphonse drew his pistol, firing it into the air to distract a bear he could not see. Moving into the brush, what he did see astonished him.

"Montoya, my grandfather's genius majordomo, utilizing the only weapon at hand, reached behind and grabbed at his steaming pile of excrement. Flinging it with accuracy, the offensive mass splattered the advancing bear in the middle of its face, stopping it in its tracks."

The shepherd's hut echoed with howls. Talking and laughing at the same time, the giggling storyteller, in fits and starts, tried to carry on.

"Turning away from Montoya, the outraged grizzly, yelping like an abandoned cub, whimpered off, crashing into the forest and running for the nearest pond. Dripping the stinking residue from its nose, the tainted animal plunged head-first into the water.

"Happy to wait for another opportunity to complete his half-finished business, Montoya giggled, thankfully in relief more than fear, then hurriedly buckled up his soiled trousers.

"Rejoining de Leon, he was greeted with belly laughs that continued all the way to Santa Barbara. It pained him listening to Alphonse retell the story over and over again, chuckling harder every time. 'The bear story,' to Montoya's regret, never died.

"And to this day, the story of 'the Brave Vaquero and the Bear' is retold around many a campfire."

Rosa tried to hide it, but the bloom on her face blushed with guilt. Manuel remembered.

"Senor Pablo," Manuel said, "my brother Jesus told that story at our table last Christmas. His presentation left nothing to the imagination, but his characters were in reverse. He said it was de Leon who was indisposed, and Montoya saved him at the last minute, lassoing the bear's foot and pulling him away with his horse."

MICHAEL ARNONE

"Different versions of this story are shared. Mine, so to speak, came from the mouth of the bear. The story lives on. I hope you enjoyed my version."

Rosa stood winking at Manuel that it was time to go.

"Senora, you have been so kind and patient; allow me to end tonight's telling with this. It will be brief. My eyes, like yours, are sleepy too."

The old married couple, holding hands, sat back down on the bed, nodding for Pablo to continue. Puffing his pipe, exhaling sweet smoke toward the open door, Pablo stared after the wispy vapors.

"Like the evening wind carrying my smoke into the night, Alphonse de Leon and Fredrico Montoya raced to end their long journey. Just before sundown, on January third, 1841, the two pioneers arrived precisely where they intended, at Mission San Miguel, outside of San Luis Obispo.

"With the help of two newly hired vaqueros, for fifteen days they drove forty head of cattle and twelve prize bulls from Rancho San Julian in Santa Barbara to the mission's presidio.

"This gift from Don Jose de la Guerra Noriega provided Rancho Piedra Blanca not only with livestock, but also its first two ranch hands—Pedro Cantinas, a Mexican soldier, and Juan Solano, a Salinan Indian.

"The breeding stock, however, was the greatest of gifts. In time, thanks to the sires out of the original twelve bulls, the rancho's herd grew to over thirty thousand head.

"At the mission, Friar Fray Tomas Sepulveda showered the trail-weary men with famed Franciscan hospitality reserved for visiting bishops, cardinals, and dons. While Alphonse and Fredrico ate and slept like royalty, the precious breeding stock lay quiet with the new hands.

"The next day, early on the fourth day of the new year 1841, they were introduced to their new world."

Pablo blinked his eyes, then closed them, resting and remembering. Rosa and Manuel took a deep breath. Yawning, he teased, "And that part of the story we shall undertake when you can oblige an old man once again.

"Now Manuel, take your beautiful bride home and rest well, knowing you have made an old man very happy."

When they were gone, Pablo tamped out his pipe, then struggling a bit in the darkness, he filled and relit his lamp.

A day destined to mourn Emilio's death turned into a coming-out party for an old man who spoke for the first time in years, sharing insight into the history Rancho Piedra Blanca. It gladdened Pablo and, for that, he liked himself again. But now his old body ached for his bed as the kerosene lamp went dark.

"Tomorrow comes quickly." He fell immediately into a delicious slumber replete with vibrant landscapes and visions of loved ones past.

Frolicking with him in the rancho's flowered meadows stood brother Vincenti, lover Yolanda, and handsome son Alejandro. As choirs of attentive angels replenished their bottomless goblets, sip by sip, they picnicked roundabout tables overflowing with luscious fruits, honey breads, and tender meats.

The enchantment blossomed until a relentless pounding sent the dreamy cast fleeing. Reaching out, trying to pull them back, Pablo pleaded with them to stay. The hammering grew louder. They were gone, and Pablo opened his eyes.

"Who is it?" he shouted from his cot. "Who has died now that you must disturb an old man?"

"Senor Pablo, I am Garcia. Mistress Annabella…she desires you to accompany me to the hacienda."

"At this hour?"

"Yes, senor. She wishes to speak to you immediately."

"Garcia…um, Garcia…you are Ronaldo's boy, no?"

"I am, senor. My father sends his regards."

"Well, my dear Garcia, tell your mistress I am sorry to disappoint her, but I will not be jumping to her whims this night or any other.

"Besides, my schedule is very full at the moment. Let me see…tell her I can see her if she comes to my house next Tuesday morning at ten," he said laughing, "That is my very first availability.

"Now, good night Garcia, and do not dare to knock on my door again."

CHAPTER 13

Rancho of the White Rock

M arch weather turned a Friday afternoon into a blustery, rain-soaked day. The culverts and gullies collected runoff, feeding the ponds and insatiable lagoons that dotted the lower concourse of the rancho.

Slowed by the mud-slick road, Manuel arrived late, picking up Pablo for the weekend visit and dinner Rosa prepared in his honor at their Cambria home.

"Senor Pablo, are you packed and ready to go?

"Old friend, what an honor you should bother with the likes of an old man like me. I have looked forward to this visit very much."

Manuel lifted Pablo's two valises, depositing them in the truck bed's toolbox. Closing the lid, he returned to help Pablo, waiting out of the rain, into the cab.

The old shepherd speculated, looking up at the threatening clouds. "Are you sure you want to fetch such a weathered old man like me to be your houseguest on such a wet and chilly day?"

Manuel beamed. "We are so happy and excited that we will have you for the entire weekend. As you look forward to our hospitality, our home awaits you. And we are anxious to hear more storytelling from your journal." Manuel took a turn speculating, "You did bring your journal?"

"How else can I pay for your bill of hospitality if not by telling a good story? My journal is in the small valise shut tightly...the rain cannot intrude."

Struggling to keep the windshield clear, the tattered wipers beat out a rhythmic percussion to accompany the raindrop staccato. For riders with an ear for music, symphonic rhapsodies were performed on the tinny hood.

"And perhaps, senor, if the roads and the rain allow, we can attend Mass at the mission on Sunday morning?"

"I would enjoy that above all things, weather and roads permitting,"

After a long silence, Manuel haltingly asked. "Senor Pablo, I hope that you will not think it an intrusion that Rosa and I have invited Jose, Conchita, and Jaime for dinner and storytelling. Once we shared with them your first stories, they begged to be invited."

"If they are welcomed by you, of course, they are welcomed by me. My concern is that my stories will bore them to sleep."

But the new listeners embraced Pablo with warm affection. And Rosa's dinner—succulent roasted lamb and honeyed sweet potatoes served warm and delicious—brought the gathering to raves. When peach compote, the feast's last course, disappeared as quickly as it was served, Conchita and Jaime cleared the table.

Jose and Manuel, along with Pablo, retired to the modest living room, smoking and speaking of things important to men, especially how the Patron came to his end.

Rosa redressed the dining room, then welcomed everyone back to the table for coffee, sopaipillas, and flan covered in her famous caramel crown.

"Senora Rosa, what a dinner...such a cook! Comparing Conchita's cooking and yours is like deciding between the angels."

Then, with a smirk, Pablo added: "Rosa, are you sure you are happily married? I am available if you can stand a man even older than your husband."

Rosa's face exploded red, and the men roared. But Conchita shook her finger chastising Pablo.

The laughter at Rosa's expense ended and, with anticipation, she handed Pablo the journal of his family and the rancho's long history.

"Now, you must pay for your dinner, Senor Pablo, and for the dinner of all these voracious ungrateful guests who, should I allow it, would eat me out of house and home," Rosa said trying to stifle her laughter. With excitement blazing in their hearts like children hearing a story for the very first time, she begged, "Senor, please tell us a tale."

The old man settled in a comfortable chair, leaned forward, and opened his tattered journal. Finding his place, he looked up at his audience with a smile on his face and a question on his lips.

"Piedra Blanca?...Piedra Blanca?...the White Rock." Pointing to Jaime, Pablo asked, "Do you know how the rancho acquired its name?"

Surprised and bit embarrassed, thinking it a simple thing that he should know, Jaime shook his head and muttered, "No, senor, I am afraid I do not."

"Good friend, the history of the rancho's name started long before the time of the missions and long before the Spaniards claimed California.

"Over many centuries, the local Indians witnessed how the outcroppings of boulders and peaks spiraling upward out of the ocean gradually changed their color. Over time, God's resident artists—seagulls and pelicans, hawks and falcons, condors and vultures—painted the offshore boulders whiter and whiter with their constant droppings, thus naming Piedra Blanca, the Rancho of the White Rock.

"What a magnificent Rancho of the White Rock it is. With sweeping coastal views, the rancho on the west dives headlong into the Pacific Ocean and to the east climbs the grassy hills and rugged Santa Lucias.

"It was a blessed land plentiful in water that kept its many creeks, lakes, and lagoons full. Its lush hills fed wild herds of unfenced cattle. Its verdant meadows brought forth a plethora of trees, grasses, and flowers from a soil so fertile.

"In the new year of 1841, when they first arrived, Alphonse and Fredrico, so astounded at the promise of the land, stayed several months before returning to Mexico, camping each night in diverse locales and taking in all the rancho's glorious wonder.

"Assisted by Cantinas and Solano, the two pioneers surveyed every waterway and mapped every plateau, hill, and valley.

"Alphonse de Leon came to realize he was the don of a very blessed and wealthy domain that ranged north from below El Sur Grande to a league southwest of the fishing village of Cambria, where today we enjoy such wonderful hospitality.

"It is said that if he had a choice of any land grant in all of California, God Himself could not have chosen one greater than Piedra Blanca.

"Humbled with gratitude, my grandfather often would ride alone to a secluded meadow or bubbling creek, or perhaps the white-crested peak of San Simeon itself. With tears streaming, he fell to his knees and gave thanks, praying that God would always be his guide."

Acknowledging Alphonse's inspired petition, Conchita and Rosa, with bowed heads, made the sign of the cross.

"Can you imagine seeing for the first time the rancho as they did?" Jaime wondered. "We see it today, and it is nothing. We take the ocean and the land for granted, but to Alphonse and Fredrico the rancho must have been like viewing heaven on earth."

"Heaven or not, how did Alphonse tame such a vast and wild kingdom?" Jose asked.

"I know a bit about mechanics. For me, the inner workings of an engine are right in front of you, but how your grandfather and all his helpers settled such a huge ranch would be a challenge too big for a hundred men."

"Senor Jaime. Senor Jose, Alphonse de Leon was not a fool. That is why he insisted Fredrico Montoya be his traveling companion and majordomo of his new world. It was his good fortune that Montoya, a seasoned vaquero, was also a genius cartographer. Fredrico's study of the terrain resulted in detailed maps, setting the rancho's boundaries.

"An expert with the transit, compass, and sextant, he measured distances and calculated elevations, setting the precise courses for water flows and plotting where roads and trails would best serve. His keen eye and common sense helped him to determine the very best locations for future housing and barns, orchards and vineyards, and pastures and meadows.

"His plan for aqueducts, from natural springs and wells, would create a steady supply of water to the rancho's inhabitants. With Montoya's invaluable assistance, grandfather considered all the factors necessary for taming this wild possession and devised a brilliant plan.

"First, to raise the necessary capital to develop Piedra Blanca while maintaining his ongoing holdings in Mexico, he chose to keep only prime sections of the rancho and sell the rest to the many settlers streaming into the region. Several of these parcels were sold over the years, keeping the rancho coffers solvent.

"Second, workers from local Indian tribes and former soldiers from the old mission system were plentiful. He ensured their loyalty by promising them a home for their families and a share of the wealth.

"For the cattle operation, he chose only the best vaqueros and Indians skilled in farming by the mission fathers. In the first five years, many small villages appeared, with the names we today know so well: Santa Lucia, Santa Maria, San Francisco, and San Xavier where Senor Jose and his family live today.

"Third, ensuring increased profitably, commerce and production flourished, satisfying both domestic and foreign demand for meat, hides, and tallow. New business development fell to my grandfather. The day-to-day operation of the rancho was entrusted to the hands of the majordomo, Fredrico Montoya.

"However, the best-laid plans conceived by the de Leon family could not foresee the turbulence about to take place in California—unforeseen events threatening the family's legal ownership rights to Piedra Blanca.

"The trouble started with the Bear Flag Revolt and continued through the end of the Mexican-American War. Mexico treasured California, but two years later it would be lost forever. The Treaty of Guadalupe Hidalgo and two laws ratified by Congress, the Land Act and the Homestead Act, forced every don of every rancho to prove their declaration of ownership.

"The cattle business in California, especially for the ranchos, flourished when gold was discovered. But when the claims played out, the Gold Rush boom fizzled. The many thousands who came west with 'yellow fever' returned home broke but wiser, and almost overnight the bottom dropped out of cattle prices. Declining demand for beef added to the problems.

"But then, in December 1858, as war winds began to blow hot between the North and South, Joaquin sent Alphonse a telegram demanding he discontinue all current and future cattle trade to all markets and return immediately to join him for a meeting in Mexico City.

"'Father...stop. Return to Mexico City immediately... stop. Discuss departure with no one...stop. Require complete discretion...stop. Cancel all existing sale of cattle... stop. Joaquin...stop.'

"The reason for the secrecy became quite apparent when Alphonse arrived at Rancho de Leon. His presence was required to ratify an agreement with the Union Army that guaranteed all current and future rancho cattle and food-stuff production be reserved exclusively for the Union western forces. In exchange, the Union Army named Rancho Piedra Blanca its exclusive supplier, guaranteeing purchase of all its products for no less than five years, or until the end of the war, whichever was longer.

"Two weeks later, as Joaquin sealed arrangements in Washington, Alphonse sailed back from Mexico City to Piedra Blanca to implement the plan.

"Through timely strategies, like the Civil War contracts, my father Joaquin assured a steady and growing flow of cash that kept the rancho coffers filled. His business savvy saved Piedra Blanca from becoming another victim of the onslaught others suffered due to the turbulent times. Unlike other ranchos forced into bankruptcy or sold for pennies on the dollar, Piedra Blanca stayed intact and solvent.

"If he had not been such a brilliant businessman we, my loving friends, would not be here…and we would never have come to know one another. All of us who love California and Piedra Blanca owe so much to him."

Putting the well-worn journal aside to rest his eyes, Pablo stopped reading momentarily. The men ran for the outhouse, welcoming the pause.

"Senor Pablo, maybe you should stop for today. You have told us so much, perhaps you are too tired to continue."

Pablo shook his gray head. "My dear Rosa, I have waited too long to tell this story. Please, brew some coffee to wake us up."

Rosa stoked the kitchen stove. "Coffee will be ready soon."

"When the men return, I will explain how my grandfather Alphonse and my father Don Joaquin led Piedra Blanca into the new century."

Conchita's basket of almonds and walnuts, with the ever-present persimmons and oranges, appeared on the dining room table. "These fruits and nuts are my thank you, Pablo, for bringing the rancho's history to life."

As the smell of fresh-brewed coffee wafted through the house, before testing it, Pablo plucked an orange from Conchita's fruit bowl. He peeled it, then carefully sectioned it into twelve separate slivers. Pointing to his throat, he answered the question in his listener's eyes.

"The wonderful orange sweetens my breath and keeps my voice strong."

After eating four slivers, Pablo stirred two teaspoons of sugar, as he always did, into his coffee, carefully sipping the steaming brew.

Listeners reassembled and Rosa filled their cups with the fresh brewed coffee as each one took his place.

Manuel picked several almonds and walnuts out of the basket and, with a small mallet, started breaking the shells and separating the meat. He piled the nutmeats into a bowl, giving the old shepherd first choice.

"How very thoughtful, Manuel. Gracias." Sampling a walnut, Pablo then continued.

"Sailing home, Alphonse stopped in San Diego, Santa Barbara, and other ports along the way, meeting several dons negotiating cattle purchases that Rancho Piedra Blanca would, in turn, sell to the Union Army.

"Finally, returning home in January, 1861, he docked in Monterey and died there two weeks later."

The casual declaration of Alphonse's death shocked everyone.

"Please, do not be sad. He died in complete happiness. Over seventy years old, and a regular patron of Margarita Sanchez, the madam of Monterey's infamous La Ida Café, Alphonse de Leon remained a ladies' man to the end."

At this confession, the woman gasped, and the men, praying for the subject to change, shifted uncomfortably in their seats. The apparent unease tickled Pablo and he laughed for a long time.

"When Alphonse went missing from the rancho, no alarms sounded. It was known exactly where he could be found. The citizens of Monterey, well acquainted with Patron Alphonse, knew sooner or later someone from the rancho would realize his absence and come looking for him.

"But on this occasion, for more than a week, he had not returned home. Concerned yet unworried, Fredrico Montoya, his trusted right-hand man, drove a team and buggy to Monterey to fetch him, only to discover Alphonse's body waiting to be claimed in the local undertaker's parlor. He had been dead for three days.

"When the madam could not roust Alphonse from his perpetual sleep, she called on her younger brother, the very obese Gerardo Sanchez, the appointed city Constable to the Café, to collect the old don's remains.

"With a smile of delight etched on his face, grandfather died in Margarita's big bed surrounded by a flock of sensual women…a contented man indeed."

Rosa stared hard at her husband. "Manuel, do you know of this Madam Sanchez and this 'house' in Monterey?"

Shaking his head, as everyone laughed and slapped the table, he squawked in embarrassment. "Rosa, she is long dead and no good to me or anyone else. And her house is now a nice restaurant with waitresses, not…you know…." he said, gesturing with his chin. "Besides, my beloved, when do I ever go to Monterey?"

Conchita patted Rosa's hand, reassuring her. Pointing a finger in Manuel's blushing face, Rosa grinned and giggled. "I almost caught a little fish!" When the laughter subsided, the group settled, and the storytelling started up again.

"Assured by a somber Madam Sanchez that his good friend died well and happy, Fredrico carted grandfather's casketed body back to Piedra Blanca. After a brief ceremony, attended by ranch hands, cowboys, and farmers, Alphonse de Leon, the rancho's founder, was buried with little formality in the family plot.

"Shaded by a banner of elm and oak, he was laid to rest next to Rosita, the woman who he confessed he would have married someday if she had not died of the typhoid years before.

"Three months later, my wonderful friend Don Joaquin de Leon stepped into the breach. To assure the rancho stayed on firm footing, he traveled to Piedra Blanca and had long meetings with Fredrico Montoya. Taking Montoya into his confidence, he placed him in charge of completing his long-range plans to extricate the de Leons from Mexico and make Piedra Blanca the permanent home for he and Mama Dolores.

"In spite of all the wars, financial crises, and political upheaval of the nineteenth century, Don Joaquin's foresight and business acumen, successfully ushered Piedra Blanca into the new century.

"A brilliant example of his foresight and business savvy, took place in 1865. The Civil War was over and the demand for cattle, once again, faded as it had for his father in the waning years of the Gold Rush. To offset the drop in cattle prices, Don Joaquin sold off twenty-eight thousand raw acres of mountainous San Simeon Peak and surrounding area to George Hearst, a gold miner who struck it rich. That was the last section of the rancho to ever be sold.

"The sale of the San Simeon acreage followed Alphonse's master plan to retain all prime sections, selling off only those parcels earmarked for disposal. Unlike neighboring ranchos, forced to sell land when cattle prices dried up, Don Joaquin upheld the founding Don's goals, and Rancho Piedra Blanca flourished.

"Don Joaquin's decision to sell bolstered the rancho's financial strength well into the twentieth century. As good as the Hearst sale proved to be, Don Joaquin's greatest accomplishment came after nineteen years of legal battles and thousands of dollars in attorney fees.

"In 1876, his dogged efforts were at last rewarded when the US Public Lands Commission upheld the de Leon petition and issued the long-sought official patent my father fought for over twenty years to win.

"After so many years of legal battles, the commission confirmed Mexico's grant of California land to Alphonse de Leon as authentic, recognizing the family's official ownership of Rancho Piedra Blanca.

"Still, today, this monumental decision is but one of a few patents ever granted to an original Mexican grantee."

SUNSET LINGERED TO PAINT LONG THIN SHADOWS ON the ceiling of the modest living room, and like the candle's flame, the listener's faces glowed bright for the next story telling.

But Pablo was exhausted.

"Rosa, could this old man please go to bed. I have spoken all the words I have for today, and this old body needs to shut down and rest."

Jose shook Manuel's hand and hugged Rosa.

"Jose, you need to return tomorrow after church. We will have a little lunch, and Pablo will resume his story."

Jose beamed, delighted with the invitation.

"I would not miss a word of it, old friend. Conchita will be here, but my son must care for his kids. The things we never knew are more than revelations, are they not?"

After receiving their gracious thanks, Rosa said goodbye to her guests and put Pablo to bed.

Jaime drove Conchita home and picked up his children left in Angelina's care.

"And to think, tomorrow the old man begins with Annabella's family," Rosa said. "With her, there is much that none of us can know...yet he does."

Removing a waxy mess on the mantle, Manuel, shook his head saying, "The children are welcome, Rosa!

"Jose tells me tomorrow Jaime will miss Pablo's telling. There is no one to care for the children, so I told him to bring the kids. They are well behaved and I am sure they will enjoy hearing the old ways."

"Yes, yes," Rosa agreed from the kitchen…

"Jose, be sure you tell Jaime I will kill him if he does not let me get my hands on Maria and little Juanito. It has been too long since I have spoiled them."

CHAPTER 14

Two Brothers—
One Woman

M orning sun sparkled, but a cold winter's day swept into the room through the door Jaime held open for his daughter Maria. She entered Rosa's living room wearing her mother's warm and comfortable peacoat. But little Juanito shivered, bounding the two-step entry once again, with no jacket or sweater in sight.

The listeners, eager to hear more from Pablo, waited patiently for late arrivals. Angelina, showing signs of motherhood on the way, looked after the children reading stories of pirates and treasure.

"Where is Conchita?" Rosa asked.

"Supervising my husband, Francisco, and his brothers. They are making good on their promise to paint her old house. Today was the day they decided to start. She sends her regrets, but could not pass up the offer."

But after a bite of lunch, a very pregnant Angelina became ill, vomiting and begging to go home. She helped Jaime gathered up Maria and Juanito, and they all drove hurriedly away, with Jaime promising to return once everyone was delivered into Conchita's care. For the others, the repast Angelina had to pass up proved a delicious opening act to the honey-drenched sopaipillas that followed for dessert.

Rosa cautioned Manuel. "So, viejo, you have eaten your share of sopaipillas…leave some for Jaime. He will be back soon."

Manuel put back the last bit of dessert, sulking to his favorite chair and hoping the storyteller would begin the Estrada family saga to take his mind off the sweets.

Watching the door, Pablo refused to start until Jaime walked through it. To everyone's surprise, Jaime arrived with a smiling, waving Conchita, who searched her purse for a brush to freshen her windblown hair.

"Hello…hello," she smiled, unsnarling a tangle. "Francisco thought it best to tend to Angelina. The good news is she is resting and feeling better at home."

Rosa jumped from her chair looking for the children. "Where are Maria and Juanito?"

Jaime laughed. "Francisco and his brothers are there too. As soon as the children arrived, they put down their paintbrushes and picked up their instruments. While Francisco teaches Maria the guitar, my little son sings along.

"So, please do not worry; the children are in good hands, and I am glad to be back with Conchita. Pablo's stories are too good to miss."

With the roll call complete, Pablo opened the journal and thumbed through several pages until he rested on the page he had marked at the top in bright red ink.

When all were assembled, sitting comfortably and sipping Rosa's coffee, Pablo raised an eyebrow with sadness in his eye.

"If I dare, now is the time to introduce the Estrada family, who, through marriage, wreaked disaster on the de Leons.

"In 1844, dangling four years on the waiting list, fifty-six-year-old Don Jorge, the Estrada patriarch, was finally granted from Governor Manuel Micheltorena his elusive California land grant."

Jose joked. "Did he win Canada de los Osos like your grandfather, in a game of chance?"

"As you will discover, nothing that romantic ever happened to poor Jorge… as if he had an aversion to happiness. Good luck evaded him like he carried the plague. In fact, as the story goes, his was a life of trial, horrible timing, and, eventually, total loss.

"Two years after receiving the land grant, Jorge settled all his business affairs in Mexico. For his interest in the Cabrera bull enterprise, jointly founded in 1829 with my grandfather, he accepted an offer tendered by Don Joaquin.

"The settlement made both former partners very happy and provided Jorge the funds he needed to transport his entire family to their new California home.

"The Estradas were very excited to leave Mexico and begin a new life at Rancho Canada de los Osos, located a four-hour ride southwest of Rancho Piedra Blanca. Rekindling their lifelong friendship, the old cohorts, Jorge and Alphonse, would reunite again as neighbors.

"Now, please remember my father Joaquin and Jose de Jesus Estrada, Jorge's boy, were raised together in Mexico from birth and, like their fathers, were very close friends as well.

"As history records, in accordance with long-standing tradition and persistent prodding of their mothers, Joaquin and Jose de Jesus promised, under traditional dowry arrangements, their firstborn son and daughter would marry, joining the two families together forever.

"They could not know this innocent pledge, promised in love, would bring devastation on both families.

"On September thirteenth, 1846, thirty-four days after setting sail from Vera Cruz, the Estradas docked in Monterey. Their voyage proved uneventful and they continued on to Mission San Miguel where Franciscan hospitality and Padre Fray Tomas awaited them.

"Don Jorge's penchant for bad timing cast a black cloud on their future. Settling in the wilds of Central California brought many trials to the newly arrived family, and they discovered fear and uncertainty were the only neighbors welcoming them to their new home.

"You see, that very week, white settlers, riled to action by Major John C. Fremont, stormed the great Sonoma rancho of General Mariano Guadalupe Vallejo. Flying the Bear Flag in Vallejo's courtyard, they claimed California's independence, declaring it a republic and freed from Mexico's authority.

"General Vallejo, a well-known advocate for California's independence, nevertheless was brutally mistreated and his family temporarily imprisoned. But the Bear Flag Revolt proved unnecessary. Unknown to the Fremont's renegades, the United States had declared war on Mexico two months earlier.

"Though this uproar proved nothing and peace temporarily returned, the Estradas, like other rancho families, lived under constant threat of invasion.

"Three years later the family's destiny turned bad with a vengeance. The United States victory forced Don Jorge and his wife to return immediately to Mexico to settle threatening unfinished business. They hurriedly booked passage to Acapulco from Monterey. Until they returned, management of the Canada de los Osos was entrusted to Jose de Jesus, the Estradas' eldest son and my father's childhood friend.

"Fortunately, the urgent matters were quickly concluded. But on the return voyage, Jorge's bad luck struck once again. When American tall ship *Mariana* ironically Jorge's wife's namesake, sank in a storm off the coast of Mazatlan, they both drowned, never to be found.

"And that, my noble listeners, is how Don Joaquin's friend came to inherit luckless Rancho Canada de los Osos to become Don Jose de Jesus Estrada."

Conchita crossed herself. "What a sad story...wars and bloodshed, revolts and shipwrecks. Senor Pablo, you are right. All their luck was bad."

"Poor Jorge! Poor Mariana! They would have been better off staying in Mexico and forgetting about the land grant. Their rancho brought them nothing but heartache. Unfortunately, my sad friend, the story does not end there. In 1853, Jose de Jesus Estrada married Isabel Zaviera. Over the years the family grew and his bride blessed him with three sons—Pedro, Carlos, and Enrique. Then, at long last, a much-desired daughter arrived. The joyous parents, deliriously happy, christened her Annabella Concepción Trinidad Gabriela Estrada.

"'Our mistress, Annabella?'" Rosa asked.

"The very same," Pablo simpered. "The very same.

"The families de Leon and Estrada, from the moment of her birth, have suffered unspeakable agony."

Looking beyond his friends' loving faces, his eyes darkened as he stared into a tortured past.

Frightening his mild-mannered listeners out of their seats, as if tormented, his face contorted and he screamed, crashing his hand down on the table.

No one spoke. No one dared. No one knew what to say.

"Senor Pablo, are you all right?" Rosa asked at last.

When he did not respond, she lifted his chin and looked into his faraway eyes.

"Manuel, hurry. Bring him some water. Conchita...Conchita…a cool cloth for his head. Jose, help me lay the old man on my bed."

Jaime broke the silence, blurting, "Should I go for the doctor?"

But Pablo stopped him with a raised hand. "No…no. Please, give me a moment…let me catch my breath…I will be all right…I will be all right."

"Give him his time," Jose whispered to his son.

THE RAINS CAME AGAIN AND THE OLD SHEPHERD SLEPT. Muttering to each other, the listeners huddled around a kitchen table Rosa piled with oranges and nuts.

"What happened?" Conchita asked. "He was fine, happy, telling his story, but when he spoke Annabella's name, he grew agitated, almost frantic."

"Thinking back to a childhood Christmas Eve," Jose said, "I think a story my Aunt Catalina told explains all of this."

With his face aglow and eyes sparkling, Jose shared with his fellows a long-forgotten story. For the next few hours, Jose settled into the storyteller's armchair and told his tale.

"Every year on the Eve of Christmas, when I was just about Juanito's age, my aged uncle and aunt walked from the rancho village of San Francisco to be overnight guests at my parents' home in San Xavier.

"Excited for Christmas morning to come, my sister Madeline and I were put to bed early after dinner. The old folks renewed their annual tradition in our little home around the fire with their coffees and desserts, late into the night, sharing favorite stories and making up new ones.

"Sometimes, I would wake up to their voices. And when I couldn't fall back to sleep, I sat listening to my father and mother laugh at my Uncle Sergio's vaquero and farmhand stories of the grand casa where he worked. A very tall and dignified man, he served as Don Joaquin's personal valet in Hacienda de Leon until he retired in his late sixties.

"He married my chubby Aunt Catalina, a former chambermaid at Canada de los Osos, who came to Hacienda de Leon when Annabella married Senor Vincenti. All the forty years of their married life, my uncle and aunt worked together for the de Leons.

"I remember now. For such a formal man, Uncle Sergio's stories were the funniest. But it was Aunt Catalina's tales of hacienda life that held everyone's attention, especially the spicy accounts of Mistress Annabella. Mama asked Catalina how Annabella came to be a de Leon." Jose chuckled remembering his Auntie's response. "Well…Auntie just rolled her eyes in disgust and spat on the kitchen floor. Sharing her sorrow for Isabel, Annabella's poor mother, Auntie told my parents the sad story.

"She said to Isabel Estrada's short-lived joy, the she-devil she delivered on her bed at Hacienda Canada de los Osos came into this world to cause as much pain as possible.

"According to Auntie, it all started April twenty-second, 1864, the day Annabella was born. You see, that day the Estradas promised her in marriage to Vincenti Emilio Barrazo de Leon, the one-year-old son of their good friends, Don Joaquin and Dolores de Leon. This fulfilled the nuptial pledge the Estradas made with the de Leons many years before.

"Three months after Annabella was born, the de Leons received a letter from the Estradas announcing the birth of their daughter and pledging a generous dowry. The de Leons accepted it with joy, sealing the promise that their son Vincenti would marry Annabella before her eighteenth birthday.

"Then Aunt Catalina started to howl. Slapping her husband on the back, she mocked. 'As Annabella took her first breath, Vincenti, her promised husband, suckled at his mother's breast thousands of miles away. Vincenti was fortunate seventeen years would pass before he had to meet his betrothed.'

"At seven years old, Annabella first became aware of the nuptial pledge. With each year that passed, the significance of the marriage arrangement crystallized more and more. By her tenth birthday, her childish acceptance turned to a shy reluctance. At thirteen, the shy reluctance revolted and she wanted to scuttle the wedding completely.

"As she grew into a beautiful young woman, her resentment grew until the very name 'Vincenti' turned sour in her mouth.

"She hated him before they ever met. Though the rancho life taught her many things, asserting self-reliance was most important. To her parents' despair, she remained strong-willed and determined to be her own person.

"She departed from genteel hacienda life too soon. Abandoning the dress and donning vaquero chaps, she refused the senorita's proper side saddle and, against her poor suffering mother's wishes, dared to ride a horse like a man, with her leg over the saddle.

"Soon her brothers, expert horsemen, were no match for her. By fourteen, she outrode and outworked them, herding, branding, and winning at the summer competitions.

"Making her mark at the Rancho Santa Margarita summer games, she earned a reputation as an expert rider and roper. Although her mother condemned her unladylike behavior, her father secretly delighted in her cowboy skills.

"Defiantly independent, she grew wily and wild flaunting the vaquero life while her parents paid the bill. Cursing traditions, she publicly refused her arranged engagement to Vincenti de Leon.

"Over the years, accompanying her father and brothers on the many trips to Monterey and San Francisco, her eyes opened to the modern era.

"As kindred souls are so often introduced by chance, with her seventeenth birthday approaching, she traveled alone to meet her father on the long coach ride from San Luis Obispo to Monterey.

"On that dusty road trip, Annabella spent many hours absorbing the gospel of wickedness according to her infamous fellow passenger, Madam Margarita, herself.

"Her chance meeting with Margarita Sanchez, the madam of Monterey's brothel, La Ida Café, pushed her all the more to break with the old ties and live her life in rebellion. The young Annabella delighted in learning all she could from this corrupted woman.

"Thanks to her brothers, Annabella was intimately aware of Madam Margarita's notorious credentials. Feigning sleep in coach rides back from Monterey to Canada de los Osos, she listened intently to her brothers sharing sordid details of their visits to Madam Margarita and La Ida Café.

"Annabella felt a strong bond and kinship with the madam, admiring and respecting her for the power and dominion she held over those working for her and the men who made her rich.

"That fateful day on the bumpy road to Monterey, Madam Margarita and Annabella formed a lifelong union. To the madam, every question Annabella asked was the same—how could she break with tradition and live as she wished?

"Then my mother raised her hand and stopped Catalina with a burning question: 'Catalina, how did you come to know all these secrets?'

"Catalina replied, 'By Annabella's own hand!'

"Reading from Annabella's faithfully kept diary, Auntie said she came to know much, much more. My nosy aunt swore she could recite Madam Margarita's advice word for word.

"Her answer delighted my parents, but a mortified Uncle Sergio pointed an accusing finger at his wife. Indignant yet dignified, he bellowed at Auntie, 'To this day, why do you not regret your guilt for reading that young girl's private words?'"

The listeners leaned forward as Jose, letting them stew in suspense, waited for just the right moment to share what Aunt Catalina said in return.

"'Sit back down and shut up, Sergio. Do not play the innocent with me or these fine people. You read it too, so before your nose starts to bleed, please come down from that high horse. Besides, for everyone's good, it would have been best for all to know well in advance what that little tart was up to.'

"Mother pleaded, 'OK, Catalina, you have gone this far. What was the whore's advice? What did she say to Annabella?'

"Like an actress playing a part, Aunt Catalina, making faces, gesturing, and acting on a make-believe stage, repeated from memory all of the madam's words.

"'Life is for the taking, Senorita Annabella. You must never allow anyone, let alone a mere man, to stand in your way. Most important is achieving that which you desire. Be ready and willing to do whatever must be done, be it good or bad, to accomplish your goals. Only you stand between your desire and your reality

"'If you were only to study the success of wealthy and powerful men, you would see that they have all followed this same path. They carved the path to freedom, wealth, and power, that if the right woman were to follow, she would quickly swallow up those men like so many candies. History is filled with victories of women over men.'

"As the first act ended, my Auntie, like a triumphant actress, bowed to her audience's applause.

"Staring triumphantly into her husband's eyes, she laughed raising the curtain on Act Two.

"Never leaving Sergio's sneering face, Auntie Catalina took up the role of Madam Margarita once again.

"'My child, if you have not already discovered, and I am sure very soon you will, men are weak. They beg to be manipulated.'

"Then my aunt moved to my uncle's good ear, shouting, 'My advice? Oblige them.'

"Nose to nose with her husband, the great actress Senora Catalina finished her lines and played out Act Three with these words.

"'Lead them by the nose right to what it is you want. Men are no match for the right women.'

"It seemed from the moment Annabella and Madam Margarita met, Annabella began devising her god-forsaken plans for power, wealth, and complete freedom from men and the old family ways.

"And the history of Piedra Blanca is the primary witness to the wide swath of dead bodies, curses, witchcraft, and corruption that can be laid at her doorstep, beginning with her marriage to her lover's brother.

"Struggling not to laugh, my mother apologized to Sergio for her irreverent giggling.

"But my father, my father I remember, he was truly shaken with this talk of brothers. Afraid to hear the answer he halfheartedly asked, 'These brothers…who are they?'

"Before Aunt Catalina could answer, Uncle Sergio cleared his throat and, with the voice of God, he said. 'They are Don Joaquin's sons, Vincenti and Pablo! The cuckold bridegroom, Vincenti, and Annabella's lover—Pablo!'

With that revelation, those listening to Jose went dead silent. Nodding toward the sleeping old man, Jose said, "Yes, the very same."

THE NIGHT PASSED SLOWLY FOR ROSA AND MANUEL, relegated to sleeping on the sun porch. They awoke often, taking turns to check on Pablo who slept fitfully on their bed.

The morning sun peering into the window prodded Pablo to cry out in his dream, "My brother, my brother!" Ashen-faced and hair-tousled, he walked quietly past his sleeping hosts, exiting the home for the outhouse. When he returned, Rosa's coffee brewed and Manuel squeezed oranges at the kitchen sink.

"Good morning, Senor Pablo. We hope you like fresh orange juice."

Self-conscious, regretting the commotion he caused the night before, Pablo tendered a timid, "Buenos dias, my loves.

"Please…I am so sorry for the drama," he apologized. "I have taken your bed and embarrassed you in front of your wonderful friends."

"No, not at all, senor…no need for apologies," Rosa assured. "Our concern is not for ourselves, nor for our friends.

"Manuel and I are most concerned for you and your health. After a good sleep, we pray you are better. We want nothing more than for you to continue being our guest for as long as you like."

Pablo began to cry.

"Such kindness and consideration I can never repay. I never intended to burden you with my sorrow. It is mine to bear alone."

Manuel bristled. "Nonsense, Senor Pablo. As a witness to the Patron's death, we all live in sorrow."

Rosa poured the coffee, filling Pablo's cup first, then her husband's.

"We are a family, senor. Your pain is our pain. We share in the joy; we share in the sorrow."

WITH THE PRIEST'S FINAL BENEDICTION, "GO IN PEACE and serve the Lord," the Sunday Mass at Mission San Miguel ended.

Through Morro Bay's shantytown toward his Cambria home, Manuel drove the tired truck slowly and deliberately on the foggy and wet coastal road. He and Rosa flanked the old man sitting between them on the flatbed's bench seat. Fingering his rosary, bead by bead, Pablo prayed his silent Hail Marys.

Breaking the cab's silence, Rosa dared to ask the questions searing her tongue from the night before.

"Senor Pablo, while you slept last evening, Jose entertained us. He shared a story he overheard as a child from his Aunt Catalina and Uncle Sergio. Do you remember them?"

Pablo smiled broadly, nodding with enthusiasm. "Oh yes. Chico and Cat were part of the hacienda household. I can still hear Catalina's constant arguing with Sergio over everything. And poor Chico never won. Not once can I think of a time he bested her. It was an amusing story, no?"

"On the contrary, Senor Pablo. It was a very sad tragedy of two brothers who loved each other very much and a woman who destroyed their lives."

Pablo began to cry again.

CHAPTER 15

Trailing North to Mission San Miguel

───※───

T he juvenile bull killed the Guernsey calf, and farmer frugality went into motion. With God's blessing, the haphazard death afforded Rosa a rare opportunity.

"I found the animal last night," Manuel said. "So today, my wonderful Rosa, sad for the loss but thankful for the gift, prepared for us her famous veal and noodle dish."

Rosa smiled. "That's right! Otherwise, the little cow would be mooing for its mother's milk…and all you gluttons would have frijoles to eat."

Amid nut-and-fruit bowls, the praise subsided and the group gathered in the usual places, ready for storytelling.

For listeners to bear witness, Pablo held up his journal— indeed, the very same keepsake given by Mama Dolores. He opened it to the page entitled "Brothers Traveling North" and resumed the telling.

"As you can see, my writing is in excellent hand, telling all the stories we shared along the way. I pray the record of this day brings to life the long journey Vincenti and I traveled from Rancho de Leon in Mexico to Rancho Piedra Blanca.

"It is written to honor Mama Dolores's request for me to record our journey's events, so she and Don Joaquin could relive our many adventures.

"You will discover, as our parents did, my many curious notations of Vincenti's growing apprehension and fear as time approached to meeting Annabella.

"Since his intimacy with females was limited to two chaperoned church gatherings, any of his experience with the senoritas, you see, had yet to happen."

Pablo smiled, looking back on his youth, drawing on his ever-present pipe.

"I, on the other hand, rode often into the villages of my boyhood to visit my many 'sisters'—daughters to the mothers who nursed me as their own. Thanks to their care and generosity, they taught me many things about women another man would not learn in a lifetime. And because they loved me so much, I became much more than a brother to them all.

"But my poor brother Vincenti asked me over and over again on our long ride, 'Pablo, what should I say to her? I do not know the words. I have none of your confidence. What do I do?'

"I reassured him that when the time came, the right words would pour from his mouth.

"I did caution him, however. With women you must always act like a man. Real women will never respect a mere boy. Bolstering him, I painted a picture of how it was done.

"Be like a bull, Vincenti. Be strong, courageous, without fear. Think of yourself as a great red Cabrera bull, standing high on top of a hill, gazing in the meadows below. You see a beautiful heifer. She is tempting. You desire her. Slowly, you stroll toward her and she lingers, waiting for you…and you whisper in her ear.

"'And…and?' Vincenti begged.

"And I would answer…'She is yours, of course. My little brother, that is how it is done.'"

"'But Pablo, what do I whisper in her ear?'

"Disgusted, I would spur my horse and ride away."

Manuel smiled at Rosa, raising his eyebrows toward their bedroom. The look of disgust on her face quickly turned to a playful grin, promising Manuel he was on to something.

"Like a noose tightening around his neck, with the passing of each mile bringing him closer to the day he would meet his bride, anxiety choked my poor brother.

"Without confidence and experience, he relied unreservedly on gifts he carried as his only hope to impress Annabella.

"With her seventeenth birthday less than a month away, Vincenti prayed the gold earrings he kept for good luck in his vest pocket would speak for him in thunderous ways. Exquisitely crafted, the earrings matched perfectly the locket he planned to present to her at the wedding altar.

"Through the last two centuries, de Leon tradition passed the prophetic wedding locket on to its newest bride. It possessed a secret revealed only if a de Leon wife's death preceded her husband's."

Conchita interrupted. "Senor Pablo. In all those years of so many marriages, has no de Leon discovered the locket's secret?"

Pablo set the journal down and reached for a freshly peeled orange.

"Conchita, there is much proof of toil and blood every de Leon husband had at one time or another, attempting to learn the locket's secret. None were successful, and every one of those husbands died before his wife's death. Preceding Annabella, twelve de Leon brides, including Mama Dolores, took possession of the locket at the wedding altar. Every one of them lived to pass the locket on to the next bride.

"I would often tell Vincenti that I prayed for his sake and mine that Annabella would never come to know the locket's secret. If she did, that would mean there were no brides left to inherit the locket, and the brother who tortured me would be too dead to ask any more questions."

The irony did not escape the listeners.

"To this very day, the secret of the locket remains an enigma in Annabella's possession. As the thirteenth and last bride to join the de Leon family, the secret dies with her."

When Jose returned from his hurried outhouse visit, Pablo took up the story of the de Leon brothers' long trek from Mexico to Mission San Miguel.

<hr />

"Seven years after Alphonse de Leon died, Vincenti and I, at the age of eighteen, trailed on horseback north from Mexico City to Central California, to begin our tenure at Rancho Piedra Blanca.

"Blessed with good weather, the mild winter allowed us to ride into the courtyard of Mission San Miguel in mid-June 1881, two weeks earlier than planned. A young boy greeted us at the presidio entry.

"'Senor, welcome to the mission. From where have you ridden?'

"I dismounted, tying my horse at the water trough. Vincenti followed Don Joaquin's instructions, seeking Friar Fray Tomas Sepulveda first, the recipient of the introduction letters our father posted months before our departure from Rancho de Leon.

"'We are from very far away. Now, run to Friar Sepulveda and inform him that Vincenti de Leon and his brother Pablo seek his hospitality.'"

"'Hurry, *niño*,' Vincenti shouted after him. 'We are tired and very hungry.'

"I can still smell the masa harina baking in the nearby hearth. The delicious aroma filled the courtyard, whetting our famished appetites.

"At the base of the quiet grinding mill, several squaws, gossiping about the just-arrived strangers, squatted in a circle, stripping corn husks into a large straw basket.

"The noon sun burned hot and sticky, and the winds from the southwest that rode with us from Santa Maria stoked the humid breeze. I watched our horses splashing the trough water and dreamed of taking a long soothing bath. And I started to say as much to Vincenti when he growled.

"'Pablo, it is midday and we haven't eaten anything but a bite of jerky all day, and you are thinking about a bath and cleaning the outside of your smelly body. The last two weeks, the jerky we had left to eat made me sick. I pray the Franciscans feed us soon, or I will be forced to raid the courtyard ovens and feast on the masa.'

"Then the noon Angelus rang out, and children of every age came running out of the sacristy of the adobe church followed by a tall, skinny priest who walked briskly toward the orange orchard after them.

"Noticing us watering the horses, he stopped and greeted us with a voice that resonated from deep within his slender frame. 'Welcome to Mission San Miguel.'

"Every syllable he uttered, every sound he made, I swear emerged from a bottomless well. 'Buenos dias, amigos. I am Friar Philippe. Has Friar Sepulveda been informed that you are here?'

"'Please excuse us, padre,' Vincenti begged. 'Our father is Don Joaquin de Leon. I am Vincenti de Leon, and this is my brother, Pablo. We have ridden from Mexico City these last six months to take up residence on our family rancho, Piedra Blanca. We believe the good Friar Sepulveda has been expecting us for several months.'

"Vincenti pointed in the direction of the little boy and said, 'A *niño* has run to let the friar know we are here.'

"Anticipating the magnificent basso profundity of his voice, I asked, 'Are you a teacher of the children?'

"He laughed. 'On the contrary, gentlemen. They are teaching me. Can you not feel their joy? The good Lord, Himself dances in their souls.'

"For a moment, he watched the kids at play, then prayed, 'Why can we not remain children like them? I am afraid it is much too difficult to be a man.'

"In the deepest octave, singing the Angus Dei, he bowed and hurried off to join the children.

"'Pablo, we have just heard singing, the Angel of God. In all my days, I do not think I will ever be so close to heaven as I am right now.'

"That is when Friar Fray Tomas Sepulveda joined us.

"'Yes, every day we praise the Lord for Friar Philippe's magnificent instrument. The friars of San Miguel believe his voice is the eternal bass long-awaited by heaven's choir.'

"Forty years before Vincenti and I arrived, Padre Fray Tomas met a younger version of our grandfather. And like his grandsons, Alphonse de Leon surely welcomed the fabled hospitality of the Franciscan fathers historically bestowed on travelers of the El Camino Real.

"'Since your father's letter arrived, the mission has awaited the day his sons would ride into our presidio. I pray your journey has been rewarding.'

"Vincenti exclaimed, 'The trail was kind, but we are bursting with excitement to see Piedra Blanca.'

"'As your grandfather did before you, I am sure you will delight in the rancho's magnificence. But come now, and please join the other friars at our midday meal. You must be starving. Miguel will care for the animals. After you rest, there will be time enough to ask questions and discuss many things.'

"The young boy Miguel, who first greeted us, took the reins and led our horses to the mission stables.

"Anticipating home cooking and the coolness of the adobe walls, we walked toward the priory until the friar, drawing pictures from his memory, stopped to study me.

"'Yes...yes. You are taller than your grandfather Alphonse. But it is easy to see that you are a de Leon. Take off your hat. Let me look at you more closely.'

"Embarrassed for the old priest, I immediately bowed in respect and whispered to the friar.

"'I beg your indulgences, padre, but your sentiments surely are intended for my brother Vincenti. He has the de Leon blood coursing through his veins. I am just the adopted orphan.'

"The friar's face flushed a burning red.

"'Please excuse an old man,' he pleaded. 'My eyes are constantly betraying me.' He laughed at himself. 'It is good the mind can still admit the mistake.'

"Pointing to each of us in turn, he righted the ship.

"'Please forgive your priest. You are Vincenti...and you are Pablo. I am sure I will get that right.'

"Then he turned and led us silently to the dining room. Seated among priests and brothers, I tried to soothe a seething Vincenti. Making a joke, I laughed, and said, 'Do not take offense with the old man. After all, our parents said we might as well be twins.'

"But still, Vincenti fumed. The meal was filling. The soup, bread, some wine, and cheese accompanying the fried chicken and spinach was a gift from the Lord and so very welcomed after days and days of hardtack and jerky.

"After lunch, we rested in priory guest rooms.

"Friar Tomas hurried to his office to read again Don Joaquin's letter sent almost a year before. But reading them again and again, his confusion only deepened."

"THE EVENING TURNED COOL AND DAMP, YET A FULL moon, shining brightly through the friar's window, reflected blurred images on a stained-glass canister resting on the pedestal next to his desk.

"Waiting for the padre's return from vespers, we sat in his office overlooking the courtyard. I toyed with an ancient relic labeled Saint Peter's shinbone that laid naked on an ornate table covered with maps. The bone acted as a paperweight, and I quickly returned it to its proper place at the sound of Vincenti's irritation.

"'Why are we here listening to this old man? He knows nothing that can help us. He is not even aware who I am…I mean, who we are.

"'I love you brother, but all this talk about you and my grandfather and the resemblance…' 'I know, I know,' I said, trying to cut him off. 'It is annoying. But his misspoken word is not what is bothering you, Vincenti. Tomorrow, for the very first time, you meet Annabella. You are flustered and nervous. What you are feeling is not anger for a careless old man.'

"Pushing himself up by the armrests, Vincenti jumped from his chair, his face a bright red. His pacing reminded me of a bull about to charge.

"'Take it easy, amigo; you are going to burst.'

"'It is easy for you to say, Pablo. It is not you who is pledged in this stupid marriage. I have never met this girl, and everyone expects me to be the perfect gentleman. I'd rather be riding a wild stallion than meeting her. What if she doesn't like me? What if I don't like her?'

"Then the crimson of his face paled to yellow. I tried to console him, saying that at a time that should be filled with great joy, he was making this a very uncomfortable situation.

"'Is it not wonderful to know what lies ahead in one's life, to have it before you like a brilliant map showing you where to find the treasures? I, for one, am very envious that your life is so well planned by parents who love you very much and want only the best for you. My brother, you possess a great gift.'

"Still, vexation continued. Seeing him in such distress, I made Vincenti an offer that would haunt me for the rest of my life.

"'If it would ease your mind, let me help you tomorrow. Maybe it would be best if I met Annabella first. You know…bearing a formal invitation from you to meet for the first time…setting the place and time. That will put you in control and show her you are a very decisive yet considerate man.'

"'She doesn't have any idea you are here yet, so I can smooth out the trail for you, so to speak, and give her an opportunity to ready herself. Who knows? Perhaps she feels the same way you do. Remember, you know nothing at all about Annabella, and she knows very little about you.'

"'You would do that for me?' Vincenti chimed. 'Oh, Pablo you would meet her, and talk to her, and do these things for me?'

"'Listen, little brother, this is nothing. We have traveled very far and done many things from our boyhood times to the long journey just completed. This is just a little thing. I do this to show my gratitude for all you have done for me.'

"Finally, his anger was gone. The meeting that followed with Friar Fray Tomas went well. And we all agreed that I would carry the introductory invitation to Annabella at Rancho Canada de los Osos the next morning.

"Their first meeting would be an intimate dinner hosted by Friar Sepulveda at the presidio one week later, inviting Annabella, her parents, and brothers to join the groom-to-be and me.

"When the meeting ended, the friar hurried back to his quarters. He kept to himself the disappointing news Vincenti and I would come to know soon enough about Annabella."

CHAPTER 16

Meeting the Three Estrada Brothers

⌁

The sun warmed Pablo's back, but the chill from the great ocean reminded him he was wise to carry his poncho that morning.

"Feeling his morning oats, my horse snorted a breath of brisk salted air and the stout winds chafed my cheeks, but I felt free for the first time since leaving Mexico. My spirits were buoyed, and I was glad to be a good brother tendering reprieve for brother Vincenti, smoothing the path to his bride-to-be. From the highest ridge the panorama that was Rancho Canada de los Osos sparkled like a brilliant gem in the morning sun. For a long time resting on my horse I watched quietly the western hills turn to gold as the sun's artistry paint shadowed flourishes on the scenic canvas that were barns, outbuildings and orchards. To the west, bordering the sleepy hacienda, creeks meandered into a funnel-shaped pond. To the east, cattle grazed the lush rolling hills. North and south, vineyards, orchards, fields, and groves speckled the landscape. Guarded by towering redwoods, a long road that cut through crop fields ran out to the south ending at the cobblestoned courtyard of Hacienda Estrada that nestled in the protective windbreak of a giant eucalyptus grove.

"The absolute magnificence of Canada de los Osos frightened and also encouraged me and I prayed Piedra Blanca could possess only half the potential and promise that lay before me.

"Leaving the ridge I bypassed many outbuildings and village homes that dotted the hills south of the orange orchards.

"Riding toward the hacienda, I leaned back in the saddle to soak up the sunshine and drink in the intoxicating orange blossoms that filled the morning air. The relaxing rhythm of my chestnut's footfalls lulled me into a hazy daydream of father Don Joaquin sharing with his sons the dream for Rancho Piedra Blanca.

"'Piedra Blanca is yours, my sons. It belongs to you. My function will be strictly advisory. But, when needed, I will not hesitate to exert my political influence and call on all my resources.

"'Vincenti will succeed me in all business affairs including banking and trade. He will be learning at my side day by day and replace me as Piedra Blanca's next don.

"'Pablo, you will be entrusted to Rodrigo and assume all the responsibility for livestock and farming production. As Vincenti's chief advisor, you will share equally in all profits and decisions.

"'From the rancho's beginnings and since his father's death, Rodrigo, following in Fredrico's footsteps, will retain his position as majordomo, overseeing all rancho operations.

"'When our Mexico holdings are sold, Mama and I will leave Mexico to make Rancho Piedra Blanca our new home.'

"Then in my daydream, Grandfather Alphonse de Leon appeared speaking to Fredrico Montoya.

"'Until my return from Mexico City, I am content to leave the rancho in your hands, Fredrico, like it is your own child. You have done magical things with Piedra Blanca.

You have always had my full confidence and respect. I am honored you are part of the de Leon family.'

"Passed down through time, the stories of Fredrico Montoya's genius flooded back. As Alphonse extolled Montoya's incalculable contributions, I prayed Don Joaquin would see fit someday to commend me in the same way. It occurred to me if Rodrigo possessed only half his father's talent through his mentoring, my hard work and dedication would repay the de Leon family for all their love and kindness.

"Desperate voices screaming, *'Hombre...Hombre!'* wrenched me out of my musing in time to avoid trampling a line of farmhands crossing the road.

"All I could say was, 'Buenos dias.'

"Walking single file into a field shed at the side of the road, the five workers said nothing. With a sign of hospitality, the last man in line turned back and, with pickax in hand, gestured 'thanks,' then quietly shut the door behind him.

"The road to the hacienda gave up its gradual decline, leveling out at a crossroad marked with the signpost *'Annabella Way.'* Another arrow pointed south, climbed a hill, and dipped into a valley out of sight. The marker *'El Camino Estrada,'* pointed west, directly at the hacienda.

"Studying the signpost, I noticed blooming dust clouds mushrooming in the north. Three charging vaqueros raced toward me, waving and shouting for me to stop.

"The first rider, a very big man, steered his gigantic horse to my left. The brim of his hat was so large it blotted out the sun. His chaps were so enormous that, if pieced together, there was leather enough for two vaqueros.

"Before his horse stopped, rider two—small, sinewy, and decisive—jumped to the ground, grabbing the halter, securing my reins, and smiling a toothless grin.

"To my right, grabbing the saddle horn for balance, the last rider reined in. When he leaned back to throw his right leg over his horse's neck, his sombrero fell till the tie sting stopped it in the middle of his back. His boots were magnificent; I had never seen the like.

"Smiles appeared on all their faces. 'Welcome, amigo, to Rancho Canada de los Osos. Please allow us to offer you the hospitality of our father, Don Jose de Jesus Estrada. I am Pedro Estrada, and these ugly things are my brothers, Carlos and Enrique.

"'Carlos, as you can see, is here for protection. Enrique sees that things move quickly. I am the eldest. I am here to do the deciding.'

"With a simper, he mumbled, 'And too soon you will meet Annabella.'

"'Gracias, gracias. I am pleased to meet you. I am your humble servant, Pablo Cabrera Barrazo de Leon, son of Don Joaquin de Leon. I count the days until I can return your hospitality at our new home, Rancho Piedra Blanca.'

"Bravely, I ventured on.

"'We have traveled these many months from Mexico City for just this day. I am here as an emissary of the de Leon family to offer a formal introduction to your sister, the beautiful Annabella, to my brother Vincenti de Leon, her betrothed.

"When I finished, the brothers stared at one another and began laughing in absolute hysterics. Throwing their heads back, they laughed and laughed and laughed…loudly, raucously, and uncontrolled.

"Enrique rolled in the dirt, Carlos wiped the tears from his face, and Pedro…Pedro could not stop howling. Slapping his knee, he jumped off his mount, bending low, laughing louder, and wheezing more like a horse than his horse.

"I just stared after them, dumbfounded and wondering…are these men loco? The joke was on me, but what was the joke?

"When the laughing played out, Pedro could only say 'You do not know what you are getting into.'

"Struggling to restrain himself, trying diligently to regain some dignity, he smiled, asking more for his edification than mine. 'Senor Pablo, you do not have any idea what I mean, do you?' And their laughter erupted anew.

"Carlos hoisted his tiny brother onto his horse. Unfortunately, Enrique sat defenseless on the horse's neck on the wrong side of the horn. Despite the sharp jabs endured from the gigantic saddle horn with each of Carlos's hugs, Enrique's giggling never stopped.

"However, at the courtyard entry, all laughter ceased. Still mounted, his brothers and I remained at the gate while Pedro entered the hacienda alone.

"Confiding that our meeting had gotten out of hand, Pedro told his father who I was and why I had come.

"Several minutes went by before a short man, immaculately groomed, walked hurriedly through the courtyard to the three of us mounted outside the huge entry gate.

"'Senor de Leon, welcome to Hacienda Estrada and Rancho Canada de los Osos. I am Don Jose de Jesus Estrada. Please forgive my sons' horrendous manners.

"'Not possessing the gift of hospitality, they are ignorant of the genteel ways. We beg your forgiveness. Please allow us to begin anew by inviting you to enter our home for rest and refreshments.'

"'My dear Senor Estrada, there is nothing to forgive. You have wonderful sons filled with the joys of life, who, like me, enjoy a good laugh from time to time. It was nothing but a good rub. And they were most kind to bring me to your door. I am honored to accept your invitation.'

"Don Jose, the most gracious of hosts, shook my hand vigorously and guided me past huge oak entry doors into an inviting parlor.

"Catalina, the chubby housemaid, waited to take my hat.

"'Please allow me to introduce my wife, Isabel.'

"Extending her hand as I entered, she rose to greet me.

"'Buenos dias, Senor de Leon.'

"I returned the greeting with a bow.

"'Buenos dias, senora. Please accept greetings of affection and salutations from my parents, Don Joaquin and Delores de Leon. How my mother and father spoke of their friendship with you both! She made me promise to tell you how much you are missed.'

"'How kind of you to say. I will be sure to tell you stories of our childhood friendship that has lasted all these years. And how are your parents? Very well, I hope.'

"'It has been almost six months since I have seen them, but at the time of our departure, they were wonderful—full of life, very anxious to join us at Rancho Piedra Blanca. I am delighted to finally meet your family.'

"'May I inquire of Annabella? I am here to offer her an introduction to my brother Vincenti. He requests her company and yours at a dinner next week at Mission San Miguel.'

"Iciness chilled the room.

"'Is she not home?'

"Isabel turned from me, and the smile faded from her face. With obvious contempt, she pointed to her husband and, with biting sarcasm, replied.

"'Ask her father. I am sure he can tell you where she is. Go on, Jose, tell him where he can find Annabella. He is here to see her, so tell him. Go on...tell him.'

"Astounded at the blatant disrespect shown to her husband, I could not conceive of a reason why Isabel would speak to him this way, especially in the presence of a guest.

"After much hesitation, a tentative Don Jose launched into the painful explanation.

"'Senor de Leon, our daughter has, how do you say... broken ranks with the family. As you can see, her mother is very unhappy with her and with me.'

"He stuttered to a stop. Needing fortification, he walked to a cabinet and removed a bottle of tequila and two glasses.

"Except for the clinking of the crystal, it was so quiet in the parlor I was afraid to move. Handing me a glass he filled his first, then mine. Without a preamble or a toast, he immediately poured the liquor down his throat.

"I tried to thank him, but was cut short when, strengthened by the alcohol, he took up his explanation.

"'It is my sad and unfortunate duty to inform you that Annabella has expressed clearly to us her refusal to honor the marriage promise to your brother, Vincenti, and she has no interest in meeting him.'

"He growled. 'She wants none of the old ways, and resents the dowry arrangement we made with your parents when she was born. Annabella prefers the company of vaqueros to her family. She now lives by herself in an outbuilding on the rancho.'

"As you might expect, this disgraceful news came too fast for me to take in.

"Don Jose limped to the window and stared blankly into the courtyard. In a voice filled with regret, he spoke to himself.

"'Oh, had she been born a boy, tradition could be broken without disgrace, but she is a full-grown woman and much too much her own person.'

"He turned to face me and shouted. 'She will not listen to me, her mother, her brothers, or anyone; only herself, and only what she wants and only what she believes. We have tried every way we know to bring her back to the family. Nothing has succeeded. Her defiance cannot be broached. What is worse, her talents support her independence, and she has no need of anything from us.'

"By then, I was collapsed in a chair, and like Senor Estrada, my drink was emptied too.

"'I have dreaded this day for a very long time, Senor de Leon. What could only be worse is telling your parents personally. The Estradas are disgraced, and all that we can do is pray for your family's forgiveness.'

"He breathed a long sigh, refilled our tumblers, weeping bitterly before he swallowed another drop."

CHAPTER 17

Glorious Rancho Piedra Blanca

"The visit ended!" Pablo shouted. "Bad news needed to be shared quickly. Thanking the Estradas for their hospitality. I excused myself, and rode away from Rancho Canada de los Osos. Racing back to the mission, I could not conceive how parental pledges could be reduced to wreckage at the whim of an adolescent girl, but that, in truth, is what had happened.

"Though Vincenti would be relieved, I felt a deep concern for the Estrada family and how my parents would take the news.

"I did not hesitate to tell Vincenti all that I heard and saw at Canada de los Osos.

"A broad smile covered his beaming face. Slowly he raised his arms into the air, and like a man hearing he had been found not guilty, he clenched his fists and broke out into hysterical laughter. It was as if a life sentence to a ball and chain had been commuted.

"No longer trapped by a despised obligation, freedom reigned! Unencumbered by the baggage of a new wife, he could settle into Piedra Blanca his own man.

"I offered my congratulations as he excitedly paced the room.

"'I am very glad for you brother. If a woman pledged to me acted as Annabella, I would be better off hanging myself than taking her on as a bride.

"'Based upon what her father told me, his untamed daughter of the stirrup and lasso possesses no dignity, no shame, nor any respect for her parents' customs or traditions.

"'You would have been miserable, brother. And thank God this has happened, for if you had become her husband, you would have badgered me unmercifully with complaints about that contrary woman.'

"But he paid me no attention at all. He stopped pacing only when a chair I purposely tipped over blocked his path.

"'It is best that all these things are in the open now, well before it went any further, especially before our parents arrive.'

"Not hearing a word I said, Vincenti yelled. 'I want to go to Piedra Blanca tomorrow, Pablo. I don't care that it is Sunday. The hell with Mass, the hell with the friar, and the hell with Annabella and the Estradas.'

"'Leave it to our parents to deal with them in any way they choose. All I want…all I want…is a fresh start at the rancho. We go tomorrow to meet Rodrigo.'

"And just like that, the pallor of his face turned rosy pink. Vincenti's burden vanished.

"Sleep did not come that night. The rooster was still asleep as we crept to the stable. Quietly saddling our horses, we rode toward San Simeon looming in the distance, wispy clouds crowning its peak.

"A massive orange moon hanging low in the morning sky brightly lit our way. The next two hours, bridling our excitement, we said nothing, riding steadily north.

"I do remember praying, 'Please, Mother Mary, may Piedra Blanca equal the splendor I witnessed yesterday from the ridge above Canada de los Osos.'

"As Rancho Piedra Blanca commanded our view, the moon fell below the horizon and the sun rose above the eastern hills.

"What we saw surpassed all expectations.

"The westward sunlight flooded sprawling valleys and the verdant hills. Ancient oak and pungent eucalyptus acting as windbreaks bordered the burgeoning orchards, graceful vineyards, gardens, and groves.

"Hastening many creeks, lakes, and ponds, the brimming marshes fed the reedy wetlands. On hills of green, long-horned cattle grazed everywhere on open range.

"Below the coastal cliffs, the roaring Pacific Ocean seemed a mere afterthought of God's benevolence and generosity.

"When our eyes could not take in another wonder, our ears heard a raucous clamoring emanating from the distant courtyard of the hacienda.

"With California and Mexico flags waving proudly, rancho hands and mariachis sang to us a jubilant Piedra Blanca welcome.

"Hosting our reception, Rodrigo Montoya, our resident majordomo, his wife, Martha, and their four children waved a warm welcome. We were overwhelmed.

"Introductions and hugs concluded, everyone, especially Rodrigo, laughed and laughed when Vincenti could not refrain from expounding on the rancho's marvels.

"Joining our gracious hosts, Vincenti and I sat at the head where everyone dove into the steak-and-eggs breakfast Martha and the trail cooks kept sizzling on the patio grills.

"I wondered how he knew who we were and when we would arrive. Commiserating over T-bones and tortillas, Rodrigo just smiled.

"'Padre Fray Tomas sent word you would be arriving today. It gave us enough time to plan a welcome.'

"But how could he know that?"

"'Pablo, the good padre knows more than you think. Just take my word and never underestimate him. He is a reservoir of history and insight.'

"I could not then know the incredible truth of Rodrigo's assessment of the good padre. If history is the judge, Fray Tomas's advice served me well over the many years that followed.

"With breakfast done and the hands to their jobs, we fledgling newcomers slipped away as quickly as we arrived.

"Vincenti and I spent the next several days drinking in the rancho's diversity much in the same way Alphonse and Fredrico did more than forty years before.

"More than either of us could have ever imagined, Piedra Blanca did not disappoint."

<hr/>

"The next four months passed into deep September, without a whisper of marriages or dowries, when a peace offering mysteriously appeared.

"At the courtyard hitching post, perfect in every way, two incredible stallions, wearing a simple note, stood tall. It read: *Courtesy of Rancho Canada de los Osos: Pinto for Vincenti, Palomino for Pablo.*

"No one witnessed their delivery.

"More than relieved by Annabella's rejection, it took some arm-twisting, but Vincenti finally agreed to accept the gifts as an Estrada apology."

CHAPTER 18

Angels from on High

⸻

"'Autumn has burst into color and our hills can only dream of wintergreen. This year, with the reservoirs so full, God's great blessing renders prayer for winter rain unwarranted.'

"Contrary to his usual terse content, Rodrigo's reports to Don Joaquin heaped high praise on his new wards.

"'I compare your sons to thirsty sponges, sucking every drop from every opportunity. By the time you arrive at Piedra Blanca, Vincenti and Pablo will be well prepared to run the rancho.'"

⸻

"THE OCEAN WINDS BLEW FRIGID THAT EARLY NOVEMBER day. Vincenti mounted his pinto, leaving the hacienda before sunrise. He rode the coast south to San Luis Obispo to meet Daniel Best for a presentation of his innovative steam-powered tractor.

"I, instead, ranged far in the opposite direction. Riding my new palomino gifted to me from the Estradas, I rode north toward El Sur Grande to camp a few days sleeping under the stars.

"To cut losses and add to our herd count, I planned on rounding up the many strays that wandered off into the Grande's lush valleys. On day one alone, I gathered up thirty head, driving them into an improvised corral at my sheltered campsite.

"At sunset I quit for the day, tired and hungry but happy. A campfire dinner of bacon, beans, and hardtack followed.

"Buffering the cold Pacific breeze under a huge rock overhang where I fed the fire and spread my bedroll, I made myself comfortable for the night. The obliging wind cleared the skies to black velvet and the star clusters in the dark canopy glittered brightly. Pointing the way to Arcturus, I smiled at the Big Dipper's defiance of the darkness. Lulled by the lowing cows, the hush drifted me into a slumber abounding with heavenly angels, wings widespread, descending from the night sky.

"Glowing from the firmament with a shimmering light, the seraph's radiance lit the camp. On motionless wings they circled over me, never touching the ground.

"Watched intently by the others, a solitary angel, the most beautiful of all, glided over my bedroll and stared down at me.

"Her black silky hair fell loosely, and a sparkle radiated her face. Gazing into mine, her emerald eyes pierced my heart, setting me on fire. Whispering my name, 'Pablo, Pablo,' her perfect rosebud lips brushed mine, flooding me with passion.

"I struggled to wake up, but her sweet breath tickled my ear, returning me to slumber.

"All through the night, the dream did not end. When daylight came, I fought the impulse to open my eyes, pleading for the dream to linger.

"Closing my eyes, I shook my head. Yet, still, the angel slept soundly under the covers.

"Ruffling the blanket, I raised a purring sigh from the sleepy cherub. Then tanned arms, with angel wings inexplicably absent, stretched from under the bedroll into the sun's light.

"When I attempted to pull back the blanket, her eyes stayed shut but the purring grew louder.

"'Leave the cover!' she scolded. 'It is too cold!' Then, she settled down again, warm and content.

"Her voice had me jumping out of the bedroll.

"'Who are you?'"

"With piercing green eyes looking up at me, she turned slowly onto her back and threw the covers off her naked body.

"'Pablo…Pablo…Pablo. If I make you so uncomfortable, perhaps you should have Vincenti formally introduce us!

"'Now, why don't you come back to bed? It is warmer in here; introductions can come later.'

"'Anyway, had I known you were an available de Leon, I should have not resented the arrangement so much. In fact, I think I would have not resented the arrangement at all!'

"Then the wayward angel, Annabella Estrada, giggled and giggled.

"I had no explanation how she happened, but when she welcomed me back to the bedroll, the erotic dreams returned. And I melted to her temptations, over and over and over again."

THE LISTENERS DID NOT KNOW WHAT TO SAY. RUMORS were rampant, accusing Annabella of many affairs, but no one ever substantiated them.

But now with Pablo's admission, here sat a credible source, verifiable eyewitness, and an active participant.

The old man searched his audience and dared to ask, "Are you too offended for me to continue?"

The assemblage would never be the same again.

What had been a history lesson and pastoral tale turned into a melodrama. Lifelong secrets never shared with parents, never shared with Vincenti—in fact, never shared with anyone—cast Pablo in an unexpected role.

Jaime and Jose looked to Manuel for direction. With a timid acknowledgment, Manuel consulted the women.

"Senor," Rosa said bravely, "what you have told us does not change our friendship or our love for you. In fact, newly married, I remember those days well."

She laughed. "If the truth be told, all of us pray for the confidence and courage, like you, to share the secrets of our youth."

Conchita intimated, with her arm around Pablo. "We are not here to throw stones, senor. If that were true, I, for one, and others who hear me now, would have been stoned to death long ago."

The men and women laughed, sharing indiscretions that broke the tension and encouraged the old man all the more.

"If that is your answer, Rosa, then pour the coffee. Jose, pull down the shades. And Manuel, light the lamps! Once I light this bowl and the smoke rises, be prepared for my next fall from grace."

--------⎯∂≈∂⎯--------

"For the next two days, Annabella and I stayed together in El Sur Grande, learning about one another, discussing many things. Since my visit to her parents at Canada de los Osos, she admitted spying on me.

"Hiding in the mudroom, she heard every word said by her father, mother, and me, especially my request to formally introduce Vincenti.

"She said the days that followed turned to weeks and then months. Though never a word was exchanged between us, she said she came to know me through persistent observation.

"'I knew what time you rose and the hour you turned in. I learned you favored your left leg mounting your horse. That you never drank any more than one glass of tequila. And I saw you sunning yourself on the rocks, swimming naked in your favorite pond.

"'You might say, my handsome friend, I learned many things about you. But what I learned the most was your kindness and loyalty you showed Vincenti.'

"Saying his name made her clench her fists.

"'And I realized Vincenti would always be a problem for me. The two of you were always and forever together. So, I waited for an opportunity to meet with you alone. I felt, for some reason, I owed you an explanation for refusing to marry Vincenti.

"'Yesterday, when Vincenti rode in the opposite directions, I decided it was time to follow you north.'

"'But why are you so interested in me, Annabella? Why was it so important to learn all these things about me? I don't understand.'

"'All my life all I ever heard was Vincenti de Leon. That you existed…that he had a brother, Pablo…that was never mentioned. At first, through you, I wanted to hurt him, but I soon forgot that plan.'

"'Why hurt Vincenti, someone you never even met?'

"'The reason? By now, Pablo, you should know. These days and nights with you have changed everything. What was just curiosity, I am afraid blossomed into something very different. I hoped that it would…and it has. All I can think of now is being with you. Do you not feel the same?'

"I sat thinking of my boyhood days shared with Vincenti, chasing the cattle on Rancho de Leon, watching the great bulls, and how his loving family took in an orphan boy as one of their own. From orphan to brother, my life changed because the de Leons fell in love with me, just as I was falling in love with Annabella.

"'Annabella, all that has happened…it puzzles me. How can it be you and I have lived a lifetime in the last few days? Were we lovers in another life?

"'Perhaps that is why we already knew each other so well. Perhaps that is why you sought me out, coercing you to come to me in the way you did.

"'Or perhaps, this is the only time we ever met and the only time we will ever spend together.'"

"She turned away without a word.

"Nothing was said for a very long time, and I knew if I broke the silence, I would be lost to her forever. With much to say and too weak to resist, I turned to her and saw tears in her green eyes.

"'All my life Annabella was just a name to me…a name that belonged to Vincenti. And because that is so, I never gave you much thought. It is not as if I wondered what you looked like, or the color of your hair, or the way you talked. Now, you come into my life, an angel in a dream, but you are real. And you stand here, a beautiful woman, flesh and blood.

"'In an instant, you turned my life upside down, and I want more, much more of you.'

"'But how is that possible? How can we be together? How can you ever become my wife? How could I do that to my brother? How could I do that to our parents?'

"The questions hung over our heads like a guillotine. No answers, no opinions were offered.

"We gathered more strays. Annabella helped me drive them back as far as San Simeon. In the sweetest sadness, she kissed me goodbye and rode south to her home at Rancho Canada de los Osos."

⚬⚬⚬

Fidgeting in their chairs, the women waited for someone to say something. The uncomfortable quiet hurt everyone's ears until Manuel relieved the tension and himself by racing to the outhouse. "Sometimes the telling makes me happy, but this time it pains my soul. My story for this evening is done. Please, Jaime, will you please drive me home?"

Pablo kissed Rosa on her cheek, and she squeezed his hand in return.

Struggling into the front seat of the two-door Chevy, Pablo said to everyone crowding around the car, "Next time, it is best to come to my hut for the story."

With one taillight broken, the coupe carried the story-teller away.

CHAPTER 19

Pain Sharpens the Blade

⸺⧟⸺

Nervous and crazy, Jose's week of dread dragged on.

On mid-Wednesday morning, he cranked up Pedro Fernandez's ancient Plymouth for a test run and found himself driving to visit Manuel at the floodgate. He felt sick and needed an advance fix on what the old man would say next.

"Amigo, you have driven from your garage, over the hardpan, through the cornfields, to this promontory, all the way to the water switches, to ask me if I know what is in the mind of the shepherd?"

"It is, how you say, a fool's errand.

"When we all meet Friday evening, after we all have heard the storyteller telling his story, I will then be much better informed to let you know what is coming next."

Thirsty, Jose broke out a bottle of wine, and the two friends took turns tipping until the bottle went dry.

"I guess, Friday will come soon enough," Jose said. "In the meantime, is Wednesday morning too early to be drunk?"

⸺⧟⸺

On Friday night, crowding the coastal road, a line of cars filled with families from San Xavier headed to Cambria for the annual carnival. Swearing at the slow drivers and making them late for Pablo's next confession, Jaime in his coupe and Manuel and Rosa in their truck struggled to the top of San Simeon, arriving well past 7:45 p.m. By eight o'clock, all the edgy listeners were finally sitting in the hut's makeshift patio, sipping Pablo's coffee and fighting over the last piece of the raspberry-filled cake Rosa brought to the party.

Conchita's ever-present fruit bowl and an assortment of fine chocolates Jose brought from Andoleto's sat on Pablo's rickety table, which Manuel moved to the patio from inside the hut.

"I am sorry for cutting our last time so short, but I am very grateful you came if only to hear my latest confession. Welcome to my immense patio and tiny home. Pray, everyone, that the weather holds; otherwise, it will be cramped quarters inside. And do not worry...tonight I will not disappoint you."

With the woodstove warming the coffee and the lanterns hanging brightly from the hut's eaves, the old shepherd puffed one last plume, then started the next telling.

"First, you must come to know a bit more about Don Joaquin and Mama Dolores's big push to leave Mexico and make Piedra Blanca their new home.

"After several years, Don Joaquin finally assembled buyers who bought up all the assets the de Leon family held in Mexico.

"Jacinta Maria Candida, owner of Rancho Refugio, a California land grant in Santa Cruz, agreed to the terms, paying handsomely for Rancho de Leon, our longheld home in Mexico.

"Luis Díaz, first cousin of Mexico's president, Porfirio Díaz, won the bid for the coveted Cabrera bull enterprise.

"Selling all remaining de Leon business interests in Mexico freed my parents to reunite with us in California and move permanently to Rancho Piedra Blanca.

"In a beautiful letter, Mama Dolores's every word spoke with joy her life's new beginning at Piedra Blanca.

"'Weather permitting!' she wrote. 'We cannot be sure the day we dock in Monterey. But the best news is that Papa assures me we will arrive in time to celebrate a Piedra Blanca Christmas with you!'

"The best estimate for their ship's arrival was mid-December, give or take seven days.

"Don Jose Boronda, Rodrigo's good friend, welcomed Vincenti and me as his guests to Los Laureles, his rancho bordering Monterey. Its nearness to the harbor provided us with easy access to monitor ship dockings.

"Until the fog lifted in the late morning of December fifteenth, our parents' arrival on the French freighter the *Parisian* remained in question. But as the sun melted the fog away, we screamed with joy seeing our parents waving frantically to us from the ship's railing.

"With rapt attention, Vincenti and I listened as Don Joaquin revisited their exciting passage. Like a roaring whirlwind, the sea stories flooded forth.

"Unexpected, especially by her husband, Mama Dolores shared with us from her daily journal their seafaring memories, which she detailed with excellent illustrations.

"Promised to Mama Dolores long ago, and to our parent's enthusiastic delight, I related exploits Vincenti and I shared dating back to the day we rode away from Rancho de Leon.

"'But did you write them down?' Mama Dolores demanded.

"As you, my listeners can testify, I assured her every word had been faithfully transcribed in this, the very same journal she gave me the day Vincenti and I left for California. We chose not to disclose Annabella's rejection of Vincenti.

No need would be served in spoiling the joyous reunion. Bad news could wait for another day.

"Suffering alone in my guilt, the bad news would come to light soon enough.

"When asked, Vincenti simply said he chose not to begin the courtship until they arrived.

"As the *Parisian* cargo was off-loaded onto teamsters' wagons that lined the wharf, the laughter of a happy reunion carried on and on.

"While the twelve teamster wagons slogged the muddy roads to Piedra Blanca, we adjourned to Los Laureles for an overnight stay.

"The next morning, with a breakfast of steak and eggs a delicious memory, the de Leons hugged and kissed the Borondas farewell, thankful for their gracious hospitality. We boarded the coach and six that would take us home, looking forward to sharing our first California Christmas together.

"Through El Sur Grande from Monterey to the Piedra Blanca, the six-hour coach ride struggled along over the rut-soaked roads. Vincenti, happy for the captive audience, boasted about the glories of the northern rancho. To my mortification, he even related to our beaming parents the results of my recent cattle roundup!

"Patting me on the back, Vincenti bragged, 'Pablo alone gathered up wandering longhorns, adding fifty-seven head to our southern herds.'

"But since Annabella graced my bedroll, a battle waged in my soul. Do I crush my family by surrendering to my desire for Annabella? Or do I give her up and remain the loyal, loving brother and son?

"In truth, my flesh burned for our next time. The thought, the smell, the touch of her filled me with longing every waking minute, hour, and day. To hide the affair, our trysts were set in the remotest places. Each meeting's secrecy flamed our passion all the more. With each parting, blinded with desire, the next time and place were prearranged.

"If a solution existed to our problem, it remained a mystery. In fact, the next rendezvous, three days after my parents settled in, only intensified the urgent resolution to the problem.

"But in God's good time and for His good purpose, the puzzle pieces fit and a final solution settled in."

"ANNABELLA WAITED FOR ME IN THIS VERY HUT.

"Remembering our last time, she peered out the window at the quarter moon anticipating her lover.

"I remember the dress she wore that chilly night. Trimmed in lace and smelling of aloes, its full length concealed the goosebumps on her naked legs. Reserved for special parties and trips to San Francisco, the dress fit tightly about her waist, rising up to expose breasts bubbling out of the deep-cut bodice.

"All was ready, from the glowing candles circling the bedroll to her favorite wine, like me, sweet to her taste. With Christmas less than a week away, the present she intended for me would be shameless pleasure.

"Stumbling badly out of the shadows, my palomino staggered onto the summit of San Simeon. Stopping the horse from falling, I trembled in the saddle for a long time. With agonizing exactness, lest a careless move retrigger more weeping, bit by bit, with minutes passing like hours, at last, I dismounted.

"Prodded by some unseen hand, moving mechanically at a snail's pace and never daring a look toward the hut, I tethered my horse. Like a messenger bearing deadly news, with each step as through a swamp, I waded to the hut.

"Even before a word was spoken, she counted her loss. The lover she expected would not be coming tonight.

"A novice to such pain and despair, the impossibility that was our love stabbed her with a lifelong wound—one she would never allow to heal, one that demanded retribution— a retribution to be dealt for the all the days of her life.

"Like you, my good friends, Annabella was an exceptional listener.

"Riding home, Madam Margarita's wicked counsel spoke loudest to her. A God-fearing woman looks for relief in the gospels or psalms. Annabella took comfort, instead, in the ungodly morality fed to her by her teacher, the wicked prostitute.

"Swallowed up in vengeance, evil contorting her face, she chanted over and over again, 'Pain sharpens the blade! Pain sharpens the blade!'"

CHAPTER 20

And for Vincenti, a Wife, the Beautiful Annabella

—⟊⟊⟊—

"O n Christmas morning, a handsome *carrado*, wearing magnificent boots and bearing an urgent message for Don Joaquin de Leon, galloped into the courtyard of Hacienda Piedra Blanca.

"Martha Montoya, the majordomo's wife, left him waiting in the parlor and entered the dining room to inform Don Joaquin.

"Celebrating the birth of the baby Jesus and the coming new year, the de Leon family, gathered round the table, enjoying Mama Dolores's traditional Christmas breakfast.

"'Don Joaquin, a vaquero has arrived and he waits in the parlor with a message for you.'

"'Today? A messenger today? Who is it, Martha?'

"'He did not introduce himself, but I believe he is one of the Estrada brothers. I remember him from the summer games in Santa Margarita'

"Christmas was about to be ruined!

"The hair on Vincenti's neck stood straight out and my heart pounded in fear that today Annabella's rejection or the disgraceful affair would be exposed.

"Don Joaquin excused himself to meet the messenger in the parlor and we waited in silent terror.

"'*Feliz Navidad*, senor.' He bowed, in greeting. 'Feliz Navidad, Don Joaquin.'

"'Thank you for allowing this intrusion on such a holy day. I am Pedro Estrada. My father is Don Jose de Jesus Estrada of Rancho Canada de los Osos. I am his eldest son.

"'It is with profound respect and affection I offer Christmas greetings from the Estrada family to the family de Leon. I am also instructed by my father to deliver this personal message to you.'

"He handed the surprised Don Joaquin an envelope bearing the waxed seal of the Estrada family.

"Holding his sombrero with both hands over his chest, he stepped back, giving the Don privacy to read the missive.

"Receiving the envelope and recognizing the Estrada seal, Don Joaquin's face beamed.

"'How are your father and mother? We, ourselves, have just recently arrived and have not had the opportunity to send our greetings or come to visit. Is all well?'

"Pedro nodded.

"'Senor, the Estrada family is fine, and we are very happy you have arrived safely from such a long journey. But it is best if you allow my father to speak to you through his message. Then I will be happy to address all of your inquiries.'

"On delicate parchment the exquisitely crafted invitation extended a formal invitation to family de Leon.

"*The Estrada family invites your family to be our guests for a New Year's Day celebration and, most importantly, for the formal introduction of our daughter, Annabella, to her future husband, Vincenti de Leon!*

"Acknowledging the invitation with great joy, Don Joaquin embraced Pedro, coaxing him into the dining room to share both the good news and the Christmas breakfast.

"Annabella's oldest brother, a man I hoped I would never again encounter, walked proudly into the dining room behind his host. Motioning for Pedro to take a seat, Don Joaquin excitedly shook Vincenti's trembling hand, slapped me on my stiffened back, and then kissed his confused wife. Laughing, shouting, and sitting all at the same time, he demanded our attention.

"'Please allow me to introduce Senor Pedro Estrada from Rancho Canada de los Osos. He brings a wonderful Christmas present from his family to ours.'

"Placing both hands firmly on the table, he stood and smiled at each of us in turn. With his eyes twinkling, he raised the invitation above his head for all to see.

"Overheard by all, he whispered to his wife, 'A daughter for us! And, yes, Pablo, a sister, for you!'

"He paused a moment to relish the greatest gift of all.

"'And for Vincenti, a wife, the beautiful Annabella.'"

CHAPTER 21

New Year's Day at Canada de los Osos

"Early on New Year's Day, 1885, the de Leon family left Piedra Blanca. The threatening cumulus hovering over the year's last evening vanished. Blowing them eastward over Santa Lucia, the westerlies left a brilliant canopy of blue to welcome the year's first sunrise.

"For each of us, dealing with different sets of emotion, the three hours' journey over forty miles of rugged rutted roads ended not a minute too soon.

"Choosing to not complain and sully the season's joy, Don Joaquin and Mama Dolores, with soreness creeping up their backsides, smiled in selfless discomfort.

"When at last our coach pulled into the Estradas' cobblestone courtyard, Vincenti whispered in my ear for the thousandth time so no one could hear.

"'I still do not know what to say to her!'

"For me, unfortunately, I remembered all too painfully the last thing I had said to Annabella that last night on San Simeon. Tears wetting my cheeks I could still hear my quivering goodbye.

"I squeezed Vincenti's arm for brotherly assurance and prayed he would never come to know the truth about my affair with his future wife. From the center of the courtyard, eager to embrace their old friends, Don Jose and Isabel Estrada waved joyously as our livery driver brought the coach to a stop.

"At first sight of each other, the husbands burst into tears crying like babies.

"Dolores and Isabel tried maintaining a more dignified demeanor, but eventually they wept too.

"It had been over twenty years since their last meeting. In happy hellos, laughing and crying, the old friends hugged each other for a long time.

"Although it was obvious Vincenti kept a nervous eye open for the first sign of Annabella, my sentimental brother delighted in their reunion, as did I.

"I cringed each time an Estrada brother appeared, not knowing what to expect and praying for a miracle when Annabella finally would.

"I surmised, since her dramatic change of heart, the brothers saw no need bringing up old business that could embarrass the couple. Later I learned Pedro, Carlos, and Enrique were under strict orders to never acknowledge their first meeting with me or divulge the discussions I had with their parents.

"The courtyard welcome ended with the host and hostess excusing themselves to give their guests time to rest and freshen up from their dusty coach trip.

"Yolanda Gomez, the Estradas' adopted daughter, showed my happy and excited family our rooms, each suite decorated with beautiful hand-carved furniture.

"When she was four years old, Yolanda's parents, traveling from Monterey for a visit to Rancho Canada de los Osos, fell victim to the highway bandit, Vasquez.

"They were poor and had no money or jewels for him to steal. Vasquez, in his usual cruelty, hung them anyway.

Taken in by the Estradas', orphaned Yolanda, abandoned and unharmed, became a beloved adopted little sister to the trio of big brothers.

"Three years after Yolanda's adoption, Annabella was born. Over the years as sisters often do, big sister Yolanda and little sister Annabella grew very close, sharing everything including many secrets.

"'Please feel at home. Catalina's fresh towels and washbowls are for your use and comfort. I hope you enjoy her delicious fruit and lemonade. Rest now, and in an hour or so, I will return and escort you to the reception.'

"When all was ready, Yolanda and Catalina brought us to the hacienda's rotunda for the formal introduction to the members of Estrada family. Don Jose took his position at the head of the reception line, followed by wife Isabel and sons Pedro, Enrique, and finally, Carlos, who towered over everyone.

"Waiting for the right moment, as the de Leon family entered the rotunda, Annabella made her entrance. Everyone, especially Vincenti, turned to see her grace the steps of the arched stairway.

"Standing regally and more beautiful than I ever remembered, she took her place next to her brother Carlos. Stabbing my heart, I realized she was wearing the same dress she wore the night of our final goodbye.

"She extended her hand and curtsied politely, greeting Don Joaquin and Dolores de Leon. While her grace and charm captivated my parents, her beauty mesmerized my brother.

"Bowing and avoiding her eyes, Vincenti turned to meet Annabella. Rising, he took her hand, kissing the back of it lightly, allowing his lips to linger to breathe in her captivating fragrance.

"In that instant, he realized the foolishness of his reluctance to meet so enticing a young woman. How fortunate for him she changed her mind. For here she stood, an incredible beauty, with her long flowing black hair and sparkling green eyes—talking to him, asking him questions, and taking a lively interest in him.

"In retrospect, it was indeed, in that instant, that very first second that Annabella took complete possession of Vincenti, to eventually do with him whatever she wished.

"Drinking in her perfect mouth, her blossoming bosom, and the tiniest feet he'd ever seen, he watched her lips moving but heard nothing she said.

"The last de Leon in the line, I waited in terror, unsure how Annabella would act with me. Vincenti's lingering didn't help; first, making small talk, then starting to leave, only to return for another word with Annabella.

"When he finally moved on to Carlos, smiling meekly, I stepped forward as she stood before me and bowed. But her hand was not offered.

"I rose to meet the once loving emerald eyes that now brimmed with anger.

"She mumbled the dismissive afterthought. 'So, you are the brother?'

"Turning her backside to me, following Carlos into the dining room, she left me dangling like the scorned lover I had made of her."

"Three weeks later, at Mission San Miguel Sunday High Mass, Padre Fray Tomas Sepulveda announced the banns of marriage for Vincenti Emilio Barrazo de Leon and Annabella Concepción Trinidad Gabriela Estrada.

"'Their blessed holy marriage will take place in six weeks in the gardens of Rancho Canada de los Osos. Any person who has reason that these two children of God should not be married, speak now, or forever hold your peace.'

"The mothers kept busy with preparations, while the proud fathers congratulated each other, relieved their ancient arrangement, after such a brief engagement, came to fruition so quickly.

"'Pablo, where do I begin? I have no idea! You know what to do with a woman. Tell me!' Vincenti pleaded.

"'Pablo, you must be my *padrino*, my sponsor, my best man. Who but you could be a better mentor?

"'You were right all along. I was nervous for nothing. She is so wonderful, and she can ride like the wind. It is difficult for me to keep up with her. And when I don't know what to say, she is never at a loss for words.'

"All I could do was smile and accept the role fate had destined me to play. I assured my lover's future husband that to be his best man and padrino would be my honor.

"But in the lonely quiet, when the dark of night swallowed the rancho, if anyone listened carefully, they could hear weeping through my bedroom door. How could anyone know my pain when no one knew my heart was broken?

"For the love of my brother and family, I surrendered Annabella.

"Not to shame them or hurt them in any way, I vowed to suffer in silence and take my love for her to the grave.

"It seemed from birth my life followed dimly lit paths. For what reason or purpose heartbreaks marked my way, I was certain I would never come to know. An abandoned child, my loneliness, like a tormenting ghost, always seemed to follow."

CHAPTER 22

Mothers' Plans and the Garden Party

M others feared March showers would wash away their wedding plans. But the rains stopped and the weather cleared, reviving hopes and dreams.

Gardens burst into blooms with tulips and daffodils. Flowers—red and pink, yellow and white—colonized dormant planters, pots, and beds. Orange poppies roosted round about the greening shrubs, while sprouting buckeye and budding anise populated the sodden roadsides.

Engorged creeks, fed by bloated ponds, gushed incessantly, rejuvenating life into low-lying silage. Molting cattle, shedding their winter coats, grazed verdant hills of tender grass and luscious succulents.

Within earshot, from millpond to floodplain, all of nature heard discordant choirs of crickets and croakers wooing, chirping, belching, and sawing, singing winter's dirge.

Returning swallows flocked the leafy hedges of the western wall, revisiting springtime havens and rekindling old friendships.

For mothers, nature turned a pleasant page, making all things well for feast and celebrant.

THE COLD COFFEE POT WITH MUDDY REMNANTS riled Manuel.

"Rosa, when the old man returns, please pour him a fresh cup of coffee. He deserves at least that much after such a miserable story."

"Brother!" Jose lamented, "to think that our old shepherd has lived so long with this nonsense...and so close to that horrible woman."

Reentering the kitchen, Pablo closed the front door. Overhearing Jose's incensed comments, he laughed and told everyone to settle in for much more wickedness.

"My friends, you are just beginning to taste the bitter appetizer. The meal is far from served. Wait, please wait. Much is left to tell. About this horror story of my life, let me give you some advice. Before deciding how to digest it, allow me to serve you every course.

"You remember Yolanda Gomez, do you not? This is a sisterly secret told to me that she witnessed firsthand, the night before Annabella's wedding. As best I can remember, this is what Yolanda said.

"'Annabella woke me from a sound sleep in the early morning hours of her wedding day. She said while she was gone, if anyone sought her, I was to tell them she rode off to a favorite place to pray.

"'But I knew her intentions had nothing to do with prayer. So that no one could hear, she very quietly walked to the stable, saddled her horse, but did not mount her sorrel until she and the horse were out of sight and riding north, well past the rancho crossroads.

"'She rode to Mission San Miguel where she and Vincenti would wed the next afternoon. But it would not be Vincenti she would meet. Her plan started to take shape at her engagement party three nights before, when she asked me to deliver a private message to Pablo.

"'Alone and apart from the festivities, from the terrace balcony that overlooked the courtyard's garden, Pablo stared blankly into the clear March night.

"'Senor, may I offer you a glass of the Estradas' finest port? Your opinion is requested.'

"'Before he could answer, I handed him a crystal goblet. He took it without looking. Distracted, he raised it to receive wine he expected I would pour. Instead, I nodded subtly for him to look at the goblet, where he discovered a tiny folded note.

"'Forgive me, senor, how foolish; this bottle is still corked! I will be back in a moment to pour the wine'

"'Minutes later, in the stable's solitude, Pablo sat alone under lantern light reading the message.'

Dearest Pablo, I must talk to you before the wedding. We have much to discuss. Annabella

"'Thoughts raced through his head. Had they been discovered? Did Annabella tell Vincenti? Why did she want to meet?'

"'The note gave no indication where the meeting would be, and as for when, "before the wedding" was all that it said. Not daring to approach Annabella, engaged in conversation with Mama Delores, Pablo returned to the parlor looking for me. Trying to find me, he walked absently into Vincenti, who stood in his way, waiting for him.

"'Amigo, where have you been?' he asked ominously. 'I have something very important to discuss with you...and it cannot wait.'

"'As Vincenti gripped his arm and walked him briskly out of the hacienda into the rose garden, I saw his troubles.

"'I followed, listening, but Vincenti said nothing. Fearing what could come, Pablo stayed calm, laughing weakly when his brother pushed him into a chair.

"'With fury in his eyes, Vincenti began his interrogation.

"'Did you think I would not find out, Pablo? Did you think you could do such a thing without my knowing?'

"'In defense, Pablo stumbled, 'Brother, I don't understand what—'"

"'Vincenti cut him off. 'You don't understand? You don't understand? He says he does not understand…. How could you understand, Pablo? I am sorry to report to you, my dear brother, the silversmith from San Luis came calling today. Can you guess what this man delivered, mistaking me for you?'

"'Hardly able to get the words out, Vincenti began to laugh. With tears filling his eyes, he pulled a very confused Pablo up from the chair, embracing him.

"'Pablo! The matching saddles! They are wonderful… such a wedding present!'

"The blood drained from Pablo's face and he took a breath in relief.

"'The rich black leather is worked so well, and the silver dressing is brilliant. They must have cost you a fortune! How can Annabella and I ever repay you?'

"'Pablo mumbled something, but Vincenti did not hear and just carried on.

"'Of course, the saddles will remain our secret; I will deny to the death that I saw them before our wedding day. They are safely stored in your room, along with the silversmith's bill of sale.

"'Many thanks, big brother. You should not have done it, but I am glad you did. And I did not look at the bill.' Vincenti joked, starting back to the party.

"'At the loud commotion, Annabella hurried into the patio.

"'Senors, is everything all right? We heard loud voices and did not know what to think.'

"'Just a bit of brotherly mischief.' Vincenti said laughing.

"'Pablo sat uncertain what to say or think. Playing along with Vincenti's explanation, he smiled and waved that everything was fine. Somewhat assured, Annabella took Vincenti's arm, then looked at Pablo.

"'Enough mischief. It is time for the garden walk you promised.'

"Vincenti feigned reluctance, forcing Annabella to drag him to the steps. Pulled down the stairway, he groaned. 'So this is what marriage is all about.'

"'I watched them enter the garden below. Then nodding at the message at the bottom of the goblet, I asked, "Senor Pablo, may I pour the wine now?"

"'He took the parchment, and I poured the wine.'

"'Gracias, Yolanda. When you return, I will give you my opinion.'"

CHAPTER 23

A Meeting in the Confessional

———⊸⊷⊶———

"**A**n hour before midnight, my way lit by the slivered moon and ears numbed by the cold wind, I reined my horse into the dark orange grove flanking Mission San Miguel. With reins secured and the palomino's leg fettered, I crept toward the mission entrance.

"Unconvinced Annabella authored the missives, I arrived early to wait in hiding to see just who would come to meet me. The church door hung open, inviting all. Slipping quietly into the vestibule, I climbed the rank bell-tower stairs that reeked of rotting flesh.

"The belfry's stench triggered memories of the foul weather huts parceled on the remote northern hills of the rancho. Fighting the bubble gurgling in my throat, the odor nauseated me in the exact same way.

"Unlike the cloistered field huts, the bell tower's open arches invited the fresh night air. There was no escape, however, from the piles of vile bat droppings covering the slippery floor.

"I thanked God the bats were absent, hunting in search of their evening meal.

"To avoid the guano, I climbed above the stinking muddle below, high into the tower housing to sit relieved on the crossbeam supporting the bell. The vantage commanded views in every direction.

"The meeting hour arrived when a lone figure, riding silently into the grove from the southwest, dismounted, tied the horse to a tree, then trotted to the entry gate.

"Retracing my steps, I waited for the rider to appear at the bottom of the stairs.

"'Pablo, Pablo…where are you?'

"I stepped into the light, raising a finger to my lips, signaling my location.

"My mind, for the hundredth time, filled with ominous possibilities, questioned why Annabella wanted to meet. Had she confided in Vincenti about our affair? Was this a warning of consequences to come? Or was she reconsidering marrying Vincenti after all?

"My fears faded instantly when she leapt the boardwalk, rushing to kiss me. The torrid kiss in the dim-lit doorway did not end, and why she wanted to meet did not seem to matter anymore.

"I carried her into the ornate confessional box and gently placed her in the priest's chair where sins were forgiven.

"I closed the solid door, pulling shut the heavy curtains, leaving us in total darkness except for the candlelight seeping under the sill.

"When my eyes adjusted, Annabella stood naked before me, her clothes a heap on the confessional floor. With her finger placed on my lips, she gave fair warning.

"'Do not say a word, Pablo. Do not spoil tonight. The angel of your dreams has returned to her lover for the last time. When this night ends, she will never return. Let us make this night last a lifetime, forever.'"

"Passions satiated, Annabella laid in my arms, weeping aloud how my rejection broke her heart.

"Deepening from a bitter melancholy, her depression raged into anger that burned for revenge. To torture me as long as I lived became her only obsession.

"She turned away from me, then like an actress embarking on her greatest performance, she began to recite a well-rehearsed dialogue of self-denial.

"'To spite you and your rejection, I changed my mind and agreed with my parents to marry Vincenti and honor the dowry arrangement I so long despised.

"'I knew you still loved me, and the gravest pain I could inflict on you would be to marry your brother.'

"Resting her naked back to my chest, she melted into me all the more, before taking up a heartbreaking story I thoroughly believed.

"'I realized you would never compromise your loyalty to Vincenti and the de Leons. Your love for them was greater than your love for me, and I would never have you for my own. You threw me away, and, oh, how I wanted you to suffer. I desired that you should die a little every day to understand how broken-hearted and hopeless I was when you deserted me.'

"But then, in all her nakedness, she stood and looked down on me with her wicked smile smugly in place.

"'I plotted and planned to give my body willingly to your brother just so I could see your life crumble into ruins… little by little…every day, living in the same casa, knowing you could never touch me again.

"'But as the wedding drew close, I realized this stupid desire for revenge made me my own prisoner. I would be the one serving a life sentence marrying a man I did not love…while you…you could forget me and be free to find a woman who loved and desired you.'

"'Annabella, if you do not love Vincenti, please…for everyone's sake, do not go through with it.'

"At that moment, seeming noble and selfless, she broke away from my attempted embrace and resumed the dialogue of her well-rehearsed, contrived answers.

"'Finally, I understood. Your decision to do what was right, regardless the loss and pain, convinced me. Faithfulness to your brother and family was sacred. I too felt obligated to honor the Estrada family in the same way.'

"I turned away, unable to look at her. Believing every word she said broke my heart, and I wept, suffering all the guilt she so skillfully intended.

"'Please, Pablo, no tears. It is the painful but honorable thing we must do. In the afternoon, Vincenti and I will marry, and the love you and I shared will be but a cherished memory.'

"Hesitating, to be sure I was watching, I think she expected applause and almost took a bow.

"Without a doubt, I am sure Madam Margarita's words reverberated in her mind.

"'Men are weak and beg to be manipulated. Lead them by the nose right to what it is you want. Men are no match for the right women.'

"We rode away to our destinies, but not unobserved. From the sacristy, Padre Fray Tomas witnessed our rendezvous. The historian of Mission San Miguel recorded for posterity everything he saw and heard that night."

CHAPTER 24
A Trickle of Absolution

W hen the ceremony ended and the church emptied, a gentle drizzle and a traditional shower of red good-luck beads christened the wedding party hurrying out of the rain into the waiting coaches.

Looking into the darkening canopy, Pablo welcomed the cool wetness, and for a very long time kept his face raised to meet the March rain.

"I needed a cleansing, and the water running off my face granted a trickle of absolution for my guilt.

"Vincenti, wearing with pride the ceremonial 'lasso' rosary around his neck, shouted, 'Pablo, your face doesn't look any better wet. Get in the coach, you fool. My bride is waiting.'

"A wry smile twisted my dampened face. I climbed grudgingly in the second of three coaches, accompanied by Annabella's cousin and *madrina*, Philomena, a recent arrival from Los Angeles.

"Passengers with us, costumed miniature versions of the bride and groom, were the flower girl and the ring bearer—the *niña*, niece Sophia, daughter of the bride's brother Pedro, and the *niño*, nephew Alejandro, Yolanda's son.

"Pretending to sleep in the corner of the coach, I distanced myself from all intrusion and avoided all contact and conversation. Desiring no more than to get through the miserable day, I fended off the torture of splintered glass stabbing my mind, picturing Annabella and Vincenti on their wedding bed.

"The bearer of the gold wedding bands, however, had different ideas. Sitting next to me, little Alejandro did not like the shoes he was made to wear for the wedding. His constant heel thumping on the seat's backboard brought me to his welcome attention.

"Trying not to be too annoyed, I sat up to ask, 'What is the matter, little fellow? Why, when you see I am trying to sleep, do you keep banging your shoes?'

"The boy complained his feet hurt because the shoes pinched his toes.

"'My toes are smashed in these shoes and hurt very much.'

"Turning the boy so that both his feet rested in my lap, I unlaced the shoes, taking them off, and discovered blisters on each of Alejandro's little toes.

"At the sight of the red blisters, the flower girl squirmed.

"'Excuse me, senorita Philomena, may I borrow your hat pin? The niño suffers from shoes that are too tight, and your pin is necessary to relieve the discomfort the blisters are causing him.'

"Smiling at the request, the maiden of honor reached into her hat, extracting a four-inch pin adorned with a silver cupid.

"Cupid-end first, she handed it to me, saying, 'Hopefully, this will do, senor.'

"'Gracias, Senorita Philomena. It is my sincere hope to return it to you in the same lovely condition with which it was offered.'

"'No, no senor. Allow me my small contribution to aiding a fellow passenger.'

"When I started the procedure, the flower girl and the maiden of honor turned away from the sight of the oozing fluid that flowed from each blister. The operation ended quickly, and I dabbed Alejandro's wounds, absorbing the fluids with my handkerchief.

"'You are very brave. Now, let the air breathe on your feet. In a day or two, you will feel better. Do not wear these or any other shoes for at least a week. I will speak to your mama when we arrive at the rancho, all right, amigo?'

"I smiled, ruffling Alejandro's hair. Through tears, he nodded, refusing to leave my lap.

"Surgery concluded, the coach returned to a restful quietness.

"Why I did not withdraw again, I could not be sure. Encouraging Alejandro and exchanging pleasantries with Philomena and little Sophia, I felt blessed all the way to the dreaded wedding reception.

"In spite of all the goodwill reaped during the coach ride, this day of misery could not end soon enough. Far away from the raucous reception and the stalking Philomena, when my "*padrino* duties" in the tedious reception line ended, I hid away from everyone. For peace and solitude, I fled to the barn, joining the animals to soothe my pain.

"I suffered my loss without resentment. From that day on, I accepted my fate, swearing to love Vincenti and Annabella like brother and sister.

"However, I discovered the loss of my angel would be the mere beginning to the many disappointments the future held for me."

CHAPTER 25

Master of Waterways, God of the Creeks

———∞∞———

"**P**raying his thanks aloud at the old mission's Easter Mass, Don Joaquin shared with the congregation his gratitude the spring flooding would never pose a problem again.

"'Due to Pablo's incredible accomplishment, thank you, God, according to your good will, the lower pastures are free of standing water and ready for early planting. We are grateful for your every blessing, especially for Pablo, our inspired son.

"'Continue to bless his heart and find favor in the title we bestow upon him this day for his prodigious achievement. From henceforth, he will bear the title Master of the Waterways, God of the Creeks.'"

———∞∞———

IN THE SPRINGTIME OF 1885, THE RANCHO EMERGED blessed from the heavy winter showers. The green hills and bursting reservoirs under the azure Santa Lucia skies would produce the richest of harvests.

During the preceding summer, fortunate to anticipate winter's heavy rain, Pablo designed a system of waterway canals to direct flooding runoff for future irrigation and livestock use into favorably located retaining pools.

"By averting the seasonal lowland flooding, we were able to plant much earlier the many fields usually left fallow due to summer's water scarcity

"I am happy to report, as our good friend Manuel can attest, the plan worked perfectly and continues to do so to this very day.

"Although I received the lion's share of congratulations, success belonged to everyone for the collective work.

"I, of course, was humbled and delighted to be recognized by Don Joaquin that Easter Sunday. But today, our very own Manuel carries this mantle and deserves our thanks and praise.

"Manuel's mastery, bringing water to the rancho's varied needs, is a testament to his love, commitment, and loyalty. It is no secret we all love him for it, and we love him more for being the noble, wonderful man we call our friend.

"Now, the time has come to break out the wine and celebrate Manuel and all he does for us. Jose, please fetch the ice buckets from under the table."

Rosa poured wine into crystal glasses Pablo had kept from his "padrino" duties, toasting Vincenti and his bride.

"To Manuel, may you always wear your title Master of the Waterways, God of the Creeks, with pride and distinction! Salud!"

Sealing the toast, the glasses clinked, and Pablo refilled glass after glass.

"Drink up. Tonight we rejoice in our friendship and our love for one another. And do not worry, I have lots of coffee to sober you before you drive home."

He and his Rosa were delighted. The next day, Manuel's back would ache from the all congratulatory slaps.

Rosa kissed Pablo's cheek. "Senor, you are so kind to

recognize my Manuel in this way." But Jose joked, "Manuel's head will be three sizes bigger tomorrow."

⸙

"MAY THE WINE KEEP FLOWING THROUGHOUT MY TELLING." The happy group settled in but waited just an instant when Pablo's next surprise came.

"Thanks to the Almighty for the splendid spring weather of '85 that provided vaqueros, hands, and tenders many avenues of escape, but most assuredly, the de Leon men who resided in the great hacienda. Don Joaquin, Vincenti, Rodrigo, and I…we were all very thankful for those fair weather days guaranteeing us work and time far away as possible from the women of Hacienda de Leon.

"I accepted and volunteered for every chore, job, and responsibility that provided the widest berth from contact from Annabella and old memories. In fact, I remember inventing extravagant excuses to distance myself.

"April and May passed into a fertile June. Assisting Rodrigo to implement his plans for crop cultivation and livestock production filled all my daylight hours.

"Rodrigo's farm operations leaned heavily on experienced hands to bring their skills and instincts to the harvests. While blending modern methods learned in their mission days, our many Salinan Indians hands shared freely their farming secrets and techniques.

"But for Rodrigo, raising and maintaining livestock was his greatest love. Delegating responsibilities to Don Joaquin, Vincenti, and me, he assigned the responsibility of overseeing the droppings of calves, foals, and pigs.

"In shifts around the clock, we stood watch, assisting the most in need, first-time mothers. Veteran cows, mares and sows usually did not require help, but Don Joaquin discovered that was not always true.

"We did suffer one casualty that foaling season. During the birthing of her coal-black colt, Don Joaquin's prized bay flailed a kick that caught him above the left knee, breaking his thigh bone.

"Rancho springtime demands, as you all know, can require everyone's waking hours—everyone, that is, except the injured and unlucky Don Joaquin.

"No matter how hard he tried or persistent his whining, his broken bone kept him hamstrung at the hacienda. In absolute desperation each morning, he pleaded with Vincenti and me. 'Take me with you today! I am begging you. Do not leave me here this beautiful day as a prisoner sentenced in this woman's hell.

"'I would easily welcome the worst discomfort of the hardest wagon bed, on the roughest roads, in the hottest sun, in heaviest rains, or the most frigid sleet, to my imprisonment at the hacienda that these hysterical women fill daily with all manner of wailing and screaming.'

"Alas, his tear-stained pleading fell on deaf ears. Laying down the law to king and prince, Mama Dolores advised no excuse conceived would be good enough to allow the don to leave the hacienda until his leg was healed.

"And she prevailed. Everyone felt for him, but not enough to challenge Mama Dolores. Instead, we strained, stifling our laughing and howling as we listened secretly to the chastening his warden wife showered on him. For early probation, she rejected every invented scheme. It was hilarious.

"'Joaquin, your broken bones must mend and to do that you must stay here in the casa. You taught your sons well enough; they can tend to things without you.

"'The good Lord never intended for you to work as a one-legged *charro*…and that, my dear husband, is my last word.'

"Restraining the recalcitrant don proved nothing compared to the constant demands of the miserable and the very pregnant Annabella.

"She drained all of Mama Dolores's strength, taxed her patience, and provided the men, especially Vincenti, ample reason to run earlier each day from the hacienda and return later each night.

"The exhausted warden cried out in total frustration, lamenting to her incarcerated husband. 'Already I would be crazy if Martha and Catalina were not here to help. And this is just Annabella's third month.'

"The hacienda always welcomed the coming morning before Annabella's pregnancy held it prisoner. Now everyone dreaded the rising sun and escalating nausea.

"The slightest of morsels offered by Catalina to Annabella turned her complexion green, followed by a mad dash to the chamber pot, the crashing of the serving tray, and the splattering of vomit all over her bedroom.

"Driving witnesses into shed, stable, and outhouse, her bouts of retching were worse still. Signs cautioning 'extreme care' for those passing through, were posted all about the casa. The game afoot was avoiding collision with clay pots strewn about the hacienda, placed strategically for deposits of, as Mama Dolores called it, 'morning sickness.'

"Poor Martha complained bitterly to her husband, Rodrigo, about Annabella's volcanic eruptions.

"'The devil from hell spews fountains of filth, leaving me the one to clean it up. See the muck she leaves behind? Her misses are legend, and when her deposits are close to a pot, they are more out than in!'

"As tears rolled down Martha's flustered cheeks, Rodrigo pulled her close, making sure she would not see his inopportune smile and happiness to be leaving soon.

"At the behest of Mama Dolores, desperate for relief, Josefina Espinoza, *curandera* of village San Xavier, came to the casa with ready 'cures' for the-mother-to-be.

"A practitioner of the ancient arts, the old witch boiled horrid things in a vinegar vat. Adding among many other bits and pieces, rotting peppers, chicken feet, and fermented vegetables, she concocted disgusting compounds, smearing them on Annabella's belly as a poultice.

"With the treatments moderately successful, the *curandera* held an open invitation to return to Annabella's bedside.

"Forging a bond with the *curandera,* for Annabella, was good business. Like Madam Margarita, Josefina Espinoza possessed position and influence. With the *curandera* as an ally, Annabella added to her arsenal a strategic tool that would help her reach goals of independence, power, and wealth.

"Her nausea continued with little relief, however, until Annabella's screaming and pleading unexpectedly presented Mama Dolores with a brilliant solution.

"'If only Yolanda were here!' Annabella wailed.

"'Yolanda will know how to care for me. Yolanda would know what to do! Catalina…tell Mama Dolores.'

"Recruiting Yolanda and eager for relief, Mama Delores conferred with Vincenti and the don. All agreed. A household position at Piedra Blanca immediately opened for Yolanda Gomez.

"The rub was convincing the Estradas to release Yolanda from her position at Canada de los Osos. Success proved as costly as it was effective.

"Before marrying Vincenti, Annabella had hoped her parents would allow Yolanda to leave their employ and accompany her to Piedra Blanca. But the Estradas could not part with her or little Alejandro, her son.

"'Annabella, losing one daughter is enough to bear,' was her father's sad reply. But now, with our household in frenzied need, the de Leons hastened to risk the Estrada ire to acquire Yolanda.

"Once again, brother Vincenti turned to me.

"'Dear brother, will you please ride? I cannot leave Annabella, and I know you are the one who can make a strong case to her parents for Yolanda to come and be at her side.' And so, I was recruited to go.

"The flowering fields and newly scythed hay perfumed the morning air. Free from the day-to-day turmoil, the next morning, happy to be away, I drove a coach and four with mount tied behind, headed southwest over a worn trail to Rancho Canada de los Osos.

"Since our first meeting on the coach ride to the wedding reception, I held an affinity for Alejandro, and often wondered how he was getting along. I remembered the little boy's admiring and grateful eyes, how relieved and comforted he felt as my patient in this same coach. Why it happened, I was not sure, but I could not stop smiling, knowing he could be coming to live at Piedra Blanca.

"Jose and Isabel Estrada welcomed me warmly and with sincere affection. They ushered me into the parlor where we first had met just a year earlier, asking excitedly about their daughter, the mother-to-be.

"When they learned the reason for my visit too soon, their goodwill turned hostile. Belligerent and spiteful, Don Jose challenged the de Leons with angry defiance.

"'Give me one good reason why I should allow the de Leons to take others from my household.'

"Playing to the grandparents' pride, I presented a long list of benefits a new baby in the family would bring.

"'My good friends, please allow me to explain. As you know, soon you will become grandparents to Annabella's first child. The talk is that if it is a boy, it will be his honor to bear your name, Don Jose.

"'And if, per chance, a little girl should arrive, the wonderful name of Isabel is being considered. And who is to say how many children Annabella and my brother Vincenti will add to the quiver of the Estrada and de Leon families?

"'Yolanda's coming to her sister's aid at Piedra Blanca will ensure your daughter wonderful and loving care. How much better it would be if the same loving care is available to the new infant as well?'

"I ended my impassioned plea, bowing respectfully and without saying another word, and sat down in the comfortable chair to sip my cold lemonade.

"Congratulating myself for such a masterful performance, I waited in silence for Don Jose's response.

"Due to their concern for Annabella's health and the promise of many other grandchildren to come, the Estradas eventually relented but not without first exacting a notable concession.

"'Isabel and I have spoken to Yolanda,' Don Jose said. 'She is sad to leave us, but she favors helping her sister and baby.

"'Mama and I will release her and little Alejandro with the following condition: Annabella, and any and all of her children, along with Yolanda and Alejandro, are to visit Canada de los Osos for a week, three times a year. And any expenses, including wages, are the de Leons' responsibility.'

"I complained that he drove too hard a bargain, holding the de Leons over a barrel, but I knew my reluctance would only compliment him for his formidable negotiating.

"Although he saw through me, he, nevertheless, smiled in triumph.

"I returned his smile, congratulating myself, once again, at my own brilliance. Don Jose saved face, Mama Dolores gained a reprieve, and the de Leons retained an old friend. Yolanda and little Alejandro joined us in the parlor as the victor, Don Jose, poured tequila formalizing the hard-fought agreement.

"With the clinking of glasses the families were saluted and peace and tranquility for Piedra Blanca were gratefully restored."

CHAPTER 26

Annabella...Yolanda... Alejandro...Emilio

———◦◦◦———

"Turbulent spring faded into mellow summer. With a deft hand, Yolanda tended Annabella, ending her morning sickness and bringing peace to the household.

"Mama Delores doted on her healing husband. And with the torment of the clay pots put to rest, Martha happily resumed her housekeeping chores.

"Sanity restored, the once skittish men plowed into the business of the rancho producing autumn harvests that repaid everyone richly for their hard work, especially the Salinan Indians.

"Ignored since the start of the Civil War, overseas markets flourished once again and continued to grow through the end of the century. Taking the don's advice, Vincenti sought out markets abroad, reestablishing lucrative international trade. Selling thousands of heads of cattle to a new the emperor of Japan delivered huge profits.

"But, for me...I held no great desire for fame or money. I was happy, of course, for the rancho's success. But until Yolanda and Alejandro came to live at Piedra Blanca, I struggled every day.

"Yolanda sought me out, asking me to mentor her little son, despite Annabella confessing I was her secret lover. And the little fellow followed me wherever I went.

"Bonding our blossoming friendship into a tender close-ness, Yolanda knew I would be good for Alejandro, and she knew I needed him more than he needed me.

"A day without Alejandro was incomplete. We were inseparable. I came to think of him as my own and a gift from God. He lifted my spirits, taught me wonderful things and freed me more and more from the past.

"Answering a steady stream of questions about 'animals,' his favorite subject, I repaid Alejandro daily for launching me into my second boyhood.

"Wherever on the rancho we went, the tiny outdoors-man displayed his affinity for wildlife. Be it the orneriest bull to the gentlest bunny, Alejandro demanded I tell him everything I knew about every animal.

"I loved him and the little boy loved me. We melded together more and more, day by day, like a father and a son.

"And over time, in the secret places of her heart, as a woman loves and desires a man, Yolanda came to love and desire me.

"One night, after putting Alejandro to bed, Yolanda sat next to me and whispered, 'My dear Pablo, my mourning for Fernando is over. To think Annabella brought you to my son…and to me…she brought a man I could love, and the man I do love is close at hand.'"

"It is sad to think Fernando never saw his child. He died at the hand of Vasquez before Alejandro was born. Seven months after his death, when Alejandro was born, a fire of joy sparked in the souls who lived at Rancho Canada de Los Osos.

"To the delight of the Estrada family, Annabella and Yolanda became close friends and confidantes. It was

Annabella who saw her adopted sister, Yolanda, through Alejandro's birth.

"In all of life's twists and turns, circumstance returned the favor. Yolanda, years later in her good turn, now sat at Annabella's bedside, nursing her through the birth of the newest de Leon, who entered the world on All Souls Day, the first of November 1885."

⸙

"A HEAVY DOWNPOUR SCATTERED THE GATHERING crowds waiting in the courtyard of Hacienda de Leon for news of the baby's arrival. In the comfort of Hacienda de Leon, the ecstatic grandparents, Jose and Isabel Estrada with Don Joaquin and Mama Dolores, waited expectantly over coffee and tequila for their first grandchild.

"As custom dictated, earlier that rainy morning Don Joaquin sent notification throughout the rancho.

"'Today is the day of new life. Mistress Annabella is in labor. Put all work aside to join the de Leon vigil awaiting the birth of our grandchild. Bring your families into the courtyard to pray and encourage the mother through her travail. When the blessed event occurs, you are invited, as our guests, to join in the celebration of our joy.'

"Walking from their homes, singing and praying, the people came, grateful for the honor extended them by Don Joaquin.

"The women and children, joining the parish priests, gathered near the hacienda entry to pray for a safe delivery. The men—smoking, laughing, trading old tales and long remembered stories—met together at the fountain.

"The rains stopped and November's cold brought out a rainbow of blankets, coats, and *rebozos*.

"Martha served tortillas and beans for lunch and roasted beef and potatoes for dinner. Everyone had enough to eat.

"Uninvited to the birthing room, the *curandera* spent the hours thumping a ceaseless beat on a hollow log until the baby was born.

"After twenty-one hours of labor, with Yolanda as her midwife and Vincenti at her side, Annabella's child arrived.

"Moments before midnight, as the sickly child coughed his way into the world, without warning, the *curandera* stopped her thumping and shouted.

"'The womb's harvest is reaped!'

"Then sleeping families awoke to hear Don Joaquin's joy.

"'Faithful friends, awaken from your sleep and hear the good news. My grandson is born this night. Happily, I can now be addressed as grandfather. His mother, father, and grandparents thank you for your prayers.'

"He hesitated, adding, 'Struggling as we all do, Emilio Jose Vincenti Barrazo de Leon comes into this world, fighting for his breath. Continue praying for him to be strong and healthy. Be it God's will he live a long and noble life.

"'Due to the late arrival, because you are so faithful, rancho work will not commence until the end of siesta time tomorrow afternoon.

"'So now, please rejoice for little Emilio, his mother, and family. Enjoy the feast, and celebrate this wonderful blessing. Gracias, amigos!'"

"A MERE FIVE POUNDS AND TWO OUNCES, EMILIO'S JAUN-diced skin contrasted sharply to the black crown of curly hair that topped his conical head. With Yolanda's encouraging care, little Emilio—weak and struggling for air—at last cried out, clearing obstructed passages, breathing as a baby should.

"Days later, when Annabella appeared to be regaining her strength, Vincenti and Mama Dolores prayed she would soon assume care for her son and relieve Yolanda.

"But Annabella insisted she was still too weak to mother her baby, and nursing him was out the question.

"Day-to-day childcare remained entrusted to Yolanda. Surviving the first two days of life on goat's milk and Yolanda's maternal care, a scrawny, battered, fragile Emilio was left to carry on his fight without a mother to nurture him.

"Purposely avoiding contact with her child, it became obvious Annabella possessed no great affinity for motherhood. Constantly feigning illness, she refused the breast pump or attendance at Emilio's baptism.

"The third month passed. Emilio stabilized his weight and strength. And as he grew stronger, Yolanda's patience grew short. Mentally and physically worn by the child's continual demand, Yolanda looked frail, lost weight, and after sleeping less than four hours a night, was totally exhausted.

"Personal time with me or Alejandro was purely imaginary. At first, Yolanda requested politely to be replaced. After the fourth month, she demanded it.

"Vincenti pleaded for her to stay on.

"'I am so grateful for the special care you have given Emilio, and so is your sister. Annabella assures me she will be ready to assume Emilio's care very soon. Please consider staying on a bit longer until that time arrives.'

"But, Yolanda had had enough. The time and situation had finally arrived to tell Vincenti the hurtful truth she kept hidden since the night of Emilio's birth."

"'Senor, you remember the night of your wife's labor? You remember also I witnessed the disrespect she showered on you that night? You remember I witnessed her shouting for you to get out of her room, banishing you from the birth?'

"'I know, I know…but Annabella was hysterical. Her pain made her crazy. It is understandable that she would act in such a bizarre way.'

"'You are too kind, senor…much too kind. What you cannot know, which I alone witnessed, was Annabella's blasphemy spewed out after she threw you out of the room.

"'What she said…I have told no one. What she claimed… I have told no one.

"'I have struggled with this, Senor Vincenti. You have been so kind to me, but for your sake, you must know, and it seems I must be the one to tell you.

"'Be strong, senor; her words are hurtful.'

"Listening to what would only break his heart, my poor brother sank into the sofa. Yolanda sat next to him to soften the blow, knowing her revelation would forever change Vincenti's belief about his wife.

"'When you closed the door behind you, she cursed and mocked you, yelling she could not wait for you to leave.

"'Screaming horrible things no wife should say about her husband, she confessed she had despised you since your wedding night. She never loved you. You were a fraud and failure and a weak little boy who possessed no manhood.

"'Then, and I will never forget, her ranting stopped, and pulling me to her side so that I would not miss a word, she smiled a horrible evil smile.

"'I would never let Vincenti touch me…never!' she said. 'Pablo, my Pablo is the only man in the de Leon family! And this child…is his!'

"What Yolanda refused to share were Annabella's threats to kill her and her son, Alejandro.

"'My dowdy sister, Pablo belongs to me!' Annabella said. 'You are a dead person if you touch him, and little Alejandro will also be joining you in hell.'

"Vincenti sat weeping. Yolanda tried to comfort him, placing her hand on his shoulder.

"'I am very sorry, Senor Vincenti. It has taken much for me to tell you these things.

"'By now, you must know that Annabella does not want to be a mother. When he was born, she would not even look at your son. Not with all my coaxing did she ever offer him her breast. I am truly sorry you had to learn these things and sad that it was I to tell you.'

"She waited, but no response came.

"'You will have to look elsewhere for Emilio's nursemaid. Today is my last day.

"'I have done all I can do. Emilio is past his colic. He is healthy and fine. My duty is done. I have seen him through his trials. I will continue no longer.

"'Tomorrow, for the first time since Emilio's birth, I will attend Sunday Mass at the mission with Pablo and my son.

"'Perhaps Mama Dolores and Martha together will assist you until Annabella is ready to embrace Emilio as her own.

"'I pray she will love you as her husband soon, senor.'

"The next morning at sunrise, Yolanda left the hacienda."

The back door slammed. Manuel started up the flatbed and sped off with Jaime sitting next to him.

Armando's oldest son, Pedro, stopped to tell Manuel someone kicked open the gate at the upper southern pasture, sending water reserved for the corn crop into a fallow field.

"I will stop the telling until Manuel and Jaime return."

Jose joked. "Senor Pablo, listen. We will be lucky if Manuel and Jaime are back before the new moon."

"What is this 'new' moon?" Rosa said. "I do not understand."

"The new moon rises tomorrow night. If the gate is damaged and not just kicked open, your husband will have his hands full trying to stop the flooding, even temporarily. Good thing Jaime went with him. Besides, the supply yard won't open for parts he could need till the morning.

"By then, my shop will be overrun with broken-down cars from the crazy Sunday drivers who will park them, blocking my garage door from here to Mexico City. I think it is best to go home and get ready for the week's work. Maybe next Friday we can get together at my house to listen to the rest of Pablo's story."

"You are right, Jose."

"I am sick, speaking of these things. Perhaps, in a few days, I can face the truth and finish this misery."

No one spoke of it again. The week passed slowly, each listener taking the time to chew over Pablo's sad admission.

When the work week ended, Manuel arrived promptly at sunset to pick up the old man. "Buenos noches, Senor Pablo."

"Good evening, Manuel. I trust Rosa is well. I have missed seeing her since my last visit to your hospitable home. Are we off to Jose's?"

"Si, senor, and eager to hear more. What we believed about the past has changed. We wonder where you will next take us. It is difficult to understand such cruel truths."

The flatbed made one stop, picking up Conchita and the dinner she planned to serve at Jose's garage. The bouquet of her cooking teased noses and whetted appetites.

"Buenos noches, Conchita. What treasures from the kitchen will delight us this fine evening?"

"Tonight, Senor Pablo, the question is what new revelations you will share with us? As for the dinner, it is specially prepared for our host, Jose. He just loves my rellenos and chili verde, and the tortillas are fresher than the *sopaipillas*. Once more, there is *mucho* to eat; no one will be hungry."

Conchita's delicious repast brought little mirth and less conversation. Despite the freely poured wine, the listeners languished in expectation.

When the dishes were cleared away, and the men returned from their smokes and outhouse visits, Rosa sidled up to Pablo to whisper in his ear.

"Everyone is anxiously waiting for you to take up where you left off. But we are scared to think of what can come next."

"Rosa, the story is not better; it only grows worse. Warn our friends. I will understand if they choose to leave."

But no one left. Instead, the gathering formed a tight circle around Pablo, hungry for the ugly facts that scarred his life.

CHAPTER 27

The Forsaken Bride

"This telling begins at the wedding altar of Vincenti and his unfaithful wife, Annabella, and ends with Yolanda and Alejandro sailing away to save their lives.

"So, Rosa and Conchita, be sure the coffee pot is full, the fruit bowl is close at hand, and you are all comfortable. If you must, now is the time for the outhouse."

All reassembled, ready for the long telling. Pablo lit his pipe and began.

"To help me remember the many events and years to be shared, my tobacco tin is full. Please save questions until my telling is done.

"As you all might guess, the wedding ceremony began with Annabella giving to Vincenti the promised dowry pledged by her parents from her birth.

"In return, according to custom, Vincenti surrendered to his wife control of all his worldly possessions and presented to her a dazzling ornate jeweled box containing 'Las Arras,' thirteen gold coins representing Jesus Christ and His twelve apostles.

"Among 'Las Arras' lay the wedding locket, the family heirloom passed on to the newest de Leon bride, its secret unknown to this day.

"More than three hundred dignitaries attended the vows honoring the union of the de Leon and Estrada families. The guests included the Alta, California, governor and his wife and the dons and families from ranchos all over California.

"Beyond generous, the wedding gifts covered the walls and every inch of the massive dining room table and twelve side chairs, spilling onto the floor and into the rotunda foyer.

"During the sumptuous dinner, notables rose, proposing toast after toast to the new husband and the hosting families, but mostly to the comely bride who astonished guests with her beauty, intellect, and charm.

"Annabella, the new mistress of Piedra Blanca, made a most indelible impression.

"The guests came together in the ballroom to witness the bride and groom's first dance, to form a huge heart that encircled the newlyweds.

"Late into the evening, the mariachis played on and on. Many celebrants stayed on drinking and dancing, long after the bride and groom retired.

"I hid away for most of the evening, praying Philomena would not find me. She gave up the search to join the mariachi musicians, who escorted the newlyweds to their suite.

"As the troubadours played love songs under the balcony window, Annabella and Vincenti were alone for the first time.

"Too humiliated to seek Don Joaquin's advice before the wedding night, Vincenti sought me out for the whys and wherefores of how to woo his bride.

"Offering generalities only, I found myself strangely reluctant to detail intimacies husbands and wives shared.

"Loving her newfound notoriety, wine spinning her round and round, Annabella started having second thoughts, reconsidering that life as Vincenti's wife might not be so terrible after all.

"'He is not Pablo, but he is a charming, handsome husband a woman like me, over time, could come to love and respect. Who knows, perhaps his lovemaking will not be so bad. He might be a better lover than his brother.'

"Of course, his position of power and the wealth did not hinder his appeal.

"Smiling alluringly at her new husband, very slowly, she began to undress. Vincenti looked on…scared and bewildered.

"Shedding her last garment, revealing her beautiful body to him for the first time, the red-faced groom looked away, paralyzed with fear.

"With head bowed and eyes averted, he begged her pardon and left his bride naked and alone, dashing out of their wedding suite for the *baño*.

"Forever dreading his wedding night, with the instincts of a seven-year-old-boy, my brother panicked. Trembling, he ran to the stables, saddled his horse, and into the hills to hide he rode far and fast.

"It was easier to run off like the coward he knew he was than confess to Annabella his anxiety.

"Patiently waiting for his return, she draped her nakedness with the bedsheet. But the few minutes his baño visit should have taken dragged on beyond an hour.

"Then the hour turned into a day, and the day turned into a week, and the week, for Annabella, turned into a lifetime.

"That night he never returned. Her confusion became anger, quickly flaming into hatred. Loathing followed right behind.

"The absurdity of a bride seeking help from anyone to find, on her wedding night, a misplaced groom would bring nothing but humiliation and disgrace. By forsaking Annabella, he surrendered his only chance she could ever love him.

"Had he the least notion the enormous price he and the de Leon family would pay for rejecting his bride, Vincenti would surely have overcome his fear and consummated the marriage.

"For you see, his cowardice brought extinction to the de Leons."

"PLEDGED TO A MARRIAGE FROM THE MOMENT OF HIS birth, Vincenti never would be a match for Annabella.

"His spinelessness forfeited all power and control to her.

"From the day he sheepishly returned, she manipulated him unmercifully, controlled him completely, and hated him all the more for it.

"And, of course, he came to hate himself so much more. The best anyone could say about Vincenti was that he muddled through his life in pitiful denial.

"About their wedding night, he lied to everyone. Annabella said nothing.

"Regardless of the cost, perfecting deceit, he saved face by denying the truth. Offering outlandish pretext for his wife's willful disrespect, he spent his life constantly rationalizing his wife's bizarre behavior.

"Vincenti chose to merely absorb the rude judgment from family and friends for every accusation registered against his intolerable wife...and there were hundreds.

"In the presence of Don Joaquin and Mama Dolores, it was my brotherly indictment shouted in anger that stung him to the quick.

"'Dealing with Annabella, have I not always advised you to be a wild stallion, the stud of all studs who roams the pasture at will that no mare would dare refuse? But, Vincenti, you are no stallion! You have no seed! No, my dear brother, you are a gelding! While the whole world laughs at you, the mare lords over the gelding and makes you the butt of all her jokes.'"

CHAPTER 28

Salvaged Manhood—
Evil Alliance

⬡

"When Yolanda departed, Vincenti was forced to resolve the obligation of Emilio's welfare. After my blistering assault, he attempted to salvage what little manhood he still possessed. Mustering his courage, delivering Emilio into her arms, he confronted Annabella at last.

"'Dear bride, Yolanda is gone, and your childhood is over!'

"With no chance to respond, he pulled Annabella out of bed to stand before him. With face calm and manner frigid, his words were hard.

"'You are not only my wife, you are Emilio's mother. The time has long since passed for you to embrace your motherly duties to your son. No one else is his mother, only you. No one else is responsible for his upbringing. He does not belong to your sister Yolanda, Mama Dolores, or Martha, nor anyone else!

"'Whether you are well or sick, happy or sad, rich or poor, there will be no more shirking your responsibility.

"'He is your child…to love, nurture, and rear.

"'He is the son you gave me, and you are his mother.

"'He is your responsibility.

"'And he will be raised as a de Leon by his mother. My duty is to provide for our family.

"'Yours is raising the children. From this moment forward, Emilio is entrusted to your care, and you alone are responsible for his well-being.

"'Now, work calls, dear. Have a good day with your son.'

"Smiling from ear to ear, he bounded out the door.

"Annabella, standing in her bedclothes with Emilio in her arms, said nothing. She had been found out.

"Refusing Emilio ended that day. She tempered her fire for only a moment. Yielding to Vincenti's demands, a momentary concession, accelerated Annabella's hatred and quickened her plan. What began as a tantrum perverted into an obsession that remained unsatisfied until all the de Leons were dead."

<hr/>

"TO EXECUTE HER BLOODLETTING, ANNABELLA SOUGHT an alliance with a powerful collaborator.

"On its southern boundary in the rancho's aged oak grove, Annabella waited that wintry day for what seemed hours—a desolate place filled with dying light and lonely shadows. Rotting in stinking ponds, the copse reeked of decaying life.

"Stomping the damp ground, she shivered fending off February's cold that rose up through soles of her boots.

"The *curandera* demanded they meet in secret, but the appointed noontime had long since passed and still Josefina Espinoza had not appeared.

"A dense fog hanging heaviest over the closest pond hid the old witch from Annabella's sight and allowed Josefina time to study her young mistress.

"When the *curandera* materialized out of the fog, a startled Annabella stumbled and stuttered her awkward apology for slighting the old witch at Emilio's birth.

"Making light of the indiscretion, putting Annabella at ease, she said, 'It was nothing more than first-child anxiety.'

"Relieved, Annabella fawned her admiration for the *curandera*, confiding her unique services and formidable powers were greatly in need. Then, Annabella gambled.

"'To enter into an intimate alliance with me, what are your requirements?'

"Acting neither surprised nor curious of her motive, the *curandera* assured Annabella that she would join in alliance with her if two simple conditions were met.

"'For my fidelity and use of my practice, for whatever your purpose, a small gesture, senora, from your considerable resource is a necessity.

"'First, senora, all my days on the rancho, I have lived in a small shack that I am made to share with disgusting farm animals. They are always going and coming, coming and going—the donkeys, cows, and horrible pigs.

"'Senora, what I desire…what I crave most…is permanency. I fancy a home to call my own, where living with an open door is not a requirement.

"'A modest home, warm from the winter, with a good floor, four walls, and sturdy roof to withstand any weather. Without that, it would be impossible for me to guarantee that someone else could not wrest away my fidelity.'

"Annabella nodded agreement. 'Once you have helped me fulfill my plans, I will gladly build you a lovely new home in a pleasant location on the rancho.'

"'Second, senora, for the use of my practice, your undivided loyalty is demanded.'

"'Senora, will you guarantee your loyalty to me?'

"'What guarantee, to your satisfaction, can I provide?'

"'The use of my practice is a solemn trust and must be honored with respect. The risk is great to me should someone become sick or injured, or even die.

"'If someone should say, "this is all the *curandera's* doing"— senora, this is a serious thing, and I would suffer greatly.

"'You see, senora, that is the dilemma for both of us, you and me.

"'And yet, to solve this dilemma of guarantees, the answer is simple.

"'First, your guarantee provides me with my own home.'

"Then, searching Annabella's eyes, she said, 'The second condition that guarantees our alliance, is this. You are a mother of a wonderful child, very precious to you, I am sure. So precious that should he get sick or injured, or even die, the loss to you would be as great as if my practice was taken from me.

"'So, you see, the solution is quite simple. Your fidelity to me will prevent a sickness for a sickness, an injury for an injury, or even a death for a death.

"'In our alliance, it is your child's well-being that guarantees fidelity to me. Should you forsake your fidelity, your son would belong to me.'"

"Emilio's life ransomed the partnership. Without hesitation, Annabella agreed.

"The shocked witch could not know Annabella had no love for her son and never would. Whatever happened to Emilio did not matter; his mother did not care. So their evil alliance was born."

"Perched in village San Xavier, gray-and-white carrier pigeons conveyed messages from Annabella to the *curandera* and back again.

"In the black night overhead, unheard and unseen, with curled missives fixed to feathered legs, the messengers on wing arrived after midnight.

"Awaiting their fluttering arrival, Annabella mused, 'They are old friends come to a visit. How fitting. They bring tormenting spells and dreadful curses, to my bedroom window.'"

CHAPTER 29

Flores de Flores and Josefina Espinoza

———— ∞∞∞ ————

"On a foggy morning ushering in the Ides of March, an odd little man knocked at Yolanda's door. Standing the height of a ten-year-old boy, he appeared without premonition or preamble. Yet his wrinkled nape and drooping ears that rested in deep folds on his flaccid cheeks told an old, old story. Common to himself, others might declare him eccentric or bizarre!

"The resurrection of an eighteenth-century sailor, his ensemble consisted of a rust-colored duster knotted tightly at the throat, covering most of a faded blue tunic. The blouse, reinforced by a wide black leather belt, cinched by a shiny silver buckle, secured tightly the grizzled knickers hovering just above his bowed knees.

With no strength to stand alone, his tattered stockings fell at his ankles, partially covering his ridiculous shoes, three sizes too large for his feet and curling to a salute at the tip of the toe.

"His head was bare save for straggled hair piled in circular layers in one lengthy braid frazzled at the ends atop his head, pointing to the sky. His eyes the color of gray stone, sharpened by the point of a nose too large for his face, seemed to flutter in a dreamy trance. Akin to a windblown weathervane, his proboscis preceded his every move. Despite the absurdity, his face glowed with kindness, his disposition with humility.

"Yolanda thought him harmless until he stood on a milking stool to whisper in her ear his terrible message.

"'At hand, an illness approaches nigh; be forewarned, too soon ye die.'

"In prepositional prose, he continued.

"'Senora, the time is now...to tend to final affairs, to make way your child's future, to then rest in your fate.

"'Heed my counsel, death is your certainty. It comes to all, some sooner, some later. Your time is more precious...now.'

"Yolanda stood unwavering.

"'Little man, who are you to deliver such dreadful news? Are you a rancho resident?'

"Bowing, he replied. 'Flores de Flores, at your service.'

"Nodding, confident, brimming with antidotes, he added, 'I am from the village of San Xavier, where sadly I have seen with my own eyes many strange things and ongoings.'

"When Yolanda did not respond, he jumped down from the milking stool and stood a head shorter than her.

"'Senora, did you not hear the direness of my words? Are you at all concerned if not for your safety, then that of your child?'

"Voicing a few prophecies of her own, Yolanda clenched her fists and confronted the prophet.

"'Listen to me, you peddler of counterfeit cures and silly enchantments. I will not buy any of your herbs or remedies. You can expect no commerce here. On your way to the next fool who might scare so easily. I am sure it is your ridiculous appearance much more than your words that frightens the naive.'

"Spitting on his pointed shoes, she warmed to the task.

"'You are nothing but a fraud, a conjurer, and a false prophet who lives on people's fear. I would not believe anything you say.'

"To stop her, he raised his hand higher and higher until she was silent.

"Certain she would not interrupt, he cleared his sagging throat and offered, 'There is no profit or joy in this enterprise for me, senora. I have no herbs or remedies for you, only my words of alarm.'

"And his eyes filled with tears as he turned away so Yolanda could not see. He stared into space and asked, 'Do you know of Josefina Espinoza?'

"Not waiting for her to reply, he stammered. 'If you live on the rancho, you know she is the *curandera*, an evil, horrible witch who is guilty of vicious and vile atrocities perpetrated on the innocent.'

"His silence ended in an explosive wail that forced Yolanda to shrink back, afraid for the first time.

"He screamed, 'She took my wife and child!'

"Sitting on the milking stool, he lowered his head and muttered in a language Yolanda did not know. After a moment, he lifted his wretched face and explained his grief.

"'We were old people who married late. This child would be our first and last.'

"With a strange language weaving in and out, he ran his words together. Yolanda, more curious than frightened, moved closer to the little man.

"'Early one morning late in her pregnancy, my Elizabeth and I rode to San Luis to see Dr. Martinez. I borrowed the church's buckboard from Padre Antonio. Happy to be away from the village that winter's day, my

Elizabeth did not complain about the bumpy road or the hard wagon seat.

"'I remember her laughing in the crispness of the January winds. She loved being out in the country, smelling the dampness of the sage, the dew on the grass, watching with a child's joy the huge white clouds above.

"'When we arrived, the doctor waved us into his office and told my Elizabeth to disrobe. During the examination, he asked my Elizabeth many questions and listened carefully to her answers.

"'After my Elizabeth dressed, he motioned for us to sit in his office chairs. He smiled confidently, congratulating us on her good care during the pregnancy. 'Your child's birth is very near and the baby should be very healthy.'

"'Explaining his concern, because of her age, my Elizabeth would have a very difficult time when the baby came in the next few days or so.

"'Do not return home,' he said. 'Stay close here in San Luis so I can be on hand to oversee the birth. I will make arrangements for you.

"'If you go back to San Xavier now, I cannot guarantee I would arrive at the rancho in time to help.'

"'But my Elizabeth feared the *curandera*, who insisted that the birth take place in our home village and nowhere else.'

"The little man turned toward Yolanda, paused as if unsure, and cried out, 'She pleaded with me to take her home. I should not have listened.'

"'Take me home to have this child, Flores. We must not make the *curandera* angry. The doctor does not know the power this witch holds over life and death. If she is my midwife, she promised me that all will be well and baby will be born with her blessing.'

"Wiping away his tears with a soaked duster, he breathed a sigh of regret and moaned. 'According to her wishes I gave in to my beautiful Elizabeth. We did not stay in San Luis, but returned home, and I prayed as I have never prayed before.

"'A few days later, when the labor pains came, my Elizabeth's became very sick. I begged the *curandera* to let me go for the doctor. But the old witch cursed me.

"'With a demon's face, red with blood, she screamed.

"'Insist on the doctor and I will see to it your Elizabeth suffers all the more. The doctor would curse even more this child's birth.'

"'Singing chants I could not understand, the *curandera*, plying her craft, brewed teas, smeared poultices, and anointed my Elizabeth's body with foul ointments.'

"'For two days and nights, the witch's treatment wore on, with no sign of my Elizabeth improving.

"'When my Elizabeth started to bleed and vomit, the witch took off her *rebozo*, wrapping it tightly around my Elizabeth's body. Tied and bound from shoulders to ankles, my Elizabeth could not move. No relief came. Her suffering worsened, and still, the child did not come.

"'Then my Elizabeth's eyes rolled back into her head. With her last burst of strength as if some invisible force ripped at her bonds, the *rebozo* binding her body shredded. In her final agony, moaning in terrible longing, with her last breath she called out, 'Flores, Flores only to die.'

"He wiped his sweating face. His body shuddered as a fetid odor permeated the air around him. Re-creating the dreadful scene, he carried on acting out each character.

"'The *curandera* ripped off what was left of the blood- and vomit-soaked *rebozo*. Then, with a surgeon's precision, she cut our child out of my Elizabeth's womb. But it was too late, too late. The birth cord had twisted tightly around his neck, and my baby son was dead. Like a butchered pig, the witch held him upside down by his tiny ankles.

"'Glowering with a despicable smile, she condemned me.

"'In her misery, Elizabeth screamed your name, blaming you for begging for the doctor. I lay these deaths at your door.'

"Re-enacting the scene, Flores lunged forward.

"'I reached out for my dead child, but the witch laughed and pulled him away.

"'Do not worry about him, Flores. This little one belongs to me now. I will take care of his ending.

"'And I never saw him again.'

"Arms outstretched, straining for his dead son, he finished his story and collapsed, exhausted, plopping down once again on the milking stool.

"'The next morning, my Elizabeth's burial took place in the graveyard next to the village church.

"'Everyone in San Xavier was there. Everyone cried. And everyone realized it unwise to ask about the child. For everyone knew the special plans the *curandera* had for him.'

"Trying to console the little man, Yolanda could not speak. She believed his incredible story, because it could not be anything but the truth.

"Her face paled, and her eyes seemed to drown in their dark brown pools. Sobbing, she begged for forgiveness.

"'Forgive me, senor. Please forgive me. What sorrow, what pain. How can you bear this murder? When did this happen?'

"He never looked up when he said, 'I shall never forget. These monstrous sins befell my family on the tenth day of the new year, fourscore days from Emilio's birth.' Reaching up, he took her hand. His touch was gentle. Cradling the back of her hand with his, he gently traced the lines in her palm and he took up his tragic tale again.

"Stabbing the duster at his wet cheeks, he spoke slowly now, rarely above a whisper."

CHAPTER 30

"I Know All Their Plans"

❦

"We were workers for the *curandera*, my Elizabeth and me. My Elizabeth gathered things; herbs and leaves, roots and sap. These were the things the *curandera* used to concoct medicine, bring spells, and create curses—her stock in trade, sold to the sick and desperate and rich and the gullible.

"'I gathered frogs and lizards, hummingbirds and owl droppings and eggs, but mostly pigeons—the pigeons I trained that carried her unholy messages.

"'My Elizabeth and I were so happy and proud to have such an important job for the *curandera*, so prominent to the villagers, well regarded, feared, and respected.

"'We assisted Josefina Espinoza for the two seasons and the rancho was such a happy place. The villagers married, the babies came, the crops were bountiful, and the newborn calves, pigs, sheep, and horses crowded the barnyards and stables.

"'When Don Vincenti announced he would be bringing his new bride home to live at Rancho Piedra Blanca, we cheered for his good fortune.

"'And when Senora Annabella entered our lives, everyone was very happy. Overnight, however, our good feelings turned to sadness. Finding fault in everything we were and did, we learned she did not care for us at all.

"'To her, we were a useless rabble living in villages at the rancho's expense. We prayed to the Blessed Mother for our mistress to love us. But she never looked our way. She held no fondness for us at all, not for her servants, nor the ranch hands, or for our loving wives, not even for our children. With each passing month of her pregnancy, it seemed her distaste for us intensified. Senora Annabella's hatred made us afraid for our place on the rancho.

"'Because of her cruelty, several of the village children were punished for merely picking up the fallen oranges in the orchards. But they had done nothing wrong. They had always been allowed to eat the fallen fruit.

"'From Martha, the majordomo's wife, we learned the mistress complained to Don Vincenti, her husband. She convinced him the villagers were stealing the hen-house eggs and the field's wheat and the vineyard's grapes, none of it the truth. We were innocent and did not know what to do.'"

"'Excuse me, Senor Pablo. I remember Aunt Catalina speaking of the villagers' grief. Was it resolved?"

"Jose, at the beginning of Advent, in fear and desperation, a contingent of the villagers called on me. They trusted my reputation for fairness, saying I was known as the working-man's friend. And I listened compassionately, promising to carry their concerns to my father and brother. We believed that Annabella's attitude would change after the baby's birth, but as Flores explained to Yolanda, that was not to be."

"'Answering Don Joaquin's call, we prayed for the senora and for her baby to be healthy and strong. Waiting long hours and holding high hopes, we attended the birth vigil in the Hacienda de Leon courtyard.

"'My Elizabeth, heavy with our child, slept with me on the pavement. Sick and exhausted, she waited all those hours, like the other villagers, praying to the Holy Mother and Jesus the senora's travail would be brief.

"'When, at last, Don Joaquin made the blessed announcement of little Emilio's birth, we gave thanks and praised God, toasting the family's good fortune at the fiesta that followed, grateful too that tomorrow's work day would not start until the next afternoon.

"'We were hopeful that now our mistress would finally have a change of heart and be happy to embrace us as the good people we are. We desired nothing more than to love her and be loved in return.

"'With the successful birth, hope filled our souls. But the answer we waited for did not come.'"

"FLORES DE FLORES AND THE VILLAGE LEADERS MET WITH me again for an update on Thanksgiving Eve. I told them the problems had been discussed with my father and brother at length, and I felt things should improve very soon.'"

"'AFTER MEETING AGAIN WITH SENOR PABLO, WE WAITED anxiously, but no answer came. No answer, no answer—that is, except for the heartless decree posted in every rancho village that Christmas Eve.

"'Christmas was forgotten. Instead of gifts, much was taken from every family. In the harshest words, the decree forbade gleaning anywhere on the rancho. But the cruelty did not stop.

"'The edict decreased the villagers' harvest share, demanded men and women to be at work before sunrise every day and stay past sunset, and forever ended the monthly new moon Fiesta of the Roasted Pig.

"'We had always been kind and respectful and never offended her in any way. We did not understand why she hated us so. All these things were happening because Senora Annabella's heart was made of stone.

"'The saddest Christmas was never forgotten.

"'Two days later, I left my Elizabeth in the care of her mother and accompanied the *curandera* to Hacienda de Leon to pick up a large cage.

"'I loaded it and moved the wagon into the courtyard to wait for the witch to finish her business. When I parked, I noticed one of the wheel blocks had been left at the hacienda entrance.

"'When I walked back to pick it up, I heard the *curandera* and Senora Annabella talking quietly in the hacienda's foyer.

"'What they were saying frightened me to my soul. But who could I share it with? Who would believe the horrible things I heard from these women?

"'At first I thought the *curandera* poisoned the senora against us, convincing the senora to beat us down.

"'The rancho would be much better off without them,' she said. 'They eat like a thousand pigs, always filling the mouths of their dirty children, stealing everything they can carry from harvest to harvest.'"

"'But Senora Annabella tired of the *curandera's* ranting. Her only concern, she said, was ridding from her life the very people she should fear losing the most.

"'Old woman, your task is to find a way to quietly dispose of my dear sister and her bastard son! Then, at this time next year, I want Vincenti and his parents out of my life!

"'I do not care how it is done. Maybe a horse kicks them in the head, or there is a drowning at sea, or perhaps a deadly sickness overtakes them. That is your job. How you do it is your concern…just so I am seen as the inconsolable and grieving widow!

"'And, as for the rabble…all those filthy peasants like Flores de Flores who stink up the villages…once your deeds are done, I will drive them out, along with Rodrigo and his bitch wife!'

"'Then, she said to the *curandera*, 'No one is to ever see us together again. Once you leave here today, our only communication will be through the air!

"'Unless I send for you, do not ever come here. Once your tasks are completed and my innocence assured, your reward will be paid. Now go, and take the dwarf away from my sight. He is the most disgusting of the entire rabble!'

"'But, senora, what of Don Pablo? What is to become of him?'

"'Pablo…yes, Pablo. He is my affair, old woman. You are not invited to that party. He is my dish to relish with every bite. It will take me many years to finish that main course.'

"And Yolanda understood she had not yet heard the worst.

"'Senor Flores, why have you waited till today to seek me out? Everything you have seen and heard happened over two months ago. Why the urgency this day?'

"Straightening his crumpled tunic, his face beamed as he stood proudly to answer her question.

"'Senora Yolanda, although I have not seen the *curandera* since the day my family was taken from me, my pigeons talk to me. Every day from the sky…they come and talk to me.'

"He looked to the sky expecting a pigeon to roost on his arm at any moment.

"'Before the witch's message is delivered and before the birds fly back to their cages to return Senora Annabella's answer, every time they are set free, they seek me out. Wherever I am, they come first to me.'

"Smiling at Yolanda, he said this like the cat that just swallowed the canary.

"'That is how I trained them. The *curandera* does not know this. And she also does not know I have read all of the messages from the first to the last, sent back and forth between her and Senora Annabella.

"'I know all their secrets, and I know all their plans.

"'I have already paid a heavy price losing my family; you need not pay again. My pleasure, senora, is to save you from their wickedness. That is why I came seeking you this foggy morning. Last midnight the witch received the senora's newest message. Not only did she order your death but also that of your son. It is to be done within the week. So, you see, there is little time.'

"'It would be best that you leave the rancho now, without anyone knowing where you are going, not even me.'"

THE MOON'S LIGHT FLITTERED THROUGH THE SMALL parlor windows, mapping shadowed trails on the listeners' faces. The audience prayed the telling would end, so they could ask their burning questions.

Sipping coffee, Pablo's silence begged their patience.

Putting a finger to his lips, he reminded them answers would come only when the telling ended.

Then, entering uncharted waters, Pablo sailed Yolanda and her son to safe harbor.

CHAPTER 31

Escape to Sanctuary

"Yolanda and I talked quietly while Alejandro slept across from us on the coach seat. Our late-night coach ride ended at Monterey's dock an hour before their ship would sail.

"I carried the sleeping Alejandro on board and into their cabin, tucking him in bed, and still he slept. Through tears, we embraced and made promises we hoped to keep, saying long goodbyes, praying to always remember.

"Alejandro would awaken, unaware why he and his mother sailed away from Rancho Piedra Blanca, never to return.

"As the *Bastille Day* made way into the dark Pacific, I rushed to send a telegram to Padre Humberto in Mexico City.

"'Padre Humberto, please provide "sanctuary" to mother and son cursed with death by evil sister and *curandera*, stop. They sail secretly today from Monterey arriving Zihuatanejo French frigate Bastille Day, stop. As I once was an orphan in your care, I ask you to please welcome Yolanda and Alejandro Gomez as your wards to live in the safety of Santa Teresa de Avila, stop. Their innocence demands sanctuary, stop. Take them in without question, stop. To remain here at Piedra Blanca means their death, stop. They are like my own, stop. Upon ship's arrival, Captain Prulette to deliver my financial guarantee and letter of introduction explaining situation, stop. More complete correspondence to follow, stop.'"

"I CONTINUED MY DAILY ROUTINE, STAYING AWAY FROM the hacienda and any contact with Annabella. Concerned, my parents asked the whereabouts of Yolanda and her son. Awaiting news of their safe arrival at Santa Teresa de Avila, I said nothing to anyone about where they went or Annabella's deadly plans.

"The good news came in late May. Padre Humberto's letter, sent in the care of Padre Fray Tomas at Mission San Miguel, confided Yolanda and Alejandro had indeed taken up residential sanctuary at the rectory of Santa Teresa de Avila.

"Two weeks later a message came to me from Annabella.

"'Pablo, do you know where my sister and nephew can be reached? No one seems to know. I have spoken to everyone and my parents are worried. Annabella'

"To Annabella's astonishment, the next morning, for the first time since early March, she found me sitting at the hacienda's breakfast table talking to Vincenti and Rodrigo.

"We stopped our conversation to stand when she entered the dining room. Except for 'buenos dias,' no one spoke.

"When breakfast ended, Rodrigo and I walked toward the stables to collect our horses for the day's work. Annabella followed us as expected.

"'Rodrigo, please excuse me for a moment. I need to speak to Senor Pablo.'

"'Of course, senora.' And he continued on to the stables.

"'I will catch up to you, Rodrigo,' I shouted after him.

"I forced a smile, and through clenched teeth, asked what it was she wanted.

"'Did you not get my note about Yolanda?'

"'Yes…but I cannot answer your question.'

"'You cannot or will not? Which is it, Pablo?'

"My face betrayed anger.

"'Take your pick. You deserve no answers from me. Perhaps the *curandera* can enlighten you? She is your good friend. Why do you not ask her? She has all the answers.'

"Then I walked away. Jolted that I somehow knew of her relationship with the witch, she feigned innocence.

"'What are you talking about?'

"In the likelihood others were watching, I forced a cordial smile and lowered my voice.

"'Do you really want to discuss this here? Or perhaps, you are not worried who hears what I know?'

"I leaned closer to her ear, and growled. 'Could it be, like me, everyone already knows of your monstrous plan.'

"She began to tremble and cry, and the color drained from her face.

"'How can he know these things?' screamed in her head.

"Regaining composure, she unconsciously reached out, gripping my wrist for support. Then, as night turns to day, a grin widened across her face and she loosened her hold. I knew the ice had returned to her veins when she said, 'There is much to discuss, Pablo, but not here. Let us meet like the old days, at week's end, at the shepherd's hut, to make sense of all of this.'"

CHAPTER 32

Entrapment

"Now that Yolanda and Alejandro were out of danger, I could not wait to confront Annabella here in this very hut Friday afternoon. Our brief courtyard meeting kindled a roaring fire in me to put her in her place. How I practiced what I would say!

"Once I finished with Annabella, I planned to put my affairs in order and leave Rancho Piedra Blanca for a new life in Mexico City with Yolanda and Alejandro.

"I remember smiling, riding past the grove of familiar pines where Annabella stood waiting for me. In the rendez-vous days of our past, the abandoned shepherd's hut had been a favorite place to meet. But today's encounter would be very different. How eager I was to clip her wings.

"I dismounted and walked slowly toward her, taking my time. Confident all the wrongs would be righted that day, with a broad smile plastered on my face, I shook my hat and brushed the trail dust from my sleeves.

"Annabella, apparently, was very happy to see me. She came running, throwing her arms around my neck, begging me to kiss her. My happy smile turned to disgust. Gritting my teeth, fighting the urge to slap her, I shoved her away.

"'How little you think of me, Annabella. Acting the whore cannot buy my silence! What you have done will not be forgotten nor forgiven. If you were not my brother's wife,

I would tie you to the courtyard post and horse-whip you for everyone to see. You are fortunate that no one has died from your nonsense. If anyone had, this mountain could not hold all the people who would rejoice, seeing you and that witch hanging from these trees.'

"But the grin never left her face. She tried to speak, but uninterested in anything she had to say, I grabbed her wrists and threw her to the ground.

"Standing over her, I demanded, 'Remove the curses now, Annabella. Remove all of them now and be glad that is all my silence will cost you.'

"She looked up at me, stifling a giggle. It was then she realized a change in tactics was in order. I laughed at her as she stared at me from the dirt.

"'My dear sister-in-law, your secrets are not so secret, are they?'

"I dangled the incrimination over her head like an ax sharpened by her guilt.

"'So that there is no misunderstanding, a witness to your plans to murder everyone has written this very detailed and incriminating letter. It charges you and the *curandera* for conspiring to kill Vincenti, Don Joaquin, Mama Dolores, Rodrigo, and Martha.'

"Holding it over her head I said, 'Before you ever consider such foolishness again, this letter is all the evidence needed to stop you cold.'

"I laughed. 'It is good insurance, no?'

"Like a wrongfully accused child, she said nothing, but the feline grin on her face, growing from ear to ear, spoke loudly that she knew something I did not.

"Her impertinence angered me all the more, and I swore on Emilio's soul. 'Should anyone of them die, Annabella, for any reason, this letter ensuring their lives will be delivered immediately to the authorities in Monterey.'

"Finished with what I had come to say, I left her sitting in the dirt and walked to my horse.

"Twirling around like a schoolgirl, she jumped up and dashed ahead, blocking my path.

"She giggled and brought her face close to mine.

"'My dear Pablo, I have no problem doing what it is you ask. I have no problem at all.'

"But sarcasm poisoned her words.

"'Is it not true, my dear Pablo, in all such negotiations, there is give and take, no?'

"I was having none of this.

"'What can you possibly negotiate, Annabella?'

"Her green eyes flamed and her body coiled as she hissed her outrageous demands.

"'So that no one should hang themselves, become sick and die from exotic illness, or fall victim to a stampede of hooves…to be quite certain nothing unfortunate like that should happen, these are the concessions required of you, my dearest Pablo. They are tiny things, but, unlike your letter, these three tiny things required of you guarantee the lives of the rabble you love so much.'

"'First,' touching her nose to mine, 'promise that I am the only wife you will ever have. Second,' she said, staring into my eyes, 'promise that only I will mother your children. Third,' shouting into my ear, 'promise me you will never leave Piedra Blanca.'"

⁙

"Any breeze that stirred the trees at that moment died, and San Simeon and I groaned in pitiful surrender.

"Scolding me, she laughed. 'You have always belonged to me, Pablo. You know you could never be without me!'

"Praying my poker face had not crumbled, in one last effort at bravado, I lunged for the reins of my horse and screamed, 'What silly game are you playing now? When I leave today, you will be out of my life and I will never see you again.'

"At my obvious misery, she squealed with delight. 'My dearest Pablo, you are so delicious and so predictable. Calm yourself and know this so there is no misunderstanding! If you should ever be foolish enough to leave me, letter or no letter, your separation would be reason enough for me to resume my business with the *curandera*. And any promised protection for your rabble would leave with you.'"

SHAKING WITH RAGE, PABLO SMASHED HIS COFFEE CUP on the kitchen floor. Rosa rushed to his side, but Manuel motioned her to stay seated and let the drama play out. Struggling to stand, the old man, in a crazed fury, yelled, "Her impudence staggered me!

"She dangled my soul; she held me captive. With hope crushed and spirit broken, I rode like a madman to Mission San Miguel. Exhausted, I arrived just as the Friday afternoon Lenten service ended.

"I lashed my horse to the water trough and ran into the chapel in time to observe a masterpiece come to life. The altar boys, with brass snuffers, extinguishing Station of the Cross candles, appeared to be walking out of a Goya painting.

"I fell on my knees, thanking God this vision was a sign.

"The bells tolled thrice, calling sinners to Lenten confession hour. With incense filling the vestibule, Padre Fray Tomas, in his ornate confessor's cassock, surplice, and stole, walked forlornly from the sacristy to the ornate confessional box, the very place of my blasphemy.

"The priest was disgusted. After presiding in the majesty of the Stations of the Cross, his power to forgive would be squandered on the trifling sins his parishioners always confessed.

"With the power of limitless absolution, absolving venial sins confessed by nuns, old women, and schoolchildren amounted to an insulting exploitation of his power to forgive.

"Those insignificant offenses justified a negligible penance; at most a handful of Hail Marys and an Act of Contrition.

"What he hungered for was the hardened sinner, a degenerate possessing a lifetime of mortal sins that festered in his soul. He prayed that today would be the day a good-for-nothing sinner would slither shamefully into his confessional, begging on his knees for forgiveness for a sinful magnitude.

"That sin-ridden penitent, fearing God's eternal damnation, could inspire the heavenly choirs to rejoice, proclaiming salvation for a sinner lost but now found!

"That kind of wretch, a true aspirant for purging, offered a momentous challenge to his right to absolve. But on every former Lenten Friday afternoon, such a sinful soul remained long-absent from his confessional box.

"Padre Fray Tomas prayed for someone like the highway bandit Vasquez to miraculously appear, kneeling, ready to confess at the window of forgiveness his litany of indiscretions.

"With hopes high, praying hard for this heavenly coup, the good padre slid the confessional curtain open and blessed his first penitent.

"'In the name of the Father, and the Son, and the Holy Ghost, what are your sins, my child?'

"'Bless me, padre, for I have sinned in thought, word, and deed. I do not remember the time of my last confession, but I am here to confess all my sins and request your guidance on a matter of grave importance.'

"'Pablo…? Is that you?'

"'Yes, padre.'

"'Are you all right? You have not made your confession with me since you arrived at the mission almost two years ago. What is your trouble, my son?'

"'I continued to confess my many sins, ending with the illicit affair carried on with Annabella the night before her marriage to my brother Vincenti.

"'I am sorry to confess, padre, the depraved act, the most despicable of my sins, took place in this very confessional box the night before my brother took her as his wife. I received a message from her. She said she had something very important to discuss and to meet her at the mission after midnight.

"'But instead of a private discussion, all she really wanted was one last time together. When she took off her clothes, I was too weak to resist. That was the last time we were ever together.'

"'Does your brother know of your relations with his wife?'

"'If he does, he has not spoken of it, nor have I.'

"'And Pablo, who is Emilio's father?'

"The question rocked me. I swallowed hard but answered truthfully.

"'Padre, the night of Emilio's birth, after Annabella delivered the boy, she refused to take her son to her breast. She wanted nothing to do with the child, screaming at Yolanda that the child was mine. She told Yolanda that she and Vincenti had never lain together, even on their wedding night, and that she would never let him touch her.'

"'Pablo, did she have any other lovers?'

"'I do not know…I do not think so, padre.'

"After a long pause, at last, the priest said to go on.

"'It is true, that after they married, I missed her.

"'But then came her pregnancy and I was happy for Vincenti, thinking he had embraced his manhood.

"'With the announcement of the coming child, I was very glad she was finally out of my hair and my life.

"'Four months before Emilio was born, Yolanda came to help Annabella through her pregnancy. She and I began courting and soon we fell in love. Already, I cared deeply for Alejandro. It all seemed so good, so right.

"'Yolanda loved me and was ready for a husband, and Alejandro needed a father.

"'Our marriage plans were well known, and everyone was happy for us except Annabella.

"'As sisters do, before she was married, Annabella confided in Yolanda about everything, including her affair with me.

"'To Yolanda, it did not matter. She knew her sister to be a greedy woman and a freebooter, always wanting what she could not have. Although Annabella told Yolanda that she still loved me, she chose to marry Vincenti and become the new mistress of Piedra Blanca for the power and wealth that came with her position.

"'The night Emilio was born, in her fury, when she claimed I was Emilio's father, Annabella threatened to kill her sister and Alejandro if Yolanda became my bride.

"'It was obvious that Annabella would stop at nothing to prevent Yolanda from marrying me.

"'Yolanda demanded to leave Emilio's care immediately, but Vincenti pleaded for her to stay on until Emilio gained strength and was out of danger. Yolanda was satisfied with Emilio's condition and left Vincenti's employ to begin her life with me.

"'When my brother forced Emilio's daily care on to Annabella, her hatred perverted into an absurd thirst for revenge. She planned to kill anyone who in any way opposed her, including Yolanda and her son, Don Joaquin, and Mama Dolores, Vincenti, and the majordomo and his wife.

"'Annabella engaged Josefina Espinoza, the village *curandera* to place the curse of death on them all.

"'Flores de Flores, the *curandera's* assistant, warned Yolanda that she and her son were first to be killed. That is when Yolanda sought my help.'

"'Excuse me, Pablo. Who is this Flores?'

"'I never met him, Padre. Yolanda described him as a tiny person, a man decimated and distraught by the death of his wife and baby in childbirth at the hands of the *curandera*. Flores became aware of Annabella's scheme. What he overheard, he confirmed by intercepting the messages Annabella and the *curandera* sent to one another by the carrier pigeons he trained.

"'He then rushed to warn Yolanda to leave with Alejandro immediately, or become victims.

"'Three months ago, on the very night I learned of Annabella's plans, I sent Yolanda and her son by ship to seek sanctuary at my boyhood home in Mexico City at Santa Teresa de Avila rectory. Annabella sent me a note asking where her sister and nephew could be found. Of course, I did not answer.

"'Sent in your care, a letter for me recently arrived, confirming they were safe and living at the church rectory, the same home I enjoyed as a child.

"'When I was sure they were out of danger, I felt the time was right to confront Annabella and stop her before someone was hurt.

"'Today was the day. And although she agreed to remove the curses, she demands my life in exchange.'

"I listed for him Annabella's required concessions.

"'To keep those cursed safe and out of harm, you can see she is forcing me to ransom my life. That is why I am here. I need your help.'

"Realizing Annabella's required concessions demanded my total compliance, the priest shook his head.

"'Oh, Pablo, my poor boy, you have played with the devil and you have lost. For your penance, you must give your life to this devil of a woman so that the ones you love remain safe. It is the price you must pay for your sinful involvement with Annabella. She has taken your earthly freedom. But be thankful to the Lord, Pablo. Fulfilling your penance assures you eternal life.

"'There can be no doubt that you are Emilio's father. I remember well that dark night you soiled my confessional with your sin. I witnessed it.

"'In that one act…conceiving a child…you committed your life to her for eternity.

"'Although I performed their wedding ceremony, by her own admission, Annabella and Vincenti never consummated their marriage, and therefore, they are not married.

"'Your relations with Annabella were, indeed, consummated, and your son Emilio is the result. Pablo, my poor unfortunate boy, even though she has chosen to live with Vincenti, your brother, in the eyes of the church, you are, indeed, her husband.

"'She is the woman to whom you are married. She is the woman who bears your child. She is a proven student of the faith, and knows the laws of the church much better than you. Pablo, with sadness, I tell you she is the woman to whom you are forever obligated.

"'I pity you, my son. Your life is not yours to give to any other woman. Although no church ceremony has taken place, the church declares you are, indeed, married to Annabella, and you are obliged to forsake all others.

"'Through your good confession, by God's grace, you are indeed blessed this day and your soul has been saved. But your sin is so great you will suffer its penance for your lifetime, or until Annabella dies.'"

IT WAS LATE...AFTER MIDNIGHT. PABLO'S AUDIENCE WAS tired, confused, heartbroken.

Questions would wait.

His face frozen in pain, his cheeks swollen from tears, Pablo sat silent, clenching in his teeth a cold pipe, like him, out of fuel.

Except for Manuel picking up pieces of the broken cup, the group sat silent for a long time before anyone moved.

At last, Rosa motioned to Conchita. Leaving the men in the parlor, the women walked into Jose's tiny kitchen, put on sweaters, and thought hard about what they just learned.

When Mother Nature intervened, Jose and Manuel donned their coats and headed behind the garage for the outhouse. Jaime sat next to Pablo, dabbing his handkerchief at his eyes and, occasionally, at Pablo, whom he would drive home that night.

As always, the world's gears ground on and on. And San Xavier refused to die. At that moment, a five-point buck and his pretty doe, craving a midnight snack, trotted down the middle of the dark village road and darted into Andoleto's hay shelter.

Bewildered, with no direction, the miserable faithful wandered aimlessly into foreign terrain, suffering in the gravity of Pablo's grief.

Bringing the evening to a torturous close, a somber Manuel, with Rosa right behind, walked out of Jose's garage to their miserable flatbed. The depressing drive home that most pitiful night brought with it a cold winter's wind that predicted a wretched spring.

CHAPTER 33

Jaime and Veronica

⟨≈≈≈⟩

A week passed…no contact with Pablo. Since that last night at Jose's, no one had seen or heard from him, including the ever-devoted Rosa, who had her own problems with a throbbing toothache.

That same afternoon, a sweating, befuddled Jose drove Poncho Madragon's 1939 Buick Roadmaster out of the supply yard. His phone calls to Manuel went unanswered. Frustrated, not knowing what else to do, Jose raced to Cambria to Manuel and Rosa's home. His urgency ignited when Jaime received a call that morning from detective Lieutenant Raymundo Muchado, to meet with him in Salinas at the police station.

Driving Highway 1, the old El Camino Real Trail, Manuel did his best to console his aching wife. On the way home from Santa Maria, he navigated past the White Rocks to Morro Bay and Rosa's favorite ice cream parlor, where he planned to treat her to a double-scooped chocolate fudge ice cream sundae, her very favorite.

He favored himself with two scoops of pistachio on a cone, served in a sundae dish, eaten slowly with an old-fashioned wooden spoon.

Cherishing him for his thoughtfulness, Rosa smiled and patted his cheek, praying the icy coldness and melting cream would bring a bit more relief to the bottom left molar, where her painful cavity had been expertly drilled and filled by legendary dentist, Dr. Johnny Regales.

"Slow down, *viejo*. The chocolate makes my tooth feel better. Driving so fast will not."

They took the Cambria turnoff in time to see a flashy green Buick up ahead, soon out of sight except for the cloud of dust it left behind.

Manuel pulled his flatbed into their yard and found Jose sitting on the bumper, with the Roadmaster parked at their front door.

"Thank God, you are home at last. Where have you been? I have been calling, but no one ever answered."

Rosa explained the emergency dentist visit and asked, "Why are you in such a huff?"

Jose blurted a continuous stream of concern for Jaime.

"Jaime told me he would call, but I have waited the entire day. No call. I tried you; no answer. Finally, I rushed over in Madragon's car to see if you were home…and if not, I was waiting till you arrived. Thank God you came so fast.

"The detective asked Jaime about Veronica's suicide, and if her death had something to do with the Patron's."

"You know how it was. When Jaime found out how the Patron accosted Veronica, he went crazy. He cried and screamed and threatened to kill every de Leon, especially the Patron.'"

"But, Jose, Jaime never acted on it. He never hurt anyone."

"Yes, I know that…you know that…and I never told anyone else about how crazy he was that day. But the words were said…I heard every one of them."

Manuel's uncorked wine bottle, ever-present, sat on the kitchen table—last year's vintage, smooth and strong. He poured Jose a glass.

"Drink, drink. Let's calm down. Now, how did the police connect the two deaths? No one else heard Jaime's threats. Rosa, what do you think?"

While Rosa sipped her wine, the answer came to her in one name. "Felicity."

"'Veronica and Felicity Morales came to work at Hacienda de Leon the very first time that day. Felicity left less than an hour after arriving. Her parents told me that she never wanted to go back there again…something about drawing a bath for the Patron and his insistence that she bathe him."

With crazed eyes bulging, both men glared at Rosa.

"Why did you not tell me about Felicity giving the Patron a bath?!"

"Viejo…she refused to bathe the old bastard. When they questioned me I never told the *policia* about it either. I felt the less attention on Veronica and Jaime the better. My guess…they most likely talked to Felicity's parents."

"Where is Jaime?" Rosa shouted.

"He should be coming back from Salinas by now. Maria and Juanito are at the crossroads waiting to be picked up."

ON THEIR LAST DAY OF SCHOOL, SITTING AT THE SCHOOL-bus stop, Maria saw her father's car long before brother Juanito fell off the bus bench. Daubing his tears with her hankie, she picked him up and wiped the blood from the small cut on his elbow.

"Juanito, stand up and stop crying. Papa is here."

With dust clouds billowing, Jaime stopped the old Chevy a distance from his kids on the gravel shoulder. Upset and shaken by the police interrogation, he sat quietly taking in his precious son and daughter.

Driving back from Salinas, living the grief of his wife's incomprehensible death all over again, he spoke to his departed Veronica, telling her all about the kids and how their love for her grew stronger each day.

"How much they miss their mama."

The children filed into the somber car without their father's customary happy greeting. He scarcely listened as Maria explained about the blood, the handkerchief, and her brother's tears. Except for Juanito's occasional whimper, not another word was spoken.

The afternoon's breeze ushered them to Jose's garage where Jaime found the note his father posted.

"Jaime, call Rosa as soon as you get home."

He slipped the paper into his shirt pocket and walked slowly across the dirt road to the phone booth at Andoleto's. What good news he had, he would gladly share.

Rosa answered. With all their ears listening at the receiver, Jaime recounted his day with Detective Muchado.

CHAPTER 34

Invitation to the Ice House

⌘

The first days of summer approached and Pablo's story languished untold. The last torturous recollection killed off all his inspiration, withering Pablo into silence. Recalling his inescapable union with Annabella merely fueled the misery and loss he suffered throughout his life.

Regardless of friendly encouragement, the old shepherd could not bring himself to take up his tragic tale again. Yet, he knew in his heart his story would not die untold.

On Friday, the sixteenth of June, 1947, seasonal heat burst into flame that blistering day. And everyone knew "Harvest Eve" was coming, a time to rejoice and have fun.

Families from every rancho, town, and village marked their calendars, eager for the fiesta to begin. From the new foals to future crop harvests, the people came together annually to give thanks for God's blessing of new life and abundance.

Village San Xavier hosted Harvest Eve the last weekend in June and the crowds that gathered in the sweltering heat would be massive.

Not telling a soul, Pablo volunteered to manage the ice house production of the tons of ice essential to keeping revelers cool and vendors in business during the searing days of Harvest Eve.

The ice facility was a large tin building at the edge of San Xavier. Formerly a hay depository, the rancho renovated it with running water, electricity, and massive ice-making equipment, purchased a dime on a dollar from a defunct Salinas ice plant. No fool, Pablo hired experienced workers from the shuttered Salinas facility, relying on their expertise.

The ice-making commenced in mid-June and continued until Harvest Eve ended. Well organized with their help, he promised to keep the ice coming.

The new challenge revitalized him. After a hard day at the factory, his old bones ached, but he slept well. The demands of this important responsibility kept him busy, happy, and most of all, creative. In the back of his mind, an ingenious plan took shape to rekindle his storytelling once again.

He personally designed hand-crafted invitations addressed individually to each of his faithful listeners, inviting them as specially selected rancho "honorees" to attend the grand opening of the Harvest Eve Ice House, Thursday, June 29, at 4 p.m., the day before the fiesta began.

"Congratulations, Honoree. After weighing the merits of all candidates, you have been chosen as the Harvest Eve's honored guests to attend the grand opening of the Harvest Eve Ice House. Come and enjoy fiesta hospitality in the cool refreshing comfort of our magnificent ice house. For your pleasure, California champagne and exotic refreshments will be served. Remember: Please keep this invitation confidential! Do not share your good fortune with anyone."

With such a large carrot dangling and dressed to the nines in his best suit, Jose was the first to arrive that stifling day. On a collar too big for his neck, his bow tie, a colorful affair, rested just under his Adam's apple. With each step he took, like a ship at sea, the gaudy tie rose and sank.

Ushering the "honorees," the tiny dancing *niña* adorned in flamenco costume and castanets, met Jose, dancing him out of the sweltering heat of the parking lot into the small, cool lobby. Arriving next in a meticulously polished and shiny Chevy coupe were Jaime and Conchita.

For the ice house grand opening, Conchita needed a new dress. Desperate for a ride, she defied the rules and confided her secret to Jaime, telling him all about the honoree invitation she received and asking "could he help her out."

Jaime admitted he too made the list and could use a new suit for the occasion as well. On a bright Friday morn, under the guise of visiting a doctor for Conchita's recurring skin rash, the two conspirators left in Jaime's coupe on a motor excursion to Salinas's finest clothing stores.

Jaime parked his coupe carefully next to a showy red 1937 Ford sedan, the only other car near the ice house entrance.

Squinting at bright afternoon sun, helping an elegant Conchita out of the coupe, Jaime pulled a hankie from his new sharkskin suit's lapel pocket to dab at his sweaty brow.

The tiny dancer with graceful pirouettes and castanet staccatos escorted the stylish couple to the coolness of the lobby and introduced them to another lucky "honoree," the startled Jose.

While Jaime wondered, "Whose car did he steal this time?" a surprised Jose wondered, "You were honorees too?"

Before Jaime could ask, his father confessed. "The Ford is Poncho Lolinda's. He owes me money."

With not a moment for father and son to rejoice their incredible luck as chosen honorees, Manuel and Rosa sauntered into the chilly lobby behind the tiny dancer. The five speechless friends could only stare at each other.

Playing Pablo's favorite on cue, the mariachi band struck up the *grito* "El Jarable Tapatio," the Mexican Hat Dance. Loud and brash, the mariachis played on as the castanet virtuoso danced the befuddled "honorees" into the ice house interior to introduce them to a mysterious host they all knew so well.

⸙

THE RUSE WORKED TO PERFECTION, AND THE VICTIMS blushed naively. When the laughing died down and the kissing turned to clutching and handshakes, Pablo cried happy tears.

In the coolness of the ice house, the musical gaiety played on and the champagne cocktails flowed. The delicious reunion made the fare filling their bellies and nurturing their souls taste all the better for the ploy.

For his ingenuity and bravado and to tell him everyone loved him very much, Jose, acting as the toastmaster, raised his glass to honor host Pablo. The house roared, "Bravo, Bravo!

"To Pablo!"

The sly old shepherd was not only the first Master of the Waterways, but now the first Master of the Ice House.

Rosa grabbed her husband's clapping hands to pull him close. She whispered tenderly in his good ear, "We both love Pablo very much, but you, my darling, in my heart, will always be the God of the Creeks!"

Patting her hand, Manuel smiled his love.

Restoring order, Jose clanked his glass and continued his tribute.

"The joke is on us. You have gathered your chicks like a mother hen, embracing us with your love. Gracias for taking us back into your heart, especially in such a clever, funny way. With this sip of champagne, your friends and devoted listeners eagerly wait for your words. And may our thirst for all you can teach us never end. Salud…Pablo!!!"

"Hear, Hear!" The glasses clinked and the beloved storyteller rose slowly to the rowdy applause to make a toast of his own.

"Now that my chicks have come home to roost...and, make no mistake...I am the old rooster...my wish for you, my wonderful people of God, is for you to enjoy this day, ever aware our friendship is a gift from the Almighty. I am eternally grateful to Him, for His faithfulness mends the broken. His mercy heals the sick. And His generosity prescribes you as my medicine and grants you my cure.

"Raise your glass to give our thanks to the Lord, who first loved us before we ever knew Him, before we were even born."

The toast brought everyone to silent prayer.

When the moment passed, Pablo stood holding his familiar journal, thumbing through its many pages.

"It seems the time has come to open the book and share the past once again with you, loyal friends.

"Get comfortable. Loosen those fancy sashes and belts. Remove those stuffy ties and sit back and enjoy the coolness. I have looked forward to telling you the rest of my life since the Lord took my pain.

"Are you ready?"

As the cheering group shouted raucously, Pablo's long silence came to its end.

To begin where he left off, as in the past, the storyteller once again lit his pipe and bathed the cool room in billows of pine-scented smoke.

CHAPTER 35

The Dam Held

‐◦◦◦‐

"As trapped as I felt...so was Annabella.

"Keeping her promises to reverse the curses, convincing the *curandera* to rescind them, brought her a dire warning from Josefina Espinoza.

"'This game you play, Senora Annabella, is a dangerous one. The damming of such a torrent, if you are not careful, risks grave consequences that could, instead, bring the curses to your doorstep.

"'I have acted in strict accord with your wishes,' Josefina said. 'Without complaint, I have waited patiently to execute what you desire.

"'Already, many things have been set into motion, but now you demand the tide be reversed, like stopping the current of a raging river. Blocking the river's course requires the building of a dam, strong enough to not only stop but reverse its flow.

"'Expense and danger in undoing what you desired are greatly heightened now. With all the time that is needed and all the risk required, though it is possible, some things are too perilous to attempt, let alone realize.

"'This change in course could cost much more than time and money. Add to it what is already owed to me, the final bill could demand payment in flesh and blood as well.

"'So you see, senora, building this dam is a worrisome gamble, and one without guarantee.

"'The retribution you risk…you will not be willing to suffer. Pray no seepage compromises its integrity.'

"Undeterred, Annabella ordered the *curandera* to move ahead.

"'Everything I wanted I accomplished without implicating myself or spilling blood. Retract the curses whatever the cost.

"'Senora Josefina, I have discovered a secret. The mere threat of death is enough. The fear the weak possess is sufficient and less incriminating than any bloodletting the curses would have wrought.'

"With not another cautionary word, the *curandera* demanded her pay."

"'According to our arrangement, senora, my compensation would be forthcoming at the fulfillment of the last curse. Now that fulfillment is no longer your requirement, my compensation comes due at once. I remind you of the consequences if my pay is withheld.

"Annabella promised to complete construction of the *curandera's* home and pay any additional cost, with one condition.

"'Josefina, I want the curse on Vincenti's life withdrawn. With that done, your home's construction will begin.'

"'It is a fair request,' she answered.

"'Senora, from the moment you sought me out, I have acted in good faith. Since it is only Vincenti, one retraction can be done without reversing the entire current. His curse will perish as the first wall of my home is erected.

"'Do not worry about him, senora. Vincenti has nothing to fear from me.

"'The freedom for the others, however, requires travel to Gehenna. I must implore the principals there.'

"'After my home's construction is underway, I will leave to meet the ones with the power to dam the cursed tide.'

"'Where is Gehenna—a nearby town?'

"The old woman chuckled. 'Someday, Senora Annabella, we two will know Gehenna very well.'"

<hr />

"THE TWO-DAY HIKE UP THE GRADUAL SLOPES OF THE Santa Lucia Mountains ended on Junipero Serra Peak.

"The early evening wind blew gently from the west, adding a mild chill to the pine-scented air. Tired and sleepy, the old witch made a simple camp, cooking her modest dinner over a tiny flame fed with twigs, leaves, and pine cones.

"She would need all her strength for the morning ahead.

"With the sun's light vanishing behind the western rim, the dark forest closed in. A nearby owl provided night music and the camp's fire, warming Josefina's aging hands, painted the setting an amber red.

"Throughout the night, the *curandera* made ready for her dawn flight to the land of the dead. The solitary owl, hooting in the nighttime woods, complemented her chanted litany of entreaties and incantations, a forewarning to primordial spirits of her descent into bowels of Sheol.

"'Ancients of iniquity, nurtured by recompense of hatred, quickened by man's sin, condemned for eternity time, arise from your primordial slumber. Claim your sovereignty as manifest.

"'Pay heed, evil sovereigns of Sheol! At the sun's first light on this peak, resound your thunder, unleash your lightning, and hasten my journey by loosening the whirlwind.

"'Imploring favor from the flames of hell, cauterize my heart, and lock within the unrequited curses of your wicked servant, Annabella.'"

"'Favored by the Ancients, the dawn is passed; the Sovereigns are content. The river's flow is shuttered. The dam constructed in my heart is holding firm.'"

"Fifteen years passed. The dam held, and no one cursed died. Annabella kept her promises. And best of all, we all were alive and eager to welcome the turn of the century.

"The *curandera,* no longer obligated to share her house with donkeys, cows, and horrible pigs, celebrated in the solitude of her new home, her reward for retracting into her heart the curses on those condemned.

"Contented, I never left the rancho. Annabella's life plodded along in a loveless toleration of her husband and son. She tried to seduce me in vain for several years, giving up entirely when an offer from an old friend arrived.

"In a registered letter, Annabella was offered a business partnership opportunity. Under the pretext of promoting international trade for tallow and hides and other beef by-products, Annabella and her so-called partner opened an office for trade in Monterey, where, for weeks at a time, she entertained prospective 'buyers' from all around the world.

"She convincingly impressed Vincenti and the de Leon family that this welcome opportunity would test her business skills and ultimately profit the rancho.

"But, as we were to discover, her business 'office' in Monterey was nothing but a posh hotel suite at the Hotel Del Monte, paid for by her business partner, Madam Margarita Sanchez.

"Annabella had her pick of the madam's richest patrons, who required women of distinction in private settings. She tested her business skills and made big profits as La Ida Café's most expensive escort.

"With buyers who came to her from all parts of the world, her new career, at last, satiated her lust.

"When he became the rancho's patron, Emilio fastened permanent shackles on his mother, a deserving reward for her misbegotten adventure in Monterey.

"As for me…I fulfilled all her demands. My residence remained Rancho Piedra Blanca and my life with Yolanda and Alejandro I sadly surrendered to another man."

CHAPTER 36

Leave Nothing Undone

⟨⟨⟨

"To complete the characters who make up this tale, I must reintroduce an old friend and tell you what he did and how we came to be intricately involved.

"In 1886, Flores de Flores left Piedra Blanca for Mexico. He was off to study with the expert practitioners of the healing arts, the fabled *curanderismo*.

"The open field was his schoolhouse and collective wisdom his library; any formal training he learned by practice. Years later, for his deep understanding and brilliant practice of the ancient craft, the title *curandero* was conferred on him. Singularly influenced by Catholic Church tradition, the *curanderismo* followed closely the Lord Jesus's instructions to His apostles.

"'Go forth, healing the sick, and casting out devils.'

"Like Christ who came to serve, Flores believed that prayer and prayer alone was the sacred power that brought forth God's healing.

"Assuring everyone seeking his help, he humbly confessed, he possessed no magic.

"'Before a healing can be considered, let alone attempted, the *curandero* must first pray in faith to God for His guidance, instruction, and will.'

"He came to understand quickly that the healing power instilled in him was a God-given gift appointed to only a chosen healer called and ordained for a *curandero's* life's work. And his work was miraculous! Unlike other students, Flores's cures and treatment brought instant healing. From his earliest beginnings, those he prayed over and touched always regained their health.

"His compassionate, faith-inspired practice, blessed with miraculous results, encouraged a growing following. And over the years, he served in Mexico, where his powers as a *curandero* became legend.

"Cities, villages, and boroughs bartered for his practice. Even the governor enticed Flores with offers to become his personal physician.

"Yet the lingering, unfinished business of Rancho Piedra Blanca weighed heavily on his heart. And as he was willed to do, he prayed to God for direction.

"'Please Lord, make it clear. Show me what it is you want me to do, and where it is you want me to go.'

"As one might expect God's answer came to Flores from above. While walking through the village of Cuajimalpa de Morelos, northwest of Mexico City, God's will for Flores fell from out of the sky. As he walked beneath it, an overhead banner spanning the roadway collapsed on him. He sustained no injury but it took a considerable time to free himself from the mass of fabric.

"The banner literally was the sign he prayed God to send. Its message answered his prayer. Although intended for an 'Alejandro,' Flores believed God spoke directly to him. *'Congratulations, Amigo   Finish All Tasks   Leave Nothing Undone.'* Invigorated by God's message from above, he grew eager to leave Mexico for California. It was true that his heart yearned to bring healing to the sick, but his first goal would bring judgment and justice to the evil that lived for so long at Rancho Piedra Blanca.

"His first act would be nothing less than an exorcism, casting out Satan that kept residence in the body and soul of the murderer of his family, the despicable Josefina Espinoza.

"In the predawn of June 15, 1900, as Flores walked briskly, crossing the stone hedge border and over the picket fence of Rancho Piedra Blanca, Josefina Espinoza slumbered comfortably in her home unaware his return would result that very day in her most horrible death."

CHAPTER 37

Death of the *Curandera*

"Long forgotten, Flores de Flores nestled sleeping that cloudless morning in the bough of the cypress tree shading my front door.

"In those days, with the coming of each new season, as the California coastal weather changed from hot to cold and dry to wet, I moved to a more clement locale and a different home built on the rancho over the years. My fairest weather shelter on the rancho's western bluff overlooked the ocean's summer horizons, where the cawing seagulls and crashing waves were the solitary sounds of my tranquil world.

"Windblown, graceful, majestically perched on a seemingly unreachable bluff, my cabin lay carefully concealed in the coastal cypress. Its location, known only to Vincenti and me, required a well-informed guide. And reaching it demanded all a body's perseverance, stamina, and strength.

"I rode my palomino to the base of a hidden knoll, stabling my horse in a thick shelter of oak and acacia trees.

"The crest of the knoll crowned a deep crevasse, making my cabin undetectable from below. To reach it necessitated climbing a series of rope ladders concealed in the hillside foliage.

"I first climbed down from the knoll's crest to the bottom of the crevasse, then on a second set of ropes, up the bluff's steep side to my cabin above.

"From the bounty of the cypress forest, the four-sided cabin, built ten years before Flores's visit that day, consisted of four walls and two rooms, with windows to witness the dazzling sunsets.

"I hoisted up everything needed, from water and food-stuffs to furniture and bedding, using block and tackle to maintain my seclusion from the landing below.

"At times a lonely windswept place, due to the remoteness, my well-being prospered and my health improved. From mid-May to late-September, until the chilling winds of winter forbade it, I stayed secretly tucked high on the bluff.

"My residence at Hacienda de Leon provided too many opportunities for Annabella's advances. With the day's work done, retiring to the bluff's peace, comfort, and solitude was a welcome alternative. Besides, by disappearing into thin air, frustrating Annabella became an enjoyable pastime.

"Except for Vincenti, who never questioned my motive for isolation, no one ever visited.

"I awoke late for a meeting with Don Joaquin the morning Flores de Flores appeared. Hurrying to the rope ladder, the little man, standing on a cypress stump, stopped me with his morning salutation.

"'Senor Pablo, how good of you to see me this fine day.'

"I stumbled backward toward the benches lining the cabin's front porch and sat down, startled and mystified.

"'Please allow me my introduction.'

"Bowing with hat in hand, he said, 'I am Flores de Flores. And I am available to you for whatever you require of me, my dear Senor Pablo Cabrera Barrazo de Leon.

"'We have never met and yet I feel that you and I have been close friends a very long time. You see, many of the people you love and care for, I have helped to protect.'

"When he jumped down off the stump, I just sat in dumb silence. Smiling, he replaced his hat and stood facing me with his hands on his hips.

"'Your reputation as a kind, thoughtful man is widespread and comes to me from many sources.

"'Excuse me my forwardness, Senor Pablo. I do not wish to embarrass you, but you, my fine fellow, are beloved.'

"'If I did not know better, I, like many others, who admire and pay you great homage, find it difficult to understand: first, that you have no woman; and second, you choose to live alone in seclusion like a hermit.'

"With a flourish, waving a long scarf pulled from the pocket of his rumpled coat, he continued.

"'That manner of living suits me much more than you, senor.'

"When I opened my mouth and nothing came out, he paused a moment waiting for me to respond, but began quickly again.

"'But I have gotten ahead of myself. I am well aware that, at your benevolent hand, the love of your life and her child were hastened to safety. Surely, Yolanda Gomez, that truly lovely senora, spoke to you that I came to call? Did she not relate to you the nature of my visit those many years ago?

"'I pray she and the young man by now have enjoyed a place far away from the dangers that so many years ago threatened them on this rancho.'

"Dumbfounded, I nodded.

"Flores shouted in happiness. 'Good, that is so good to know, senor. I have waited all this time to learn they are safe.'

"Choosing carefully what he would next say, the miniature fellow stopped his laughter and rubbed his chin, thinking.

"'Before I speak another word, it is with deepest affection and gratitude that I offer you my praise and admiration for the care and speed in which you acted to protect Senora Yolanda and little her child. Your noble actions were quite remarkable.'

"I remember uttering a weak expression of thanks, but Flores de Flores cut me off, sweeping his hat and bowing in humble admiration.

"'You need not thank me, Senor Pablo. Bringing a warning to Senora Yolanda was my pleasure and obligation.

"'You see, since my very innocence was usurped in an instant by the likes of the *curandera* of this very village...the honest truth...I am required to always protect the innocent.'

"Restoring composure, but astonished still at his very presence, I invited Flores to join me on the benches I carved from weathered cypress years before.

"'Senor Flores, please do not take this as ill-mannered or disrespectful. But...how did you find me? And how did you climb to these heights?'

"'My dear Senor Pablo, do not let my diminutiveness call to question my ingenuity.

"'To discover where you live, my very special friends hovered high above searching the rancho in vain for your location, until I suggested to them they should follow you.

"'When they discovered your splendid, and may I add, clandestine quarters, they rejoiced telling me they have returned often to visit you, senor!

"'If you had only been listening, I am sure you would have enjoyed their lovely songs.'

"'Senor Flores, the birds speak to you?'

"Flores de Flores beamed. 'The creatures of the air are my friends. They speak to me, and I speak to them. Much is said all-around and much can be learned from them.'

"Accentuating his point, Flores whistled a melody that brought a red-breasted robin flying onto his hand."

"'Like this feisty fellow…my feathered companions not only converse with those who listen, they also are eager to serve when called upon. And that is why I have come to visit with you this glorious day. You see, senor, the world today rejoices the long-anticipated elimination of an evil too long allowed its occupancy.

"'Those who have suffered at the hands of such a one, today are at last at peace. Suffering ended! Justice complete! Here at your beautiful rancho this very day, the wicked *curandera* is no more.'

"Doffing his hat, sweeping it low, he bowed and went on.

"'A dreadful death was inflicted upon her for the evil and suffering she wrought on so many, including your humble servant.'"

CHAPTER 38

The Bleeding Heart

⸺⚬⚬⚬⚬⸺

"Unleashed, Annabella's curses descended onto Piedra Blanca, demanding its first victim.

"On the crisp Good Friday morning in April 1901, my father, Don Joaquin, left Mama Dolores forever. After devouring a much-appreciated breakfast of green chili and eggs, Don Joaquin walked jauntily to the stable to mount his much-beloved Indigo for a ride to Cambria and a meeting with Vincenti.

"A proposal by Vincenti to cultivate the rancho's southernmost section for grape production required Don Joaquin's approval. After a sumptuous breakfast, the old don looked forward to riding the rolling hills and meadows to the future vineyards, especially on the back of his old friend.

"The history of the rider and horse originated the day of Indigo's birth, when the mother mare's flailed kick fractured Don Joaquin's leg. Through the years, the don paid special attention to the colt, watching closely as he grew into a glossy black stallion, pleasurable to ride and full of fire.

"Soon rider and horse became one.

"Mounted atop the stallion, an unexpected cough welled up deep in his chest. Wheezing, Don Joaquin labored for his breath. His retching grew violent and uncontrolled.

"Panicked and alone, he flung himself from the saddle, hoping to break up the cough with a hard landing on the stable floor. But his fall failed to clear his right boot that stayed stubbornly wedged in the stirrup.

"Indigo spooked. Racing toward the opened door, the big stallion dragged the helpless Don Joaquin through the dim stable into the morning's sun.

"Late for breakfast, Rodrigo rode in from his morning rounds, hungry and eager for Mama Dolores's green chili and eggs. He spurred his sorrel into the courtyard in time to see Don Joaquin's bay race past him, running away from Hacienda de Leon on the gravel road toward the fields to the south.

"He heard the old man screaming before he realized it was Don Joaquin dangling from the bay's right flank. Spurring his horse, he raced to catch the runaway already well beyond the entry gates and speeding away.

"Dragging my helpless father, Indigo sprinted out of control toward an oncoming buckboard, slowly approaching the hacienda entry two hundred yards ahead.

"Unable to understand why the wagon's driver was so slow to recognize and react to the situation before him, Rodrigo shouted frantically to the buckboard driver. Had the driver sensed the danger there, he had ample time to move the rig off the narrow road onto the field to his right, permitting the fast-approaching horse a way to easily pass. Instead, as if asleep, the teamster plodded straight ahead, the wagon held fast in wheel ruts cut deep in the weathered road.

"Don Joaquin struggled to free his imprisoned boot. Still, the rutted road pounded his head and back unmercifully. What strength remained left him quickly.

"Avoiding the advancing buckboard, the runaway horse veered to the right and entered a gully running along the newly planted field and bordering fence line.

"Don Joaquin's limp body smashed into a fence post, causing the stallion Indigo to stumble, flipping head over hoofs.

"The fall broke Indigo's neck and flung the tethered don high into the air, hurling his battered body toward the ground with such velocity he impaled on a fence post, his body split in two.

"After Don Joaquin's death, Mama Delores fell fatally ill. Dr. Ruben Alvarez, a family physician from Monterey, told me there was nothing to be done.

"'Her cancer has no cure and a quick death would be the best answer to prayer.'

"The day she died, heavy May rains came late, painting the hills a pastel green.

"Gazing out her bedroom through the misty blanket of rain left enveloping the valley floor, she smiled knowingly. Out of the fog, her husband would soon arrive to gather her home.

"Standing vigil, Mama Dolores in eternal reunion embraced her husband, happy the don came so quickly.

"The horror of Don Joaquin's death and Mama Dolores's suffering haunted the rancho's majordomo every hour of the day. Rodrigo dreaded sleep for the terrible nightmares that came.

"In mid-August, on a quiet Sunday morning before his children awoke, distraught with melancholy and fatigue, Rodrigo strangled to death Martha, his sleeping wife. Walking calmly into the stables, he closed the door behind him, shutting out the dawning light. With great forethought, as if rehearsed a thousand times, he placed the pulley rope dangling over Indigo's stall around his neck and hung himself.

"After sleeping fifteen years, the reawakened curses claimed four lives in three months. Cursed and still living, only three remained—Vincenti, Yolanda, and Alejandro."

CHAPTER 39

Concentric Circles of Ruin

❧

"Living in the soil and contaminating the air, the summer of 1901 saw death take up residence at Rancho Piedra Blanca.

"The unseen intruder poisoned the wells.

"Hundreds of cattle, victims of the oak grove's putrid ponds, died overnight, as did every rabbit, raccoon, field mouse, and owl.

"The grove browned in rancid tinge. Ancient oaks withered overnight into brittleness and decay. These stalwart guardians, diseased, splintered and uprooted, collected in grotesque heaps in the poisoned pools.

"Meadows turned into carnage as lightning strikes from crystal clear skies burned to cinders the hills and fields.

"From a hilltop's vantage, the destruction could be seen widening in an ever-expanding circle.

"Once the hiding place of the *curandera's* heart, geometric rings emanated from the well like an insatiable cancer destroying everything they touched.

"Winter crops failed to root. Foals, calves, colts, and pigs died at birth. Those that survived were dropped tragically deformed.

"Mown hay, freshly cut, reeked like a fetid corpse.

"Newly buried occupants from rancho cemetery plots beckoned to others, 'Come, reside in our earthen vaults.'

"The don's glory, his prized stable that boasted an array of champion equines, became a boneyard of standing skeletons. Livestock passed to lifeless. Vineyards shriveled to raisins. Orchards bloomed dead rot.

"Determined to destroy all of Piedra Blanca life, the spreading death slithered silently into every bunkhouse, village home, and hacienda.

"Villages vacated. At the first ranch hand's death, farmer and vaquero families fled.

"Grief-stricken, inept, and paralyzed with fear, Vincenti deserted his position as patron, hiding away from the curse that took our parents and now stalked him.

"He refused to leave his barricaded bedroom. Prohibiting entrance to everyone, he lived alone with an armory of weapons.

"His rancho, Piedra Blanca, lay in ruins.

"Following his petrified father's example, sixteen-year-old Emilio's first experience with death left him incapable of taking on even the most minor responsibility.

"Immature and overindulged, he wept for himself, mourning his grandparents, now gone, who had coddled him from birth. Who would dote on him now? Abandoned by his reclusive father, Emilio was forced to seek his mother for comfort.

"Delighted by the unexpected deaths of Emilio's grandparents, Annabella laughed at her son's whining and snickered at his pleas. Comfort she would not provide.

"'It is time for you to grow into a man, Emilio. No one eludes death, not your grandparents, not your father, and not you. It is time, Emilio, for you to learn that life always chases after death. The time in between birth and death... that is all the time you possess.

"'And death comes too quickly putting an end to the time squandered. Do not waste it by crying and feeling sorry for yourself like your stupid and weak father.

"'Time is too valuable for sadness and pity. All your time must be spent being strong, taking from life what it is you want. Do whatever you must to achieve your desires, regardless of the costs.

"'Let no one dictate your life. If you do, when you die it is too late. And you have no one to blame but yourself.

"'So when death arrives—and understand it will come—you must not be sorry or have regrets. In the end, you must say with pride, you did what you most desired to do.'

"Confused at first, he quickly came to appreciate the new-found attention his mother never showed before. She rarely spoke to him at all. But now, she flooded him with a torrent of advice and direction. He may have not understood what she said, but his attachment to her was swift and complete.

"With no one to intervene and Emilio hanging on her every word, Annabella indoctrinated him into her corrupt world of expediency. As time passed, Emilio proved to be a stellar student, surpassing even his mother's penchant for evil."

"DEEP INTO 1903, THE RANCHO STILL LAY IN RUINS.

"The massive desolation graphically confirmed the center of the unleashed curses. Where there had been a well, the quake gouged a deep symmetrical crater blackened with brimstone, rupturing the earth for many acres. The old standing grove was erased, with no trace to be found.

"Reversing its effects presented the new *curandero* with but one solution. According to *curanderismo* doctrine, if restoration and permanent victory against evil were to be secured, a leader, sealed by God's own appointment, must command the war.

"'Because Vincenti is unwilling, son Emilio is immature, and all other candidates are dead, I am afraid, Senor Pablo, God's path ends at your door.

"'With God's help, it is you who must resurrect the rancho to life and return the evil to hell. With *curanderismo* assistance, this sacred responsibility falls clearly to you. God answered your prayers for Yolanda and Alejandro's safety. Now, He requires you to put away your sorrow and anoints you the crusade's chosen leader. It is time for you to muster all your courage and strength if the de Leon legacy is to continue.'"

"I HUMBLY ACCEPTED GOD'S CHARGE. THROUGH FLORES de Flores and his *curanderismo* brethren, my most effective weapon was faith in God and His power that, I prayed, He would impart to me.

"Without opposition, Annabella encouraged my appointment and accepted my leadership. The intercession of a strong hand was necessary to reclaim the wealth and power lost to bygone days.

"And I am sure, she thought access to me could provide an opportunity for the intimacy she still desired.

"But Annabella's acceptance of my authority lasted only until time and experience calloused the body and soul of Emilio into the rancho's next patron."

CHAPTER 40

Mr. Merrell F. Small and His Calabash

"Despite Flores de Flores's warning, I could not believe speaking to my brother would be a waste of time. His blessing was essential before I assumed this massive undertaking.

"My enthusiasm rapidly diminished at the distinct cocking sound of a large caliber shotgun as I entered the hallway leading to his fortified bedroom.

"Vincenti, it is me, Pablo. If you shoot me, I will be dead, and you will be very sorry indeed.

"A long silence ensued. Then a weak voice strained out, 'Be sure you are alone, Pablo. If anyone should follow you through the door, they will regret it.'

"'Brother! There is only me, no one else. Put down your gun, please. I miss you, and we must talk.'

"Thankfully, the hollow release of the shotgun hammers echoed down the empty hall. Saying a silent prayer, I took a deep breath, crossed myself, and slowly opened the door. I walked cautiously into the blackness of the room, fearing what I might see.

"All the windows were shuttered and draperies drawn. Not even a sliver of light appeared. When the heavy door slammed shut, my silhouette framed in the doorway was swallowed in the room's stifling rank air.

"Afraid to breathe, I said, 'You can see it is me, but I can see nothing in the stinking black hole of your dungeon. Where are you?'

"To my right, a tiny spark glowed, and a disembodied command followed.

"'Bolt the door.'

"With the latch secured, Vincenti, to my relief, set a match to the wick of a small lamp. For an instant, the pungency of sulfur masked the room's disgusting stench. The sight and smell of my brother shocked and repulsed me.

"Hanging below his shoulders, the length of his filthy matted hair matched the scruffy beard that covered cheeks shrunken into hollow holes. His eyes were creviced slits. But the nose persisted, remaining a lone vestige of de Leon lineage. Not a glimmer of former dignity remained.

"Vincenti stood naked in the middle of the room, clutching the shotgun. With the sulfur dissipated, I found myself gagging on his putrid smell.

"'Am I that bad?' he asked.

"Embarrassed with indignity, I stammered an apology, smearing on my sleeve the sewage that vaulted from my mouth.

"'Please forgive me. This is not the way I thought our visit would begin.'

"Vincenti's laughter lightened the moment and there was an attempt at an embrace.

"'You have been in this hole much too long. It is time to join the family again, or at least what is left of it. Your wife and son need you…I need you…the rancho needs you.'

"With the mention of Annabella, Vincenti stepped back into the darkness, losing himself in the blackened perimeter.

"'Where have you gone now? Please do not shrink away. You are the don and have the responsibility to bring the rancho back to life. I cannot do it by myself, and Emilio is too young.'

"'The de Leon family is cursed, the rancho is cursed, and everyone I love, aside from you, my adopted brother, is dead. My wife is a witch, and I am not sure what or who Emilio is. And I know that if I venture outside this room, my life will be over. So, please, do not ask me again.

"'I will not leave this sanctuary until I know with certainty Annabella is dead.

"'Go now, Pablo,' he said. 'Pray you never lose your immunity to this damning. Be thankful that no de Leon blood courses through your veins.'

"His prophetic death was realized the next month when Father Luis Mendoza, a spirited priest from the San Xavier's parish church, came to convince my brother he had nothing to fear.

"Through the closed door, he spoke passionately to Vincenti, but the young friar swallowed both barrels of my brother's shotgun. He died before his innocence emptied out onto the hallway floor.

"Authorities were summoned. Blasting away the remnants of the shattered door, Vincenti let the buckshot fly. Before he could reload, the *policia* relieved him of his shotgun and dragged him away to the Salinas jail.

"His screams that first night kept the jailhouse wide awake. Trying his best to calm him, the jailer watched helplessly as my brother wrestled with an unseen force that lifted his terrified prisoner high in the air hurling him again and again into the cell bars.

"The next morning Vincenti lay dead. A crossbar, wrenched from the jail door, protruded out of each side of his head. No one could venture how that was done."

THE COOL OF THE ICE HOUSE SUSTAINED PABLO, BUT THE teller of the story faded in mumbled confusion. Depressed and exhausted, Pablo's telling trickled to a standstill.

"My words do not come," he cried.

Flustered, the old man reached for his coffee cup, spilling the contents Jose had poured hours before. Thankful for a respite from the anguish, the sympathetic listeners dispersed to clear their heads.

Conchita and Rosa, in the sanctuary of the ice house kitchen, counted the heartaches and deaths shared by Pablo that day. Between outhouse visits, the men smoked and thought but said nothing.

Reassembled, Jose begged apologetically. "Senor, do you not think it best if you take up the story another day?'"

In truth, Pablo's tragedies wore heavily on his listeners. Looking into each of his listener's faces, he realized his torment became theirs as well. Tears filled Pablo's eyes.

"Forgive me, please, good friends. Although this day in the comfort of the ice house was intended to show you my love, past sins are too great a burden to share with you."

MANUEL AND ROSA DROVE THE DESPONDENT MAN HOME. It was quiet in the cab. The late hour and emotional exhaustion ruled out any conversation

Rosa and Manuel were afraid the lonely shepherd's hut would do nothing to soothe the old man's heartbreak.

Praying the Lord to comfort him, Rosa stroked his hair and lovingly kissed his cheek, putting her fragile friend to bed.

Dreaming of his mother's tender touch, he drifted off. But the lovely dreamscape of maternal care distorted too soon into the recurring nightmare of his life.

Making way for the collective soul's healing, many days passed.

Rosa was surprised to find Pablo's pipe wedged in the seat of their truck. Returning the pipe was an excellent excuse to break the ice. That day she, with Manuel and Jose in the old flatbed, climbed the San Simeon hill. They returned his precious pipe and the old man said his thanks by filling his bowl and striking a match.

Pablo laughed and shook his head. With no room in his cramped quarters Jose was left to stand in the open doorway while Rosa and Manuel managed a seat on the shepherd's cot. "Thank you all for coming all this way, finding my burl. But as you see, I am sorry my home is too small for so many guests."

"Old shepherd, for you we would gladly pitch a tent in the rain and snow and sleet to be with you. Be ready Friday. Manuel will come for you to join the rest of us at the Fourth of July picnic in San Xavier. Come hungry and ready to tell your story to those who love you very much, wherever it leads."

Only after Rosa assured him his shared pain could never be enough to separate him from his friends, he agreed.

———⁂———

LATER THAT DAY, MR. MERRELL F. SMALL, AN OFFICIAL in the governor's office, knocked on Pablo's door. Sworn to deliver it to no one but Pablo Cabrera Barrazo de Leon, Small carried with him an official dossier from California Governor Earl Warren.

Dilapidated, cluttered, and tiny, for all its faults, the hut's scent was not one of them. A pipe man himself, Small knocked a bit louder, delighting in the tobacco aroma gusting from inside. With introductions done, bowls filled and lit, the two men settled down to the business of the dossier.

Small smiled at his good fortune to be the one to meet this well-regarded old man in this tiny hut bursting with aromatic smoke. Leaning back, drawing on his calabash, Small thanked his host.

"Gracias, Senor de Leon. The taste, the aroma, the setting—they are so delicious. Do you cure the leaves yourself, senor? I would very much enjoy knowing your recipe, if I may."

Pablo set down his precious burl to retrieve a tin from the shelf above his cot.

"Allow me to present you with this fresh mixture; I hope you enjoy it. The blend, however, is my secret. I will have to come to know you much better before I share that with you, Senor Small."

"The governor, indeed, demanded I personally bear you this good news. Let us hope your confidence in me improves with the information presented. Perhaps you will feel justified then in sharing the secrets of your tobacco?"

CHAPTER 41

Homecoming Hero

〜〜〜

That blistering summer morning Independence Day heat could not compare to Manuel's burning passion for his beloved Rosa.

He awoke finding himself peering out their bedroom window, blessing the dawning of this memorable day.

"Rosa…Rosa, dear. We are alive…we are alive. Let us rejoice in this glorious day God has given us. The sun is shining hot in a clear blue sky, flowers are blooming, and you and I, my love, should rekindle memories of our wild youth."

"Quiet down, you old fool. I am still sleeping. Besides, what wild days are you talking about? Wild days? Wild days? Are still you dreaming?"

"Oh, no. Oh no. Today of all days, this is no dream.

"This day I remember very well. For on this very day, in the hayloft of your grandfather's drafty barn, we came together for the first time.

"Ahhh! I can still smell the new hay and the sweet-smelling aloes of your skin, a forty-year-old anniversary that the mere thought of your beautiful nakedness stirs in me the same urges, the same desires!

"But do not fear, my love. That day of lovemaking stays our secret—unless, of course, you are the one to share it today at the picnic with Conchita and the rest of the senoras."

Fluttering wide-opened eyes, the coy senorita of bygone years, remembered that day, and welcomed her husband back into bed. "Just now, Manuel, the way you look, greeting this special day, you are that eighteen-year-old boy in that windy old barn who made love to me for the very first time."

In that moment, without hesitation, he surrendered unconditionally to the bride of his youth.

⸺◦∞◦⸺

PABLO SMILED AT THE SOUND OF THE GRINDING GEARS of Manuel's ancient truck trudging up the hill. He looked forward to the morning drive to San Xavier and the July Fourth picnic at his favorite rancho village.

Complimenting Rosa for the tantalizing aroma of her picnic cooking that filled the flatbed's cramped cab, he sat proudly in between husband and wife, honored to be entrusted with Rosa's confectionary dessert sitting on his lap. The cake of all cakes, the triple-layered sweet milk masterpiece *tres leches*, for which everyone would happily give up every other item on the picnic menu.

Mama Dolores reserved this delicacy for Cinco de Mayo, but Rosa created her tres leches as a new tradition to celebrate America's freedom from old King George.

With the noon chiming of the chapel bells, picnickers began arriving at San Xavier's tiny village square.

Setting up chairs and tables early that sunny morning, Francisco and Angelina reserved a shaded lawn area, thankful to be out of the sun. Jaime, Conchita, and Rosa arrived in time to cheer Juanito and Maria and the other children with streamers in hand, dancing merrily around the red, white, and blue liberty pole. When his sister Madeline was seven and he was a strapping young boy of twelve, Jose thought back on the mischievous prank celebrated in this same park on this same Fourth of July day.

"Manuel…Rosa…I do not think you were here that Independence Day, when no one in the village could break open the piñata."

From her brother's opening line, Madeline chomped at the bit to spice up this, her favorite childhood story.

"Oh yes," he jumped in. "I witnessed every *niño* and *niña*, from oldest to youngest, taking turns whacking the piñata, trying to break it open to free the candy and prizes inside. But nobody could.

"Then it was my turn. At seven years old and the youngest of all the kids, with a blindfold covering my eyes, I took firm hold of the broom handle, thumping the unbreakable piñata as hard as I could, but with no success.

"Then Papa took off my blindfold and held the piñata steady and let me go at it again. Still, the goodies remained inside."

Laughing like a big brother would, Jose chided her. "My poor little sister tired so quickly."

Madeline laughed. "Jose, you just love being the bad big brother!"

"Then Papa took a turn, swinging the handle, lashing heavy blows, but the stubborn piñata would not give up the treasure.

"Finally, after several adults tried their luck, Moochy Mendoza, the village drunk, began laughing and laughing at the practical joke played on all of us.

"On closer inspection, the papier-mache piñata was actually a painted cowhide. Worse yet, there was no candy, money, or prizes. Instead, it was stuffed with clumps of hay wrapped around river stone.

"Who made off with the piñata prizes stayed a mystery for several months, until one day in October, when I tried finding where my cat hid her new litter. I found a large tin someone buried under our back porch. When Papa confronted him, Jose admitted to the larceny.

"By then, except for the doll, all the toys still in the tin were broken," Jose said, joining in. "I had eaten all the candy long ago, and the money was spent at Andeleto's for more candy and comic books.

"Getting away with it for so long was my greatest secret and a joke I enjoyed very much—that is, until Papa took a broom handle to me just like the piñata!"

The picnickers roared. And the rellenos and the tacos, the beer and the wine, the melon and the apricots, and candy and tres leches tasted all the better with the laughter.

After lunch, a short walk and brief siesta ensued. Francisco and Angelina, in the waning afternoon, collected the children and drove home.

While the taste of tres leches still tantalized their tongues, the listeners came together for Pablo's telling. With cypress burl heavy on his lip and everyone comfortably in place, the storyteller took one last puff. The smoke curled above his snow-white hair and, once again, Pablo traveled back in time.

"Amigos, the time has come to tell you what became of Yolanda Gomez and her wonderful son, Alejandro."

———— ✦ ————

"On calm seas early on a brisk Sunday morning, the French clipper *Bastille Day* sailed southward from the bustling Monterey port. Well out to sea with the clanging of ten bells, Yolanda, at last, woke her sleepy little son.

"With widening eyes and his first glimpse of the sea, he wondered if it had an end. The pleasant weather of the first week ended with the tyrannical ocean changing Alejandro's awestruck wonder to sheer terror.

"Entering Baja waters at five bells, the sleeping wind awakened in a violent squall and, in an instant, a rain blew sideways so hard the raindrops welted the little boy's skin.

"Wave after wave, higher and higher, the sailing ship struggled on. Trimmed in royal blue, the billowing sails puffed cheeks of white to match the massive cloudscapes that filled the skies east to west and north to south, as far as he could see.

"Through a battle-scarred horn, the sailing master bristled orders, sending drenched seamen scurrying about the decks in surreal blurs.

"Pummeled deckhands tied on harnesses to keep from being blown into the sea, while their untethered mates bravely climbed rope ladders, risking their lives to lower the mizzen foresail and relieve tension on the riggings and mast.

"Peeking through hatch covers from below deck, scared yet exhilarated, Alejandro imagined himself aloft, side by side with fearless sailors, trimming sails and saving the ship from the roiling sea.

"By twelve bells, the squall blew out, with the capricious wind dying to a breath. Like a toy boat after a soothing bath, the clipper lay motionless on a glassy sea, with mountainous sprawls of sailcloth hanging from the riggings.

"Stillness befell the ship.

"The blow that threatened their lives yielded to a stifling calm, with mutinous temperatures stoking a muggy heat.

"Searing sun blistered the new day forcing dolphin pods that daily frolicked the bow to deeper cooler waters.

"The oppressive heat evaporated any remnant of shadow and shade. Like the dolphins, scorched men scurried to the darkness deep within the ship's hull.

"The sun set, yet night brought no relief. Without breeze or ripple, burning temperatures prevailed.

"Five days slithered away. Hovering overhead, the relentless sun grew larger and larger, its unquenchable appetite swallowing up the sky.

"Parched lips prayed for thirst to be quenched and the sun to dim. Still, the days did not end, and the wind would not blow.

"The endless days forced Alejandro and Yolanda below decks and to the ship's cook. Famous for the bristly black mat prominent on a sailor's chest, shirtless Felipe La Berge welcomed son and mother to the shade of his galley domain. Gregarious La Berge's tender care and warm heart loved their company, and falling in love with him came easy for his new galley hands.

"On the sixth day, the doldrums relented. The winds revived, filling limp sails and blowing the ship south. With deck privileges reinstated, the crew and passengers returned to their daily routine.

"Free to move about, Alejandro chose, instead, to spend his time below, laughing at Felipe, peeling potatoes, and listening to the cook's stirring stories of the sea.

"Enchanted by his newest friend and staunchest admirer, Felipe introduced Alejandro to the crew as 'my little brother.' Taking to Alejandro, the crew, in turn, schooled him in a bit of their trade. The little sailor, a good student, learned the art of knot-tying and the proper way to scrape barnacles.

"To five-year-old Alejandro, it was all good fun.

"Captain Francois Prulette took special interest, honoring Alejandro, the crew's newest member, promoting him to the rank of honorary bosun.

With mates beaming and the boy's mother at his side, the captain placed a bosun's hat on Alejandro's head, pinning ribbon after ribbon on his chest. Prizing the awards, Yolanda kept them safe in her memory trunk.

"But to Alejandro, his most cherished memory of that long-ago voyage would always be the thrilling visits to Captain Prulette's private quarters, where he and his mother were spellbound by the wonders there enshrined.

"The spectacular entry harbored in marble pillars a quartet of medieval crusaders who stood their ground, guarding the oak door carved with mermaids and sirens ministering to a trident-flaunting King Neptune.

"Above this cast of the deep, embellishing the transom, hung a Louis XIV crested shield, bedecked with pearl-handled sabers, razor-sharp, shining like the sun.

"The colossal charting table covering the floor lay festooned with charts and maps, secured by a protractor and compass. A Ramsden sextant hung astride a century-old telescope crafted by the famous Dutchman, Jan Van Der Bildt.

"Every cranny and nook spoke to Alejandro of spellbinding exploits, from the ancient alabaster-carved Indian chests to the hangman's noose that executed Barbados pirate Stede Bonnet, to the huge ivory tusks arching the captain's chair.

"Exotic treasures populating the good captain's wall opened a world of adventure for the little boy—a bloodied warrior's shield from a Zulu uprising, Bedouin torture whips of knotted camel hair, a foursome of harpoon poles wrested from a Russian whaler, and the jewel-encrusted dagger piercing a tattered Union Jack."

"Two weeks overdue, *Bastille Day* made its way through the obstinate spring waters of Mexico's coastline, docking at last in Zihuatanejo on April 17, 1886. And yet, the ship's arrival was much too soon for bosun mate Alejandro Gomez. Holding his mother's hand in no hurry to disembark, he cried when the memorable voyage ended.

"Fifteen years later, in 1901, as Alejandro boarded the extreme clipper ship *Rainbow*, his mind trumpeted loudly the treasured adventures remembered of his childhood *Bastille Day* voyage, when he and his mother sailed out of Monterey and away from Rancho Piedra Blanca forever.

"The *Rainbow*, a new innovation in clipper ship design, was Alejandro's first choice over all other craft to sail him to his home port of Vera Cruz, Mexico, from Boston Harbor.

"Alejandro earned a six-month sabbatical, his reward for graduating with the highest honors from Georgetown Preparatory School in Maryland, a respected Jesuit boarding school he attended for the past four years. Content to relax in his cabin and not open a book, he looked forward to the homecoming planned for him by his parents in their beautiful casa, high above the lights of Mexico City.

"A student of modern shipbuilding anxious to witness for himself the shipwright's claims, he marveled at the design of the 450-ton, American-built clipper. Sacrificing cargo capacity for speed, the boatwright lengthened the bow above the waterline, tapering the forward body and fashioning the widest breadth in her aft. This radical design accelerated the clipper to fly over the water at astounding speeds.

"The feel of *Rainbow* differed completely from his first voyage many years before on *Bastille Day*, as it did from his sailing four years before on the Dutch frigate, *Nordan*, on this same voyage from Boston Harbor to Vera Cruz.

"The speedy *Rainbow* reduced the usual twelve-week round trip to eight, adding four extra weeks at home before his required return to enter Harvard University Law School in Cambridge.

"The shipbuilder did not exaggerate the ship's speed. Four weeks from departure, the *Rainbow* docked in Vera Cruz.

"Alejandro telegraphed home that he safely arrived and would be boarding the train to Cuajimalpa de Morelos the next day.

Mama and Papa stop Arrived Vera Cruz stop Will arrive Morelos tomorrow noon by train stop Alejandro

"Cuajimalpa de Morelos, in rural Santa Fe, had no train station. But the climb of twenty-nine-hundred feet up the rugged hills from Mexico City necessitated the ancient boiler to stop and take on water, thus allowing Alejandro to disembark in his hometown.

"At ten minutes past noon, he stepped down into the glaring sunlight of Cuajimalpa de Morelos.

"Even though no one else got off the train, his mother could not be sure it was really him.

"'He has grown so much since we sent him to Maryland. He stands so tall, and he is so thin. What do they feed him at that fancy American school?'

"Musing that the boy they sent off to school four years before had returned a man, his stepfather merely smiled.

"A gentleman in manner and of a noble stature, Alejandro arrived impeccably dressed in a stiff-collared shirt, black tie, and tailored English suit. The creases of his pants stood at crisp attention, and his new leather oxfords gleamed in the brightness of the Mexican sun. With a black derby on his head, in his right hand he carried an attaché and in the other, a travel-battered valise.

"Smiling happily, brimming cordiality, he walked the length of the train toward his reception party, tipping his hat as he passed, acknowledging Helena, the senorita who sat waving goodbye to him from the seat they had shared.

"From the dirt, a gentle breeze blew up a minuscule whirlwind and just as quickly settled its pillow of dust on the waiting carriage a short stroll away.

"At the mayor's insistence, his parents were obliged to fetch the pride of Morelos in the town's official horse-drawn carriage.

"Fitted in gala décor, four perfectly matched stallions, sparkling in silver brocade, stood harnessed to the ostentatious rig. In the finest leathers and canvas spats, the dignified driver, reins in hand, sat proudly in the carriage seat, while in matching attire, the coach valet stood waiting in the road to welcome the man of the hour.

"Leaning far outside the carriage window, Yolanda fluttered her hankie at Alejandro, who strolled at a casual pace toward her commotion.

"In the dusty road, holding the coach door opened for his handsome stepson, stood Captain Francois Prulette.

"Immediately relieving Alejandro's valise and attaché, the valet carefully stowed both in the posh luggage bin.

"Alejandro let out a low whistle, examining with a critical eye the magnificent carriage and impeccable personnel. With affection, shaking his stepfather's hand, he whispered, 'Papa, how good of you to meet me.'

"Poking his head into the cab window, he gushed, 'Hello Mama, how are you?'

"He then stepped back for one last look at the impressive conveyance and, with a twinkle in his eye, behind the back of his hand, he asked Prulette, 'Does the mayor know his carriage is missing?'

"All at once, they laughed, kissed, and squealed, so happy to be together again.

"For his seafaring stepfather, Alejandro's return was timely.

"'I sail again before you return to university, so let us not waste a moment together. As you look forward to my sea stories, I am anxious for you to share your adventures in America.'

"The happy family roared with laughter, as the coach rushed the prodigal to the waiting celebration—the greatest thing to happen in Morelos since the marriage of the mayor's daughter five years before.

"Mariachis blaring, the happy citizens of Cuajimalpa de Morelos greeted their hometown hero with cheers, chants, and congratulatory song.

"Before the driver reined in the team at the town's center and the carriage valet raced to open the door, the prancing stallions negotiated three revolutions around the monument dedicated to Miguel Hidalgo y Costilla, Mexico's champion of independence.

"With dignitaries and a joyous crowd cheering the hometown hero, the carriage, at last, stopped in front of the crowded stage filled with flowers and set in a lush garden backdrop. 'Alejandro...Alejandro...Alejandro!'

"Graduating at the top of his class from a school in faraway America, Alejandro Gomez showered glory on Morelos. For the honor and privilege to celebrate one of their own, the proud citizenry extolled their hometown hero, celebrating his achievement on a huge banner that waved proudly over the dais.

"After the mayor's lengthy speech and in a brief one of his own, hero Alejandro in his usual humble fashion gratefully accepted the town's adulation.

"He later joked with his mother, 'You know, I shall expect this kind of reception with every homecoming.'

"The proud mother squeezed his hand.

"'My dear son, when you come home from law school, all these people, including your stepfather and I, will hide, fearing you bear us a summons!'

"And so on it went, his sabbatical became a never-ending fiesta. When the speeches ended, parties were ongoing for the entire summer. But the wise young man, who often with fondness thought of Helena, kept a safe distance from the many other beautiful señoritas."

CHAPTER 42

Reunion at Santa Teresa de Avila

꧀꧀

True to his word, on June 18, 1901, Captain Prulette sailed on the morning tide. If all went according to plan, the six-month voyage to China and Japan would bring him home to Yolanda in time to celebrate Christmas.

"Instilling a fierce independence in Yolanda and Alejandro, the captain's commissions kept him from home many months at a time, affording him little time to husband his wife or father his stepson.

"Alejandro stayed close to his mother that summer. To avoid the constant female distractions ever-present in Morelos, Yolanda suggested they revisit memories and old friends at Santa Teresa de Avila in Mexico City.

"Alejandro looked forward to traveling to Mexico City and Santa Teresa to share his Georgetown Preparatory School adventures with Sister Juan Dominic, his favorite teacher, and Padre Humberto, the loving Franciscan, who provided his mother and him a home for more than fifteen years.

"Yolanda's dinner, like so many prepared over the years for the Franciscan fathers, was welcomed and delicious.

"'I learned from the very best,' Yolanda said, pointing to Juanita's portrait hung in the place of prominence on the dining room wall.

"Shedding a tear, Padre Humberto's words were bittersweet.

"'Indeed, I grieve still for Juanita. Sorry too, the mother of every orphan and the proprietor of the biggest heart could not come down from the angels tonight to see how well her understudy has done.'

"It was in 1886 when Alejandro entered Santa Teresa de Avila school and Yolanda joined the rectory as Juanita's apprentice. When Juanita died during the flu epidemic two years later, Yolanda became the rectory's new cook and housekeeper.

"Four years later a proposal of marriage came from Captain Francois Prulette, with whom Yolanda maintained correspondence from their first meeting aboard the *Bastille Day*.

After a brief courtship and much consideration, Yolanda accepted and they were married by Padre Humberto in the Santa Teresa's sanctuary in the summer of 1892.

"Continuing her residency at the rectory, Yolanda stayed on as a cook and housekeeper, awaiting Captain Prulette's return from a commission that took him to France and the Netherlands. He returned in the spring of 1894.

"It was a man from his early childhood, however, who haunted Alejandro's memories. And he would not understand until years later why his mother married Francois Prulette."

"'Senor, that man Alejandro recalled could only be you, is that not the case?' Manuel asked.

Exhaling sweet briar, Pablo nodded.

"He could not forget it was I who carried him onto the great sailing ship, shushing him back to sleep.

"And it was I who took off his shoes to soothe his pain on a long coach ride from a wedding. It was I who taught him about the birds and other animals that lived on a great rancho in faraway California. He remembered his mother saying how much I loved them both and how I would be leaving California to join them in Mexico.

"Alejandro carried the hope that someday I would marry his mother and become the father he never had. But that day would never come.

"After dinner their last night in the rectory, Padre Humberto and Alejandro headed south. They rode in the same antiquated buckboard that had long ago carried Alejandro and the other schoolchildren to the parish cemetery to celebrate All Souls Day.

"At dusk, the western sun flamed low on the horizon, coloring the landscape a golden red. A rugged road leading to Mexico City's southern gate choked in horse and buggy traffic and moved in starts and stops.

"Alejandro wondered, as they rode in the quiet countryside, what the priest had on his mind. Before long, Padre Humberto stopped the dapple-gray near a tiny pond surrounded by a cluster of willow trees. Covered in early evening shadows, the peaceful knoll overlooked the entire city. 'Such a pleasant spot,' Alejandro thought, as the coolness of the evening made its home there.

"Before climbing down from the buckboard, the old priest paused, taking in the refreshing evening air. He then spread a blanket on the grass under the silhouetted willows and hung a brightly lit oil lantern on the rear gate.

"From under his robes, a small wooden box appeared.

"Looking up from the box and into Alejandro's face, he recited Proverbs 4, verses 1-6:

"'*Young men, listen to me as you would to your father. Listen, and grow wise, for I speak the truth...do not turn away. For I too was once a son tenderly loved by my mother as an only child and the companion of my father.'*

"He told me never to forget his words.

"'If you follow them,' he said, 'you will have a long and happy life. Learn to be wise and develop good judgment and common sense. I cannot overemphasize this point. Cling to wisdom, she will protect you. Love her, she will guard you.'

"'Before you leave for Morelos in the morning, you and I must this night discuss many important things.

"'Since my life's end is according to God's goodwill, and since I may never have this opportunity again, it is right to speak to you now, so that you will know the truth about all things.'

"Motioning for Alejandro to join him, he sat down on the blanket, carefully placing the box in its center.

"'You are a very blessed young man, Alejandro. Everyone you know and some people who you do not think very highly of you and love you very much. So much has been done to protect you and your mother. So much has been done to nurture you.'

"'Did you know that your life, as it were, has been diligently guarded since the moment you arrived in Mexico?

"'Do you know why your mother brought you here to Santa Teresa de Avila from the California rancho?'

"Alejandro gathered his knees to his chest and looked deeply into childhood memories for the answer. 'I had many questions and only vague memories of the people and the rancho. Through the years, when I tried to remember, I would ask my mother about who they were.'

"Taking his time to make clear exactly what his mother had told him, he gazed at the failing light filtering through the branches.

"'I remember, as time passed, her answers became a thin recollection, with little, if any, detail. That was true of everything except when I asked about Pablo.

"'At the mention of his name, a blush of pink filled her face and tears welled in her eyes. But all she said was Pablo was a good man who cared for her and loved me very much. She never explained why he never joined us or if he was still alive.

"'Time passed, and as I made new memories, I asked fewer and fewer questions about our old life and my childhood friend.

"'Then Francois entered my mother's life and became the father I never had. Studies filled my days and my life took new directions.

"'The old curiosities about Pablo and the rancho and California seemed to become less and less important.'"

"He pointed up at the remnant of the sun. 'Just like our old friend up there sinking in the west, those old memories seemed to fade away.

"'Of those you say protected us, is Pablo a man to whom I should be indebted?'

"Padre Humberto picked up the box and handed it to Alejandro.

"'Open it, my child.'

CHAPTER 43

The Forbidden Child

⁓⊕⁓

"Arranged by date, letters addressed to Padre Humberto filled the satin-lined box. Alejandro opened the first letter dated the twelfth day of August 1880.

"'These are the letters of Pablo Cabrera Barrazo de Leon. The letter you hold was written to me more than twenty years ago by the very same Pablo you remember from your childhood.

"'I have known him all his life. He remains faithful in his correspondence to me since the day of his adoption.

"'These letters tell the story of his life.

"Then his eyes drifted into the darkening sky and his voice lowered.

"'They tell the story of your life as well. Read them and you will come to know who Pablo is and what he has done for you. A casual reader of his letters would say his story speaks of noble sacrifice.

"'To you, Alejandro, his letters tell a very personal story of ensuring your safety and guarding your life.

"'It has been many years since he last saw you.

"'It is a wonderful love story. It speaks of the love he has always held for you and your mother, a story I am sure he would tell you himself if only he could.'

"Discovering I had been his unseen guardian for most of his life, uneasiness covered Alejandro's innocent face.

Nervously, he placed the unread letter back into the box and took a deep breath, a technique he used to fend off nervousness when delivering oral reports at preparatory school.

"Carefully placing his hands softly on Padre Humberto's shoulders, he searched the priest's eyes to better understand. Anxiously, he dared to ask the questions, the answers to which would shatter his naiveté and strand his life on an uncertain path.

"'Padre, I do not understand. How have our lives, my mother's and mine, been guarded? And what is this 'story of love' of which you speak?'

"'From the beginning, Alejandro, I have been witness to this saga. Listen a little longer. It will become clear and you will understand. Then your heart will tell you what you must do.'

"The tiny arc of light at the top of the western hills blinked shut, and a full moon rose in the east, brightening the darkness.

"'It is best you know everything from the beginning.'"

"'PABLO WAS AN ORPHAN, NEVER KNOWING HIS MOTHER or father. The rectory at Santa Teresa de Avila became his only home. From the first day he came into my life, God directed that his upbringing fall to Juanita, our housekeeper, and to me.

"'During the years that followed, we were his only parents, holding him in our arms, nurturing his body with food and his soul with prayer, rocking him to sleep when he was tired, encouraging him in his despair, nursing him when the sickness came and always, loving him very much.

"'He was a very quiet child, and like you, Alejandro, when he was old enough, he entered the convent school at Santa Teresa.

"'Loneliness for his parents tormented him until, in God's good time, a classmate, Vincenti de Leon, entered his life. Inseparable, the two boys grew to be good friends, loving each other like brothers. Don Joaquin and Dolores de Leon, Vincenti's parents, fell in love with Pablo. Through all the school years, they embraced him as their own, officially adopting him when he and Vincenti completed secondary school.'

"Not wanting to interrupt, Alejandro held back the questions for which he required answers. The long narrative of my winter trail ride from Mexico City to Central California continued.

"'Pioneered by grandfather and founder, Alphonse de Leon, forty years before, the two brothers mirrored the famous El Camino Real trail from Mexico City all the way to Piedra Blanca.'"

"His tale spoke of our eagerness to reach Mission San Miguel in San Luis Obispo and the welcoming hospitality of the Franciscan padre Fray Tomas, who anticipated our arrival for over a year.'

"In great detail, Padre Humberto recounted our parents' emigration when they left Mexico forever, sailing in the winter of 1884 from Zihuatanejo to Monterey.

"'The *Parisian*, five days overdue from Los Angeles, the last port of call, worried the brothers for their parents' safety. Neither one wanted to admit how much they feared losing their parents at sea, passing the time in nervous chatter about their parents' joy celebrating Christmas at the rancho.

"'But keeping the wagons in line while waiting for the ship to dock caused Pablo serious concerns. After hiring many wagons and teams to remain on hand to load his parents' cargo, when the ship's docking was late, the teamsters threatened to leave for another job.

"'Pablo's promise of double pay convinced the drivers to stand fast. So effective was the salary, the wagons stood ready for four days and nights to transport the de Leon cargo to Piedra Blanca.

"'Thanks to God, indeed, with all their earthly possessions, Mama Dolores and Don Joaquin arrived to enjoy their first Christmas at the rancho.

"'Three months after they settled in, what should have been a joyous event brought disaster into Pablo's life.

"'That was the infamous day the de Leon and Estrada families were joined by marriage. On that day, a little boy named Alejandro, dressed in a new suit and shoes too small for his feet, hobbled to the altar carrying the wedding rings for the bride and groom.'

"Remembering how he wobbled unsteadily down the church aisle, balancing the rings on the bearer's silk pillow, Alejandro laughed imagining the spectacle he must have presented.

"'Sorry to laugh, Padre. I remember when I fell over, this big hand grabbed me by the collar and stood me up. The huge man smiled, patted my behind, and then kept me upright at the altar.'

"He chuckled and said, 'I can see his face but I can't remember who he was.'

"Anxious to make his point, the agitated priest shouted, 'It was Carlos, the bride's huge brother. He was the one who saved you.'

"'Now, do you remember the groom?'

"Alejandro nodded. 'Of course, Vincenti de Leon. That day he took his wife, and brother Pablo was his sponsor.'

"'And the bride, do you remember her name?'

"'Yes. Recently Mama and I spoke of that day. Vincenti de Leon married Annabella Estrada, my mother's stepsister.

I haven't seen Aunt Annabella or my uncles, Pedro, Enrique, and the big one, Carlos, since I was six years old.'

"'Before I was born, my father was killed. Mama was grateful the Estradas took us in. They were very good to us. And when Aunt Annabella needed Mama, we left Canada de los Osos to live at Piedra Blanca.'

"'Alejandro, think back. Can you see Annabella in her gown of white, standing at the wedding altar?'

"'I remember,' he said. 'She was very beautiful.'"

"At Alejandro's description of the 'beautiful' bride,' Padre Humberto went into a tirade. Shouting into the heavens, ensuring God witnessed his anger, he trembled, spewing forth vile condemnations aimed at Annabella.

"Tongue in cheek, he said, 'I am sure everyone believed she was the picture of beauty and charm, the perfect bride, pure and unblemished.'

"'Oh, and I am sure her naive husband saw her as the picture of holiness.

"'But, Alejandro, what you are unaware of, and what everyone was soon to learn, under her veil of purity, below her appearance of perfection and beneath her profession of piety, lay an evil, ruthless immorality.

"'The epitome of the wanton, sinful, and deceitful bride, with every breath, she defiled the holy sacrament of marriage.

"'A bride possessing such hate and wickedness, she enlisted the village *curandera* to curse her sister, her husband, his parents, and yes, even her little nephew with death.

"'You are a man now. Your mother agrees it is time you know these unholy things! Know your enemy and be constantly wary.'

"'You must know the man who has always been your benefactor, Pablo Cabrera Barrazo de Leon.

"'You see, to guarantee your lives, Pablo promised Anna-bella he would never leave Piedra Blanca, never be married, and never have children of his own.

"'The curse still holds Pablo to his word, the price he pays every day to keep you and your mother alive. Especially now, since this past February, four of the cursed victims have died.

"'That is why he could never join your mother as planned.

"'That is the reason he freed and encouraged your mother to accept Francois's proposal of marriage.

"'Alejandro…it is Pablo who protects and supports you.

"'From that day, many years ago, as a sleepy five-year-old who sailed from Monterey to Mexico, Pablo has paid for your care and education. He will continue to do so until you are financially independent, in your own career, married with your family. This is his pledge to you and your mother.

"'Everything I have claimed is written in his letters. Read them. Then you will understand. This is the love story of which I speak. And it is Pablo who guards your safety and well-being, as he always will.

"'Alejandro, you are the forbidden child he could never have. And he loves you above all things.'"

CHAPTER 44

The Road of a Thousand Wonders

"In 1903, the European flu took Capitan Francois Prulette's life as he sailed home from Marseille to Vera Cruz.

When Yolanda's time for mourning ended a year later, at Padre Humberto's request, she left her Morelos home to return to Santa Teresa de Avila and her former cook and housekeeping position.

"The Morelos's mayor introduced Yolanda to prospective tenants interested in renting her home.

"She warmed to a recently immigrated German family. Its patriarch, Raleigh Wirth, an impassioned man of God and founder of the First Evangelical Lutheran Church in Mexico, made her feel her home would be in good hands.

"With her hacienda rented and the animals sold, she packed her few belongings and left to reunite with Padre Humberto to await Alejandro's graduation from law school and his possible return to Morelos.

"I enjoyed acclaimed stature as the patron of Rancho Piedra Blanca over the next three-and-a-half years as the rancho came to life and restoration accomplished. Most appreciative and notably grateful was Annabella.

"She and Emilio hired Poncho Cervantes, a talented caballero and first cousin to Rodrigo Montoya as the new majordomo. Young but experienced, Poncho proved a great teacher, and Emilio followed him doggedly. What mattered is that Annabella accepted him.

"By winter of 1906, the choir of *curandera* led in prayerful harmony by Flores de Flores, reversed all the curses released on the rancho from the *curandera's* pricked heart. As a safety measure, beloved Flores stayed on, overseeing the rancho's *curandero* duties to make certain the rancho's reestablished stability.

"With the rancho on the right footing and, most importantly, the curses dispelled, I felt free for the first time in years. I planned to travel east in the late spring to surprise Alejandro and attend his Harvard University graduation.

"Being completely honest, I not only wanted to congratulate the graduate. But after learning that Yolanda would attend the ceremony, I longed to see her once again. Twenty years had passed since she sailed out of my life to save her own.

"I lived at that time in my secluded home overlooking the ocean, high on the coastal bluffs. Telling no one, setting my affairs in order, the workweek ended, and I left for Boston undetected.

"Confounding attempts to track my whereabouts, I sailed from Monterey to San Francisco on a midnight fisherman's skiff, disguised as a merchant marine under the registered name Miguel Fuentes.

"Two days later, on Tuesday, April seventeenth, 1906, I ferried across the bay from San Francisco to Oakland to board the 9 p.m. Union Pacific & Southern Pacific Railroad train eastbound for Chicago.

"And thus began my rail adventure on the famous 'Overland Route to the Road of a Thousand Wonders,' a journey of eighteen hundred miles through the great West where once the bison and the Indians reigned.

"The next morning my excitement turned to dread when the train stopped in Reno for water and fuel. The newspaper boy shouted of a great earthquake that had struck San Francisco that morning, destroying the city almost completely by the ensuing fires."

Jose whistled. "Old man, to think, if you decided to stay another day, you could have died just another man burnt to death in some downtown hotel sleeping your life away. And no one would have ever known what happened to you."

"I have often thought of my good fortune, Jose. Checking out of the Palace Hotel, leaving for Oakland just eight hours before the calamity, I have come to believe God willed my escape for other plans he had for me in Boston. In later reports I learned the quake damage reached a bit north of King City. Relieved the rancho had not been affected, I prayed for the best and carried on with my plans.

"The first four-day leg took me east to Omaha, Nebraska. There I boarded the Chicago and North Western Railway. Reaching Chicago, I connected to an eastbound liner that took me to Albany, New York. Then, it was on through New York City and along the Eastern Seaboard to Boston, Massachusetts.

"I had often traveled by rail with Vincenti, south over the Cuesta from San Luis Obispo into Los Angeles and on the northern coastal route to San Francisco, but never east. Now, I crossed the entire country in less than two weeks.

"Senor Pablo, how did you sleep? Did you sit up?"

"No, no, Jaime. My fare included comfortable sleeping quarters, an extensive library, a well-stocked bar and smoking car, a handy barbershop, and dining cars with all the food you could ever want and where I dressed formally every night.

"If I remember, my ticket, not exceeding five hundred dollars, included travel and accommodations to Boston and back to Oakland. An overhead sign in every rail car, posted as a reminder to riders of their great bargain, read:

"'Enjoy All the Comforts of Home…Ride the Rails.'

"And before you ask, Rosa, the privy accommodations were wonderful—private and clean.

"And oh, the wonders I saw…the country, especially the Western states where the Indian chiefs reigned. Rich in history, the mountainous vistas over the Rockies and then the expansive prairies of grass as far as the eye could see. Ah, what beautiful treasures.

"Then came the cities and people and the bustle of crowds and civilization, with everyone hurrying everywhere, on foot, on horseback, or in horseless carriages with the constant clanging of the bells of the horse-drawn trolley cars—such large crowds and traffic that a policeman stood on every corner to direct it all.

"I had never seen so many people in one place at one time; there was no end to them, especially in Chicago and Boston."

Francisco asked, "How could anyone know his neighbor?"

"My dear Francisco, those cities were like nothing I had ever seen. Even your namesake, San Francisco, dwarfed in comparison. Paved roads in all directions filled with an assortment of motor vehicles, one in particular that bowled me.

"Imagine a motorized carriage large enough to hold twelve passengers on the top and twelve more on the bottom, with a driver calling out street names, and thousands of people coming and going, trying to stay out of its way.

"No one seemed to have time to stop and greet anyone. Everyone was too busy; no one was very friendly. In the modern world of the big city, no one seemed to have time to care very much about his neighbor."

As the sun disappeared, Jaime wrapped a coat around Conchita's shoulders, and Manuel walked to the flatbed to retrieve Rosa's shawl.

With its accompanying dampness, a fog seeped in from the west, emptying the square quickly. The chill told everyone the picnic was over.

Rosa helped Manuel pack up the picnic's remnants and joined Pablo, already safely deposited in the cab. Testing his high beams for the coast road ahead, Manuel turned from the village square, leaving the July Fourth picnic a good memory.

"My dear lovebirds, thank you for today. For me, these good days are fewer and fewer, and this one I reserve as a sweet-smelling rose."

Waiting for a quiet moment, Rosa waylaid into Pablo.

"What do you mean stopping the telling at such an interesting moment in time? I now will not be able to sleep until I know what happened when you arrived in Boston, to surprise the woman and child you had not seen in years. It might be polite for others to let you go off to sleep and rest without knowing. But I am not polite, old man! I need to know…I must know, please?"

Driving at a snail's pace through the fog, praying victory for frayed wipers, Manuel joined Pablo in a muffled laugh.

Rosa looked on, waiting as the storyteller rummaged his pocket for his pipe and then opened the passenger window a crack. Like a man considering which priority to serve, methodically filling the pipe bowl, he struck a match, then slowly exhaled the smoke. With smoke drifting out the crack, realizing renewed energy, Pablo cleared his throat and said, "Rosa,

Rosa, the story does not have a happy ending. I wish it did, but I cannot bear guilt for your sleepless night."

Praying a thank-you for the desired outcome, Rosa closed her eyes. "Now you are talking, now you are talking!" Then the old man took up where he had left off.

"I disembarked in New York, arriving four days before the graduation ceremony. Within a few hours' delay, I connected with a train bound for Boston."

Fog turned to a drizzle. Manuel maintained a safe, steady pace on what had become a dangerous, slippery road.

"To you good friends, I will admit, even after all the life that had flowed under the bridge for the both of us, a giddiness welled up in me thinking about seeing Yolanda again.

"But, did I hold out hope for something more than a renewed friendship? Not at all. Her husband had died. She had mourned a respectable period, living in the confines of a religious rectory, counseled daily by the priests living there."

More to assure himself than his listeners, Pablo paused, looking into Rosa's expectant face, sorry to disappoint her.

"I had no illusions that our meeting would be anything more than a lovely reminiscing. Yet, for both of us, as it turned out, our reunion proved delightful and hopeful. I had corresponded with Alejandro over the previous year. Contacting him at his dormitory by phone, he believed I called to wish him congratulations. Even assuring him his grateful words unnecessary, to say the least, his words spilled out, and our conversation was very touching, indeed.

"After such intimate words, I could stand suspense no longer, confessing to Alejandro my train had arrived. I was calling him from Boston's South Station and needed to see him as soon as possible. He screamed and shouted.

"'Stay put, I will pick you up within the hour.'

"As he had, like that little boy who insisted on naming each rabbit, squirrel, and animal on the rancho, with tears and sobs he embraced me for a long time. Sipping coffees at the university commissary, our memories flooded back. As if no time had passed at all, the hours spent together that day reaffirmed our bond for life. Our love for the other had never diminished despite the thief who stole the other's company for too long a time.

"Like schoolboys, we giggled, catching up, answering each other's questions. I asked about his mother to learn he had put her up at the new Hotel Buckminster in Kenmore Square. She had been sightseeing all day. When I suggested we join her for dinner that evening, his face turned iridescent with inspiration.

"'Senor Pablo, this is too good! This is too good! Mama always dreamed about the day the two of you would meet again. How many years has it been? At least twenty years? Correct?

"'I have, what I think is a wonderful idea. Please, I beg you, allow me the honor and the pleasure of making that first reunion for you and Mama a very special surprise for her and a wonderful delight for you.'

"I would, the next day, be attending the commencement, not as a parent, relative, or friend of an honored graduate. No, Alejandro had other plans for me. I would be sitting next to him in the graduate section of the audience.

"After dinner at a student haunt, Alejandro and I spent the time planning the celebration the three of us would enjoy after the ceremony. A Harvard education had not been wasted on him. A brilliant, unselfish fellow charged with bringing in this new age, he possessed, even in his youth, the rare attributes of wisdom and maturity that would serve him handsomely throughout his noble life.

"Alejandro, a young man of such character, upon graduation set aside every personal opportunity to honor the promise made to his saddened mother to come home to Morelos at the news of his stepfather's death. He turned down offers that came from national and international law firms, including Elisha Root's invitation to join the US Department of State.

"He handed me a package and waited impatiently for me to open it.

"'Hurry Pablo, this is your graduation day too.'

"Like one of his fellows, I donned cap and gown, to walk with Alejandro in the grand promenade.

"I was so proud, sitting there in the Harvard Law Library witnessing Alejandro's graduation. I beamed, watching him bending down to give his mother a kiss as he seated her and flashed his mischievous smile from across the graduate hall, waving to me while sitting with his fellow graduates.

"The proud mother had no idea that she and I would be that day celebrating together Alejandro's graduation.

"With a musical flourish, the university symphonic struck up Elgar's 'Pomp and Circumstance,' and the grand promenade began. When speeches concluded, the seated graduates, one by one, were invited to the podium to receive their respective diplomas and address the audience.

"When Alejandro's name was called, he ran to accept his diploma, shaking hands enthusiastically with the law school dean. Waving to her, he cleared his throat, thanking his mother. She waved back a handheld hankie used to dab her tears.

"Then, he surprised everyone, announcing he had received permission from the graduation committee to present a special award of gratitude to a man who was his secret benefactor for many years.

"'It gives me great honor to bestow my graduation diploma, as a small token of my gratitude, to the man most deserving. He gave up his life to save not only mine but my mother's as well.

"'His physical presence in my life was very short, yet he taught me much and loved me well. Although he has not seen his beloved in over twenty years, today he still holds fast his love for my mother, Yolanda.

"'Everyone would count it fortune, to come to know a man blessed by God of such noble character and selflessness. I present such a man, with my deepest love and appreciation, Senor Pablo Cabrera Barrazo de Leon!'"

"I was completely ambushed. Sitting there in my cap and gown my tears spouted as a man I hoped someday would be my son beckoned me to the podium.

"'I also invite my mother, his beloved Yolanda….Please come up and join Pablo in accepting my thanks and this, my diploma, the symbol of my success, accomplished only through his faith and love for me and my mother, Yolanda Gomez.'

"I staggered to the podium in my silly masquerade to meet a sobbing woman named Yolanda who I realized I still loved very much, and we embraced a long time.

"The well-wishers joined in our joy and the audience shouted and clapped. Yolanda and I still embraced when Alejandro handed me his diploma and began hugging both of us, kissing our cheeks.

"That night would be a night we would never forget. We three joined in graduation celebrations taking place throughout the city. At every party we attended, toasts were raised not only to the Harvard graduates but to Alejandro's benefactor, Pablo, and his lifelong love, Yolanda.

"When Boston's mayor, John Francis Fitzgerald, and his wife, Josie, arrived at the Hotel Buckminster in their round of the parties, the three of us were introduced as honored guests. Yolanda and Josie struck up a wonderful friendship from their first hello. Whether champagne or giddiness of the moment, the two graceful women came together as fast friends. Before the end of the evening, the mayor's wife insisted the three of us accept an invitation to dinner at the mayor's mansion the next night.

"At the mansion the next night, we met a parade of notables including P. J. Kennedy, the mayor's chief political rival. Polite and refined, Kennedy kissed Yolanda's hand, shook mine, and presented his son Joseph, who fidgeted with distraction, shaking my hand dismissively. It was obvious his gaze rested heavily on sixteen-year-old Rose Fitzgerald, Josie's daughter standing in the reception line next to her father, 'Honey Fitz.'"

Manuel's hand shot up. "A moment, please, is this not the same Joe Kennedy who ran whiskey during Prohibition?"

"One and the same, Manuel. And by the way, whiskey runner Joe married lovely Rose, the apple of his eye. And like the marriage that bound the de Leons and Estradas, theirs cemented the Kennedy and Fitzgerald families for life."

———— ❧ ————

STARING OUT AT THE CREEPING MIST, REMEMBERING that glorious night, the old man paused in revelry, reliving each precious moment shared with his beloved Yolanda and Alejandro.

Unexpectedly, he slapped the bowl of his pipe into his palm, collected the tobacco ashes, and carefully tossed them out the window into the fog. With sadness and pain, in a voice filled with regret, he continued.

"The week flew by and then it was time for Yolanda and Alejandro to sail home. I thought a very long time about joining them, sailing to Mexico and a new life with a beautiful woman and a son blessed with wonderful gifts, forsaking the rancho, clearing the way for Annabella and Emilio. After all, I disappeared without a word and my going back held no guarantees. For all I knew I had already been counted and gone like Josefina Espinoza, or worse.

"But Rosa, the hour is late, and I am tired. Hopefully, you are satisfied enough with this story to sleep well tonight. As for this old shepherd, take me home to my bed. I am weary of this telling. I need to sleep. Besides, others not here deserve to know what happened next."

Closing his eyes, resting his head on the windowpane, his voice trailed off. And not a syllable emanated from passenger or driver after that. For the silent monks, the old truck took on a monastic hush as they listened to the drone of slick tires squeal an opus all the way to the shepherd's hut.

Manuel brought Pablo to his cot. Once settled, Rosa stood at the door, praying for Pablo to rest and sleep well.

"Rosa, Rosa," Pablo called out. "I must put you to rest." Tears filled his eyes.

"A moment please. Forgive an old man his long-lost vanity. I confess, my fear, selfishness, and shame would not allow me to admit my horrendous error in judgment, allowing Yolanda and Alejandro to sail away from me that dreadful day."

THE OLD MAN SLEPT LATE THE NEXT MORNING. THERE would be no walk to the ridge today. Each step to the outhouse triggered a throbbing pain he gladly endured if only his mind's torment surrendered to it. That was not to be.

Sitting outside the hut, dazed and filled with regret, he looked absently at the horizon. The story told to Rosa and Manuel broke their hearts as living through it crushed his.

CHAPTER 45

A Drowning Soul in a Rising Tide

⸺◈⸺

In the shepherd's hut, late into the night, Pablo weaved his miserable tale.

"Making good friends with their daughter Rose, as her guest I lodged at the Fitzgeralds for two weeks. She possessed a hunger to discuss life with someone like me who was far removed from Boston and her privileged family—someone, she said, 'who gifted their life to help others.'

"Rose fancied knowing what it meant to be raised in the 'Wild West,' as she called any place west of Chicago. With difficulty, she grappled to understand how I could, from such a tender age, perform all the responsibilities my position at Piedra Blanca entailed.

"A member of an aristocratic family, raised in provincial Catholic Boston, she queried outsiders to learn about the outside world. She desired mostly to feel the humanity of common man, how they thought, and what was important to him.

"'I need to broaden my understanding and sharpen my insight into the common man to not only benefit my family, but society as a whole. Unburdened by society's expectations and demands, that happy fellow seems to lead such an idyllic happy life.'

"And the tours she hosted on the Eastern Seaboard opened my eyes to the modern world and gave her time to ask her questions.

"The twenty-two-story triangular Flatiron Building, reaching high into the New York sky, raised goosebumps all over my body. Even though its celebrated crack silenced its tolling years before, Philadelphia's Independence Hall, with its historic Liberty Bell, left an indelible impression.

"But the Boston Commons, home for more than a century to faithful city dwellers, remained our favorite place to exchange thoughts and ideas on our many memorable walks. When the tours ended and I expressed my gratitude, she instead thanked me for sharing my insights. 'Senor Pablo, our time together, knowing the man you are and the perspective generously shared, more than compensated me for the tours.'"

"Before wearing thin the Fitzgerald hospitality, anxious to rejoin Yolanda and Alejandro in Mexico and sever all ties to Rancho Piedra Blanca, my time in Boston came to an end.

"On a beautiful New England morning, Rose, my ever-faithful companion, saw me off. As I boarded my train, she patted her eyes with a silk hanky, chiding me never to forget her. Waving a long goodbye, the train started out of the station.

"Then, in a very unladylike fashion that made me laugh, she shouted for the world to hear: 'Do not forget, Senor Pablo. Our paths will cross again. We meet next in the Wild West.'"

"Unannounced, I arrived home three months to the day I had left. Home to my summer cabin high on the Pacific bluff, I found a sealed envelope from Flores de Flores, with the day's date embossed in black, posted on my door.

"Hesitating to open it, I wondered how he could possibly know I would be home that very day.

"His terse prose read predictably:

"'In your absence, Annabella leapt at the opportunity, convincing everyone you were not only missing but surely dead. Her lawyers filed documents with the county, proclaiming Emilio as the only living de Leon and, therefore, legal heir to Rancho Piedra Blanca estate.'

"Basking in the Pacific sunshine, I smiled at how surprised mother and son would be seeing me sitting at the hacienda's breakfast table the next morning.

"But the ravens, one after the next, started landing on my cabin roof. Hundreds perched in stillness, staring down on me. I waited for the Grand Raven to take his place on the roof's peak.

"Was I to suffer Josefina Espinoza's fate?

"A shrill whistle shattered the silence and the ravens, in unison, turned and faced away from me. The whistler prayed fervently, sitting in the clutches of a giant cypress, clothed in black priest vestments worn when saying the Mass for the Dead. The solemnity disturbing, I cried out, "'*Curandero*, why do you pray? You can see I am home safe and sound.'

"Tears filled Flores de Flores's eyes, my safety apart. A groan of such agony burst forth from his grief-stricken face that no comfort on earth could ever salve.

"'Not your safety, senor, but others journeying homeward. Some, I fear, fared badly, reaching not their destination.'

"He slid down from the tree and walked to where I stood. Choking on dread, I prayed he had no more to say.

"'Unlike you, one is lost at sea and dwells in the deep.'

"With tears falling to the ground, he shook his head. Nudging me toward the porch bench. He stood as I sat. His stature allowed him to stare directly into my eyes.

"I was shaking, fearing what would come.

"'The truth is, in you, Senor Pablo, I see your strength, your goodness. I see also how the anguish of my sad news will affect your life to its end.

"'My good and faithful friend, curses are strange things! To fulfill curses? I, for one, have seen dead men rise! But this curse, this childish, dead, and spent abomination, buried forever, is somehow not yet still.

"'Young Alejandro is spared, but not so your love. Cherished Yolanda is with the angels now.

"'From calm to torrential, bypassing Alejandro, standing innocently beside her on the ship's deck, a monstrous spout rose up out of the sea to pluck the sweetest rose with such premeditation, Saint Christopher could not have saved her.

"'Helpless, beset, Alejandro watched devils carry his mother away. As our Lord commanded the sea, Alejandro's cries stilled the wind, but the burden of his anguish made the ocean rise.

"'Dear Pablo…now your soul drowns in that rising tide.'"

"THAT WARM SUMMER EVENING IN 1906, ALEJANDRO found his old home exactly as he remembered it. If the ill-fated deaths of his parents had not enraged his soul,

Alejandro would have no quarrel with the 'intruders' occupying his parent's hacienda estate high on the valley wall overlooking hamlet Morelos.

"From Mexico City, he drove there in a horseless carriage to execute the eviction. With a heart of stone, to him, the occupants of the hacienda were nothing but weeds in the garden to be plucked and thrown in the fire.

"His beloved mother, the recent victim of Annabella's long-suffering curse, had not occupied the hacienda for years. And long silent were the treasured sea stories of his stepfather.

"In his first act as an attorney, he served the eviction notice to Pastor Wirth at his old home's front door.

"Introducing himself as 'the late landlord's son,' the notice informed the pastor and his family they had thirty days to vacate the property. Alejandro would be moving back.

"To Alejandro's surprise, knowing this day would come, the pastor accepted the notice without rancor. The mild clergyman, consoling him for the loss of his parents, gently gripped his hand and held Alejandro to his breast. Comforting his confounded landlord, the pastor patiently explained.

"'My son, although my congregation is small, plans to provide my family with a parsonage are nearing completion. In God's good time, give or take a week or two, my family will be moving into our new home. I posted a letter over a month ago giving you notice of our long-awaited move. I mailed it to the Santa Teresa de Avila's rectory, addressed to you.'

"Chagrined and foolish, Alejandro realized he carried that letter and others still unread with him from Santa Teresa's, collected at the rectory the day before.

"'Alejandro, my beloved fellow, God is faithful and we can plainly see His hand at work in both life and death.

"'First, we rejoice that He restores life, welcoming you back home to your cherished hacienda and to people here who love and honor you. Second, we rejoice that He provides a new home for my family and congregation. And third, we rejoice also in death. The Creator holds your mother and stepfather in His loving arms. Joyously, they are in heavenly company, receiving eternal rewards for their faithful love, a promise in which we all share. No more pain, suffering, or death, only life and life eternal.'

"The pastor introduced his wife and children, inviting the broken-hearted Alejandro to dinner, offering Alejandro his old room to stay in as long as he wished.

"'I promised several of your old friends who called I would let them know when you would be arriving. Your loving friends in Morelos...they all are here and waiting for you.'

"From the Wirth family's humble example, Alejandro would draw on this profound lesson for the rest of his life. God's grace can be found in the worst of tragedies.

"Hanging his lawyer shingle for all to see, Alejandro took up residence in his old Morelos home three months later."

CHAPTER 46

Alphonse and the Grand Plan

The parlor filled with familiar faces and the old man settled in the armchair reserved for him. The tea kettle let out a shriek as Rosa and Manuel were busy preparing the orange sauce for the flan. Jaime waved to his father to hurry.

"Andale. Manuel told everyone the telling would be very special today. The old man is about to start, I do not want to miss a word."

Jose ran back from the outhouse, oblivious his shoe bore witness to the place he last visited. Full of himself with mischief in his voice, he rejoined the listening circle, begging a question.

"Senor Pablo, now that Rosa's roasted chicken and tender green beans have satisfied our hunger, and dessert will soon be served, perhaps you have a short story to share before the telling begins?"

Struggling for an appropriate narrative, annoyed at Jose for asking, the old shepherd frowned and puffed hard on his pipe.

"All right, Jose, all right. I do believe I have a tale.

"This story concerns a man, very much like you, who lived in a village and worked with his hands.

"In the morning he would arise, stoke the fire, make his breakfast, and tend to his laundry.

"You see, he lived alone.

"Each morning he had the choice of exiting to his work-place from either his front or back door. The front door led to the village; the back door to the pasture. Before leaving for work, he would pray to the saints the door he chose that day would lead him to God's most desired blessing, a loving wife."

An alarm bell started to ring in Jose's mind, not a loud clang, just a tingle.

"One day the Lord answered his prayer, for indeed the old bachelor had fallen in love with a beautiful female. A true beauty, with glowing brown eyes and ripe red hair and legs so long, standing tall, the short man reached but her shoulders. But it did not matter to him, for the first time in his life, he was in love.

"After several months of courtship, nervous though he was, the old bachelor decided to pop the question. Embracing his beloved, he kissed her. Responding affectionately, she snuggled close to his chest to caress his lips.

"'My darling' he whispered, 'our long courtship must end. The people of the village are talking. And I do not want what they say to make you sad.'

"With that, he dropped to his knees, reached into his pocket, and said, 'Today at this moment, so that no one has any doubt of my intentions, here is my ring of engagement. Accept my proposal and say you will be my wife and lover.'

"Rhonda, that was her name. Rhonda scarcely knew what to say. In fact, scratching her head on the door jamb, which she liked to do, she said nothing at all.

"'Oh my Rhonda, now is not the time to play coy. Please say yes. I promise you a wonderful life. You will never want for anything.'

"Rhonda began swaying back and forth, keeping rhythm with the guitar-playing troubadour hired to stand outside the window for just this tender moment.

"Rhonda joined in the chorus, wiggling her ears and twitching her nose to the troubadour's lovely refrain.

"'Hee-haw, hee-haw, hee-haw, hee-haw.' The would-be groom beamed at her melodious voice and the two began to dance. And for the happy couple, all was fine until Rhonda noticed, dragging behind him, a three-foot trail of toilet paper dangling from her partner's boot, careless residue from his recent outhouse visit.

"Sickened by his total lack of manners and grace, Rhonda, with noble dignity, lifted her head, pointed her ears, and with a final 'hee-haw,' headed in a huff for the pasture to rejoin the other donkeys, cows, and horrible pigs, absolutely assured to never find soiled toilet paper stuck to any of their hooves."

While the mortified Jose raced to the outhouse to remove the evidence, the room erupted. Everyone roared hysterically, happy the joke was not about any of them.

On his way back, Jose, the good sport, shouted to his son Jaime waiting for him, laughing doubled-over in the doorway.

"'Whew, that was close. Good thing I married your mother and not that donkey. Your ears would be too long.'"

WHEN THE UPROAR SETTLED, ROSA AND MANUEL, giggling still, tried to serve the flan without spilling the coffee. Fueled by saucy donkey jokes at Jose's expense, the light-hearted mood carried on until Pablo held up his hand.

The group quieted, waiting while the pipe smoker carefully tamped his bowl, relit his burl, and filled the room with its intoxicating sweetness, signaling the telling would begin.

"Hombres, senoras and senoritas, before the resumption of my story, I must take this time to correct historical inaccuracies related to you by me in my many tellings."

The air buzzed as the puzzled listeners searched each other's eyes for a hint of what the old man could possibly mean.

Pablo sipped his coffee, cleared his throat, then delivered like heavy blows, declarations that made his audience afraid to inhale any more of the mesmerizing smoke.

"After the Patron's death, an official from, of all places, the office of California Governor Earl Warren, paid me a visit.

"His administrative secretary, a Mr. Merrell Small—a pipe smoker with a penchant for the finer tobacco blends—hand-carried an important report, or dossier, as he called it, intended 'for my eyes only.'

"He told me that an exhaustive study of the origins and history of the de Leon family and the Mexican land grant, Rancho Piedra Blanca, had been recently completed. Information uncovered, he said, 'affected the legal standing of one Pablo Cabrera Barrazo de Leon.'"

Apprehension ablaze, he looked at each of his friends reassuring them. Then he embarked on a series of revelations, changing everything they ever believed.

From his pouch, Pablo retrieved official papers displaying them to the room of fidgeting listeners.

"Of all things, the most incredible discovery concerned my lineage. After all these years, these documents I present to you now, establish my birth parents, and yes, much more."

Fidgeting abruptly stopped. Rosa, Manuel, Jose, Jaime, Conchita, Francisco, and Angelina collectively moved to the edge of their respective seats.

"The dossier conclusions took me back to my lonely years. I was astonished that the answer to the question I asked myself every day shone like a beacon's light.

"Those wonderful people who took in this lonely orphan were not a stepfamily. They were, in fact, the flesh of my flesh. They were the blood of my blood. My family who loved me and from before my birth were privy to my origins.

"Yet for reasons to be explained, they never ever told me.

"Too close to the obvious all along, not until the dossier did I see the connection.

"My friends, documents held in trust by Padre Humberto at Santa Teresa de Avila since the day of my birth, change the past you and I trusted to be true.

"So now, to make my story right, clear your minds of fallacies and replace them with these historical facts.

"You well remember, do you not, the orphan's plight, when I introduced to you my adopted father, Don Joaquin?

"In truth, Don Joaquin was not my adopted father, no.

"He, instead, was my blood brother!

"Mama Dolores, his wife, was my sister-in-law!

"Beloved brother Vincenti was my nephew!

"My father, who never claimed me, in fact, was the don of dons, Alphonse de Leon!

"And his lifelong wife, Lorena, the mother I always wanted to know and love!"

The bewildered listeners were momentarily distracted from digesting these revelations when a thunderous backfire from a passing truck set off from the stabled cows a mooing pandemonium.

The cows' song prodded a flaming question.

"Senor, has it not always been our understanding that Lorena and Alphonse were long ago divorced?"

"Yes, yes, that understanding I held all my life. They did separately seek divorce, but the record tells a different story. The church never allowed the divorce and rejected their request without consideration. It seems as turbulent as their marriage appeared, in truth, it never ended. Neither of the two ever remarried for one simple reason—'till death do they part.'

"They were always man and wife.

"After Joaquin's birth and for all those many years after their divorce had been denied, my mother and father continued to secretly come together, ultimately conceiving me.

"Their marriage only ended when Alphonse died.

"A roustabout to the end, true to his nature, he died disgraced in the bed of a harlot at Madam Margarita's La Ida Café. Four years later, in a Vera Cruz convent, the nunnery attending Lorena's deathbed, sang praises to God for a wife's faithfulness to a husband so disgustingly unfaithful.

"It was true; everyone believed Alphonse and Lorena had indeed divorced. And this forced my father, the villain and savior, to do a very noble thing. He protected his wife's reputation and spared public scandal of a child born out of wedlock.

"Orchestrating with the Franciscan fathers, a 'behind closed doors residency' for the last six months of her pregnancy, Alphonse hid Lorena away at the Santa Teresa de Avila rectory. Relying on her often-used ploy to secretly rendezvous with Alphonse, Lorena convinced her parents that, at age forty, she 'burned, once again, with a passion' to renew her commitment to the Lord.

"Her parents, my grandparents from my mother Lorena's side, who never knew I existed, happily gave their blessing.

"They saw her off to attend a Franciscan convent course in 'spiritual disciplines,' conducted in far-off Mexico City. By the way, the time frame coincided nicely with my mother's last and most obvious months before my birth.

"This well-worn ploy worked to perfection. Sworn to secrecy, Juanita, the rectory housekeeper and village midwife, saw my mother through labor and childbirth. And her parents never knew!

"On September twentieth, 1862, in the quiet of Juanita's rectory bedroom, wrapped in my mother's hand-sewn blanket bearing my name, I entered the world a healthy boy.

"And my 'orphan story' became reality.

"Hiding the truth of my birth from all but a few conspirators, my father's 'grand plan' locked into perfect place.

"Lorena, old friends of Padre Humberto and Juanita, traveled regularly from Vera Cruz to Santa Teresa de Avila to watch me grow and oversee my care."

Tears filling his eyes, he whispered: "From birth to school age, I vaguely remember the kind and loving lady who came often to the rectory with candy and presents. All the time, my mother was in my life and I did not know her."

The women, of course, wept, but most upset was Angelina, the mother-to-be. The men hid their sobs, retreating hastily to the outhouse, to return only after careful inspection of their shoes, to the teary women.

Composures restored, coffee cup filled, burl on fire, the old shepherd carried on.

"My brother Don Joaquin always knew our relationship. His agreement to adopt me years later was central to Alphonse's 'grand plan.' And rascal Alphonse came away unscathed.

"All of Mexico, in fact, heralded his son, Don Joaquin, and the noble de Leon family's gracious act, publicly recognizing the family for opening their hearts and welcoming into their home the orphan classmate of their son.

"A charming story, perfect and seamless. Vincenti and I bonded in convent school, became brothers in secondary, and grew into manhood at Rancho Piedra Blanca.

"Until the dossier, only benevolent schemers Alphonse, Lorena, Padre Humberto, Juanita, Don Joaquin, and Mama Dolores, knew the truth.

"The 'grand plan' succeeded. No one ever suspected! Not even me!

"I do believe, however, others knew the truth. Thinking back those many years when Vincenti and I first arrived at Mission San Miguel and introductions were made, Friar Fray Tomas Sepulveda doted on me, noting the resemblance, recognizing in me his old friend Alphonse.

"At the time, I thought his old eyes betrayed him. Begging the priest's pardon, I told him he had our identities reversed. More confused than embarrassed, he acknowledged his blunder and apologized. Yet I know now his doubts and second thoughts about 'just who this fellow Pablo is,' were real and justified.

"Now that it is too late to embrace my parents, you might be wondering what my consolation is.

"Soon, I think I will be joining them and others long dead, all those who protected my mother's virtue, keeping the secret of my birth from everyone, even me. Rest assured, my discussions with them in heaven will be eternal.

"What matters most to me now is that you, my good friends, know my real story."

"But Senor Pablo," Rosa insisted, "someone else surely knows. Who researched the de Leons and the rancho?"

"And who found the evidence of your birth?" Jose asked.

"And why was it important for Mr. Small to make his way from the governor of California to you with these revelations?"

"No, Senor Pablo," Manuel argued. "Someone else knows…somebody who cares about you, very much indeed."

"You, of course, are right. You are all very right. The answer in one word—Alejandro."

CHAPTER 47

A Son for a Son

Sitting in the steamy parlor, the listeners, daubing sweating brows, had more than Cambria's heat to overcome. Like a peace offering for the blistering day, twilight's gentle wind stirred window curtains, bringing respite to the edgy group.

With questions smoldering, Conchita and Rosa approached the old man.

"Senor Pablo, are you, indeed, Emilio's father?"

For a long time, the old man stared in silence at his pipe's wispy trail. With a trickle of tears, he let out a long sigh of self-condemnation, stuttering his lurid confession.

Straining to hear the penitent's words, the listeners leaned in closer, not wanting to miss a syllable.

"As much as I wished to deny it, the truth is the truth.

"On her marriage eve, amid shed clothes strewn on the confessional floor, the unfaithful bride coupled with the loathsome best man and brought forth a son.

"So there is no mistake. She named the bastard Emilio.

"And as life would have it, Padre Fray Tomas bore witness to the wickedness, seeing and hearing everything that terrible night. He, in fact, immortalized the depravity, in chapter and verse, in the Mission San Miguel log for the edification of all future generations.

"Oh yes, the depravity has followed me my entire life."

Still, his confession begged for more answers.

"But, senor, all those years before Vincenti's death, how could you not acknowledge Emilio?"

"Senora Rosa, Annabella feared the day his repentant father would take Emilio into confidence and tell him the truth. That is the reason she worked diligently to keep Emilio out of my reach, constantly threatening to expose me to Vincenti.

"I cared for Emilio. But as he grew older and drew closer to becoming the patron, he was poisoned against me. And I loved Vincenti much more, realizing the truth would drive him into retreating from the world all the more.

"Deep in my heart, I believe he knew. In fact, he always knew, but to protect the family, he took his pain to the grave saying nothing. A noble man, a faithful son, brother, and nephew, he deserved much more than life gave him.

"When Vincenti died and the years passed, Annabella's constant influence and demented manipulation warped Emilio into a brutal monster no one wanted to claim, most of all me.

"Flores de Flores's words of wisdom were a constant reminder: 'Emilio is his mother's son. There is no part of him that she does not own; there is no part of him left for you, Pablo, to occupy or influence.'

"When Vincenti died, Emilio's path to becoming patron was clear-sailing, with one exception.

"Annabella waited for an opportunity, which I provided, to remove me as Emilio's only obstacle. In my long absence from the rancho when I traveled to Boston, Annabella's lawyers convinced the courts to declare me legally dead. When I returned to the rancho from the East Coast, I no longer existed, and all my rights had been confiscated. I was dead.

"After Yolanda's death, I had nothing left to fight for and nothing left to say.

"I am sure, at the urging of his mother, in the new patron's sardonic generosity, Emilio tolerated my staying on the rancho as a hired hand, nothing more.

"At Emilio's funeral, surrounded by friends, I woke up from my nightmare and years of silence realizing the cursed that had bypassed Alejandro and Annabella no longer held power or control over me!

"In this irony, finally, I understood.

"Alejandro was no longer the one cursed. By fulfilling the *curandera's* demand, 'a son for a son,' the Patron took Alejandro's place to suffer the curse of death. And retribution was Annabella's price to pay for reversing the curses.

"In the end, with Emilio's death, Alejandro was spared, triggering the curse to come crashing down on Annabella.

"I was reborn. Finding my voice, eager to tell my story I reclaimed my identity. For all these reasons and so many others, truly, truly, I praised God that Alejandro's life was spared, while rejoicing in Emilio's death."

———⸙———

"This is an old story, this tale of two sons, an adopted son, a gift of love, endowed with good blood and a son conceived in sin and corrupted in evil.

"First, let us consider Emilio. His story is not noble. Socially respectable as he might have appeared, his associates, however, who he misappropriated and manipulated, knew him for an unscrupulous coward and thief.

"Victims, including me, prayed to see him in the grave. His list of enemies grew long. The number of those who despised him will make his death impossible to solve.

"Despite the fact Flores and his fellow *curanderismo*

restored the rancho's devastation, they all were fired by Emilio in his first official act as patron.

"More disgustingly, he instituted Annabella's plan to eliminate, the 'riff-raff,' the humble workers who enjoyed the rancho's care and protection. He immediately imposed unfair rent increases on occupants traditionally provided rancho homes.

"He forced family after family to move out without compensation or consideration. Those who stayed were obliged to sign long-term commitments. Old established families who lost their homes either moved away or became indentured farmhands.

"The new patron choked nearby ranches and farms dependent on the rancho for their freshwater source. He revised old water use pacts, coercing his neighbors into long-term lease arrangements at exorbitant rates.

"Neighboring owners, unable to pay, were forced to abandon their homesteads as back payment. He foreclosed on many neighboring ranchers and farmers, adding thousands of acres to the Piedra Blanca.

"Annabella was delighted ranch hands were obligated to buy exclusively from the rancho store, where easy credit trapped workers into an impossible servitude never able to earn enough to pay their debt.

"When local business owners balked, the Patron demanded kickbacks from them to allow rancho hands to patronize their businesses away from the rancho.

"The house-building boom exploded as post-war GIs came home to get married and buy a new home. But developers in Monterey and San Luis counties were required to submit housing plans to the county planning commissions for approval.

"But approvals cost them tribute payment to Emilio, who chaired both county commissions. The larger the kickback, the faster the approval. A few desperate companies were forced into paying the Patron a percentage of sales.

"Then there was the matter of the Patron's folly. Huge lumber shortages caused by the Patron's demand for lumber from local suppliers forced to pledge all available and future shipments of lumber for the "Patron's Folly" picket fence project.

"Costing developers time, labor, and money, Central California new home construction starts were delayed. Many smaller builders, unable to compete, were forced to sell their land to the Patron for pennies on the dollar.

"But my anger and sadness mounted as each disgusting story came to light of rape and physical abuse of girls and women hired to work at the Hacienda de Leon."

Jaime started crying for his wife, Veronica, a victim of Emilio de Leon's debauchery.

ON A HOT STICKY AUGUST EVENING, YEARS BEFORE THE Patron's death, when Maria and Juanito were very young, Jaime's wife, Veronica, took her life in the cornfield behind their home. Young and beautiful, full of hope, grateful for the opportunity to add to the household income, Veronica accepted a service position at Hacienda de Leon.

Veronica reported to work promptly that first Monday morning, dropped off by her husband at 7 a.m. Waving goodbye to Jaime, dreaming of benefits to share with her family, she entered the hacienda, her heart light with happy anticipation. But her position as housemaid lasted all of one day.

When the work day ended, Jaime picked up his wife, anxious to hear what he thought would be her nonstop conversation. Instead, she was silent, sullen, and weepy. He did not know what to think.

Knowing Veronica as he did, his stomach turned over, worrying what could have caused such a drastic change in the happy woman he said 'adios' to that morning.

She said nothing all the way home, sitting as far from Jaime as she could. That night, making dinner for the family, she wept, eating nothing herself. After washing the dishes, she kissed her worried husband and children, excusing herself, seeking time to think and the need for fresh air.

At a chosen spot, walking far into the tall corn crop behind their home, she took off her apron and clean dress, folding them neatly before removing her shoes. Placing everything neatly in a corn crib, she sat down on a harvest box.

Whispering her goodbyes to husband and family, she wept, staring at the dying sun. She begged their forgiveness before slitting both her wrists. With the final flicker of the sun, she bled out, slumping to the ground.

"THE APPALLING STORIES ARE MANY, AND THOSE WHO know of this evil firsthand need not be reminded to revisit their pain all over again. For all those he abused, every day I suffer everlasting pain and penance for fathering Emilio."

CHAPTER 48

The Champion of Cuajimalpa de Morelos

⁓

"Now, please allow me the delight of telling you about Alejandro, the good son whose father was murdered by a bandit, whose stepfather died at sea, and whose mother fell victim to Annabella's curse."

⁓

"The Champion of Cuajimalpa de Morelos, the well-deserved title bestowed on the forty-three-year-old Alejandro Gomez, dialed the number for the fourth time…still no answer. 'Felicita,' he sang to his secretary, 'are you listening in again?'

"When no answer came, the second-term mayor walked out of his office into the reception area to discover everyone had gone home.

"The grandfather clock, standing prominently in the waiting area, showed well past seven p.m. Alejandro was embarrassed. Time had gotten away again.

"'Now I have done it! I should have met her at five-thirty! This time Helena will be *vamanos*!'

"He ran from the office to his Model T Ford, a flashy, new 1924 touring convertible parked with the top down at the curb outside city hall. With two cranks, the four-cylinder motor came alive.

"Stepping into the sporty two-door, he slid across its hand-sewn black leather seats to adjust the mirror before donning gloves and cap. The car's first gear, with a bit of a grind, moved the vehicle slowly off the curb and into a street filled with traffic. The Model T, a present from his adoring constituency, showed brightly in the springtime's dusk against a menagerie of horse- and donkey-drawn buggies and carts and other autos clogging Avenida Constituyentes.

"Ten minutes later, working through the congestion with high hopes she might still be there, he switched into second gear, propelling twelve-spoke wooden wheels dressed in Firestone gum-dipped tires to a breakneck speed of thirty miles per hour.

"He sped to The Lion's Den, a favorite cantina on the outskirts of The Desert of the Lions, *Desierto de los Leones*, the city's massive forest reserve and freshwater source.

"Quite a feather in his cap it was too. In 1917, to the joy of the Federal District of Mexico City, Morelos's new mayor, Alejandro Gomez, through political leverage and back-door intrigue, convinced Venustiano Carranzalt, Mexico's president, to name the site a national park.

"For his exemplary service to the people of Mexico City and the Federal District, the good mayor received the coveted Citizenry Award, given to the elected official making the greatest contribution to the people of Mexico. Alejandro's political stock soared. He won a second term as Cuajimalpa de Morelos's mayor. As that term wound to its end, there was talk of a possible run as Federal District governor.

"Helena, the first lady of Morelos, left a note with their favorite waiter, Jose Mondragon, a third-generation Spaniard whose family emigrated in 1851 from Barcelona.

"'Jose, do not give the mayor this message until he is desperate, yelling, and screaming and in a cold sweat. Let him suffer a bit. And whatever you do, do not tell him while I waited that I had fun in the company of our friends.'

'Alejandro, my tardy husband, if I did not love you so much, the very first time you stood me up I would have left you, alone and miserable, to return to Santa Fe, New Mexico, my old home.

'Instead, here I am, stuck with you in Old Morelos, Mexico, much too far away from my mother and father.

'I am sure you had a reason for your late arrival. Too bad when you arrive, I will not be there to hear it.

'Now, hurry home, darling. By the way, I had my dinner at Casitas. It was delicious. Do not expect any leftovers.

'Your patient and loving wife, Helena.'

"Driving home, her note laying on the passenger seat stared back at him. He laughed. 'I feel sorry for myself, already. When I arrive, Helena will hold court. She will have no mercy—no mercy!

"'I will be ruined. She will drain all the fight out of me. The children will no longer respect me. She will take my manhood from me. She will make me grovel like a dog. The doghouse will be my eternal casa.

"'Hungry and afraid—no dinner, no love—the price I pay for my duty to the citizens of Morelos.'

"As a husband and father, but especially as a politician, 'catastrophizing' was Alejandro's game of choice, poking fun at himself, creating in his mind the worst possible scenarios resulting from an error in judgment, outright mistake, or complete omission. The game taught him valuable lessons. Dooming himself always lessened the blow, he discovered consequences were never as heinous as he made them out to be.

"Catastrophizing gave him time, the most precious commodity. That usually simmered and settled things down and offered him the chance to make sense out of chaos and find an opportunity to benefit from the situation.

"This time he would have welcomed the scolding from his wife instead of the confounding news that changed his family's life and transformed his destiny.

"Ready to take whatever kind of torture Helena had in store for him, he parked the Model T in the shady courtyard.

"Entering the foyer, anticipating a thorough ribbing, he giggled until he found his ten-year-old son, Miguel, comforting Rebecca, his sobbing twelve-year-old sister."

"'Dad' Miguel shouted, 'Mama…she needs you now. Something bad happened to Grandpa!'"

"THREE MONTHS AFTER HELENA RECEIVED THE TELEgram announcing her father's heart attack, the beleaguered train carrying Alejandro, pummeled by a 'gypsy' windstorm, limped into the Santa Fe, New Mexico, rail yard.

"The desert sand pelting the window made it impossible for him to see his wife and children waiting for him sheltered safely on the platform. Windblown, the reunion was happy but brief. Rebecca and Helena, holding Alejandro's hand, hurriedly walked to the car. Miguel struggled with his father's valise.

"On the ride to her parents' home, Helena updated Alejandro on her father's progress and her mother's faltering condition, sharing all she learned about infarctions and dementia, the maladies suffered by her aging parents.

"Her father, Antonio Silva, survived the heart attack, but a blood clot rendered his left side paralyzed. Mother,

Juanita did not remember her daughter, her husband, or anyone else. What remained of her life, she lived giggling in the blissful maturity of a nine-year-old girl.

"For the next eight years, Helena took care of her parents. Rational and alert, yet slow to recover, her bedridden father required constant care. The wandering Juanita commanded perpetual surveillance.

"Attending a private school, making new friends, Rebecca and Miguel adjusted nobly to the challenge of a new environment. Devoted to the care of their grandparents, they helped their mother when classes allowed.

"Alejandro never hesitated. Making the selfless decision to resign his mayoral office in Mexico and move to Santa Fe, he surrendered lovingly to Helena's appeal to personally care for her failing parents.

"He and all the members of the Gomez family were American-born. Citizenship was not a problem. A Harvard graduate with a law degree, plus stellar careers in public service and political office, Alejandro's résumé attracted every law firm in New Mexico.

"The numerous letters of recommendation penned by Mexico's president, cabinet members, and other political officials amplified his value, adding considerable remuneration to the many employment offers he received.

"But Helena encouraged her husband to stay the course of public service over private practice.

"Turning down several lucrative offers from the finest law firms, Alejandro joined Santa Fe's District Attorney's Office, following his Helena's advice.

"After four years as a prosecuting attorney, with residency requirements fulfilled, he entered the race for the Superior Court judge and won handily.

"Mama Juanita, unable to remember her name, withered away to sixty-eight pounds before her death. Five months later, on his birthday, Antonio joined his bride for eternity after suffering a massive heart attack.

"At the time of their deaths, Alejandro worked in Washington as an elected representative for the New Mexico State Assembly.

"From representative he vaulted to the Office of Attorney General. His advancement in New Mexico was meteoric.

"Twenty-two years after resigning his mayoral office in Cuajimalpa de Morelos, Mexico, Alejandro Gomez won, in a landslide victory, the New Mexico governor's office.

"In 1940, her father's inaugural year as New Mexico's governor, Rebecca, with her husband and two young children, lived in Palo Alto, California. A year later, just before Christmas and Japan's attack on Pearl Harbor, Martin Hauser, Rebecca's husband and a Stanford law student, enlisted in the Navy.

"At the Battle of Guadalcanal, two years later, Martin lost his right eye. A long rehabilitation ensued in Hawaii. The Purple Heart recipient and petty officer third class returned home to his family, securing employment in the mayor's office in San Francisco.

"His brother-in-law, Miguel, a sophomore at New Mexico State University, enlisted in the Navy as well. For the duration of the war, he served in Naval Intelligence in Washington, DC.

"Discharged with honors, Miguel returned to his Palo Alto home to finish his education like many other GIs. He married Barbara Gaines, his high school sweetheart a year later. Graduating with a degree in political science, he moved his family to Washington and began a notable career in the Pentagon. They had a boy and named him Alejandro.

"First Lady Helena Gomez was driven. During her husband's terms, she chaired and organized chapters of the Red Cross and championed her state's 'Woman of the War' movement that encouraged New Mexico's wartime industries to hire and train women as replacements for men serving in the military.

"The governor and first lady's popularity flourished. Their popularity ranked close behind the Roosevelts.

"Throughout his political life, Alejandro and I kept in contact through weekly correspondence. In all our letters, I encouraged him to 'always be fair in his judgments' and 'never-changing in his convictions.'

"His response to my advice honored me very much.

"'When in doubt, I mine the reservoir of your advice and philosophy, assured to find the golden course.'

"And you are all correct. Mr. Small's knocking on my door that fateful day came to pass only through Alejandro's passion to right my life's misfortunes and bring justice to all those who caused it."

CHAPTER 49

Pablo Presents His Case

﹏⟋⟋∾﹏

The year 1947 marked the tenth anniversary of the Depression-era courthouse, but the city of Salinas had no plans for a commemorative.

Crossing Church Street on that hot June day, the second-term governor, seeing the courthouse for the first time, understood why. Noted in some reviews he read, the courthouse's rectangular shape offered a fleeting resemblance to the ancient parliamentary building in Mexico City, but that is where the similarity ended.

Less than ornate, without a bell tower to accent its severe lines, the Monterey Courthouse was "architecturally irrelevant" to Alejandro Gomez. For all its practicality, the structure was nothing but a "stonecutter's nightmare."

With New Mexico's first lady, the governor entered the courthouse foyer greeting members of Governor Warren's staff. Arm in arm with his wife, following Mr. Small and his staff to Court Room 100, Alejandro's initial view of the courthouse foyer and hall triggered a less than kind critique shared discreetly with his wife.

He said: "To contrast Diego Rivera's integrated murals that flowed gracefully in Parliament's chambers, to these halls, where Joseph Jacinto Mora's sculptures are terribly misplaced, I am afraid this mess is architect Stanton's failed attempt to mitigate the edifice's tastelessness. If he was a chef, this bungled pot roast of a building would surely corrupt a diner's appetite."

In a woman's silent wisdom, Helena merely nodded, more to acknowledge her husband's opinion, than to agree. When the entourage entered the courtroom, Alejandro kissed his wife, directing her to seats behind the plaintiff's table. Then he took his chair next to Mr. Small.

A waving Rosa invited Helena to join a group of friendly rancho workers, who seemed to know and like her very much.

The slender bailiff with long black hair called the court to attention, announcing, "All rise. The Honorable Superior Court Judge Bradley Moody presiding."

Middle-aged, broad-shouldered and fit, Judge Moody showed a stern face to the attorneys, then strode to his bench smiling warmly at the gallery. With a surgeon's hands, he fixed his glasses at the end of his nose. Looking out at the half-filled courtroom, he took up his gavel and called the proceedings to order promptly at 2 p.m.

Except for her army of defense attorneys, Annabella, matriarch of Piedra Blanca, sat friendless, looking at the empty gallery behind her.

She demanded Pancho Cervantes, her majordomo, join her, but since he was not subpoenaed, his attorney advised him not to get involved.

Governor Warren's contingent, a veritable who's-who of California politics, filled the other half of the courtroom.

Co-counsels Governor Gomez and Mr. Small flanked the plaintiff while his faithful listeners grouped tightly together in the gallery.

Opening statements ensued, each side calling witnesses and entering into evidence testimony, documents, diaries, and letters.

After each side presented and rested its case, three hours evaporated. Promptly at 5 p.m., Judge Moody, robes flowing behind him, adjourned the proceedings until the next day when he would render his decision at 3 p.m.

CHAPTER 50

Celebrating Victory

—◦◦◦—

Judge Moody found most compelling the dossier's exhaustive research of the de Leon family history, which provided irrefutable proof of Pablo's lineage as the legitimate heir to Rancho Piedra Blanca.

That night, California Governor Warren, in *absentia*, hosted a victory party in the Grand Ballroom of the Hotel Del Monte. Paying special tribute to Pablo and Governor Gomez and his wife, Pablo's loyal friends Manuel and Rosa, Jaime and Jose, Conchita, Angelina, and Francisco were also recognized.

With many famous Pablo stories revisited, the celebration continued into the wee hours. Prominent among the many others, "The Vaquero and the Bear," and "Rhonda the Donkey" enjoyed a special retelling. Pablo's tales bound together Helena, Alejandro, and the loyal listeners as an intimate family sharing in their hero's joy.

At the party's end, the happy but sleepy attendees retired.

Governor Gomez and his wife, Helena, were registered in the hotel's famous bridal suite. The office of the governor honored Alejandro's dossier and co-counsel participation, thanking the couple with the honeymoon accommodations, a pre-celebration of their upcoming wedding anniversary. To Helena's delight, accented by beautiful flowers and sumptuous desserts, the suite abounded in fine California wines.

Everyone attending the party likewise had a suite of rooms.

While Rosa and Manuel laughed, loved, and slept for the first time in the slipperiness of a hotel's silk sheets, Francisco and pregnant Angelina cuddled warm in a bed more expansive than any they had ever seen. In no hurry to say goodnight, Conchita and Jaime chose to snuggle together in the comfort and privacy of her luxurious suite, enjoying all night the romantic view of Monterey Bay.

Caring not what others would say, Jose invited Melba, Judge Moody's tall, slender, blond court recorder, to the celebration. At the party's end, Jose brought to his sixth-floor suite a chilled bottle of champagne and a very tipsy stenographer who helped him to take notes all night.

Happy and exhausted, Pablo retired to his room. He thanked his creator and praised God for sending such wonderful blessings his way.

Sleeping in the posh room, a heavenly vision of lush vineyards filled with seraphim and guardian angels livened his dreams. In a banquet of delicacies, Yolanda and Vincenti, Don Joaquin, Mama Dolores, Rodrigo, and Martha feasted with him, singing and dancing and praising God's providence.

The next morning, except for Pablo and Mr. Small, other celebrants nursing the "curse of the bubbly" suffered. With buzzing hangovers, the smarting partiers wandered in a daze to the dining room to play very quietly with their bacon and eggs.

With dishes cleared and several pots of coffee later, Mr. Small, vying for the room's attention, clanked his water glass over and over again to the detriment of most.

Exuberant and cheerful, in a buoyantly congratulatory mood, Mr. Small took the opportunity to pay a final tribute to Pablo, who for the crowd was likewise all too chipper.

"To our wonderful friend, Pablo. We delight in his good fortune and it is now, with his consent and my pleasure, to share with you a personal letter from the governor.

"'Dear Mr. de Leon,

"'It has been our honor to assist you in bringing this long-standing injustice to an end. The state of California, for me personally and all your devoted friends, I am sure, are delighted with the court's decision to restore Rancho Piedra Blanca to its rightful heir, one Senor Pablo Cabrera Barrazo de Leon.

"'My office is at your disposal for any future issues or concerns that may arise. Mr. Small's reports speak highly of you, and should you need further assistance, please feel free to contact Mr. Small at my office directly.

"'With sincere congratulations, I remain,

Earl Warren, Governor of the State of California.'"

CHAPTER 51

Nailing Him to the Cross Again

That September, the rains of Indian summer fell hard on the rancho. Sheltered in the barn's soppy pens, the farm animals—donkeys, cows, and horrible pigs—waited patiently. Late to arrive and soaked from the downpour, Alfredo sheepishly skirted past the angry drunk searching for the senora's bridle and stirrups. In the dark stable, after adjusting his glasses, he found the tack and brought it to Montez.

Wrenching it out of Alfredo's hands under a whisky breath, Montez barked a slur of Spanish profanities at the sweet but diminished stable boy.

Alfredo—compliant, abused, eager to please—watched as Montez fit the bridle and hoisted the silver saddle onto the stallion's back. Stirrups buckled, the stable bully pulled a bottle from his bib.

He drank a mouthful of tequila, "To senora, the bitch!"

"Today, of all days, she wants to ride. It is wet, it is miserable, and yet she demands…this day…to ride the fence.

"These days the devil plays with us, Alfredo."

Soaked by the leaking roof, the hay bales rotted and reeked. Rodrigo's death noose, still hanging from the stable's rafter, streamed rainwater puddles into Indigo's long-deserted stall.

Montez made the sign of the cross, shaking his head at the dangling line. He pulled the horse close to his face, lamenting in Rojo Grande's ear, "The curse killed Rodrigo, a sorry end to a good man."

The stable boy walked the horse to the barn door. Montez looked at the sky and cursed again—this time at the rain. Splashing muddy puddles, the flighty horse pulled the stablemen out of the barn toward his mistress.

<hr />

BRADLEY MOODY, SUPERIOR COURT JUDGE FOR THE County of Monterey, ruled for the plaintiff. He stripped Annabella of all ownership claims to Rancho Piedra Blanca, setting aside previous judgments based on misrepresentation and fraud.

To the jubilant gallery that filled the courtroom, their friend and champion, Senor Pablo Cabrera Barrazo de Leon, won clear title as the rancho's rightful heir. Evicting Annabella from rancho's premises forever, Moody's court order was to be executed at noon that rainy day.

With Canada de los Osos sold off to creditors years before and Madam Sanchez long since dead, Annabella's supporting cast, including her three brothers, were absent for any curtain calls. Pablo did allow her one accommodation, however. She could stay on at the rancho in the old shepherd's hut.

Annabella refused.

Proudly, in later life she maintained her beauty: complexion clear, face without wrinkles. She sat on the stallion handsomely, her black leather outfit a match to the aging silver saddle, a wedding gift from a former lover. To commemorate her long reign at Piedra Blanca, Annabella chose to ride through the narrows of the picket fence and stone hedge on the back of the patron's stallion, Rojo Grande.

Waving goodbye to her through the windy drizzle, Alfredo bid her *adios*.

She mounted the huge horse ignoring Alfredo. Yanking the bridle she steered the horse toward the restricted trail. Daydreaming of Pablo swimming naked in a spring pond, she turned her face into the rain and never looked back.

When Emilio died, influence over Pablo vanished, and her power and stature were obliterated. The lifelong games she played to keep Pablo close were no more. His love for others endured while her manipulations came to nothing. The only man she ever truly loved marched free from her torture and coercion.

Future uncertain, reluctant to admit defeat, she planned to board an evening train to Monterey, hoping the big city held an answer. A room at Hotel Del Monte was reserved and meetings with commercial agents were scheduled to view local hotels offered for sale—for her, an occupation that held some possibilities.

Riding in the damp air dulled her senses. With immense black clouds turning daylight to a grayish pall, without notice, she spurred the big horse steadily through the six-foot strip toward the confluence of the creeks.

Eyes trained ahead, she felt this last fence-line ride would help sort out her next move. For a half-hour, one with the horse, riding rhythmically, she barely glanced at the horizon.

Annabella rode on, unaware alighting one by one behind her, an army of ravens steadily populated Patron's Folly. Perching as she passed, the black-muted soldiers, one after the next, took position on each spire of the picket fence.

Near the confluence, standing in the muddy track, a diminutive man dressed entirely in black inexplicably appeared blocking her way.

Why would anyone be out here on foot?

Drawing closer, the tiny figure reminded her of someone from long ago. Aware, finally, it was indeed the rancho's old *curandera*, she spurred Rojo Grande to run him over.

By simply raising his hand before harm would be done, Flores de Flores halted the stallion's charge at his feet.

"Buenos dias, senora. I see it is a fine day for a ride in God's glorious rain. Please, excuse my manners. Allow me please to reintroduce myself, for we do know each other all too well, but it has been years.

"Once again, I am Flores de Flores, at your service."

Saying nothing, Annabella spurred the horse harder, but Rojo Grande would not budge.

"Senora, it is my understanding your entitlement to the rancho has been revoked, and you need a permanent place of residency. If that is correct, senora, I believe I can be of assistance with your need."

Saddle whip in hand, she dismounted to confront the little man.

"I thought you were dead."

Scratching his chin, he looked to the sky for an answer.

"Those reports are…let me see…yes, of course, you are right. Those reports are indeed accurate. I gave up the ghost, so to speak, shortly after your son fired me as Piedra Blanca *curandero*.

"But, as *curanderos* do, as you can see, I have returned on, how you say, 'special assignment.' Yes, yes, I am dead. Yet here I am, speaking to you the same way as a gentle person does.

"Senora de Leon, are you a gentle person? If you are, my service to you is invaluable. If you are not, I am afraid your next residency is a sadder place. Now, senora, with patience and forethought, please answer this question. Your future is depending on it."

"I should have squashed you when I had the chance. Give me the way, you toad."

"Senora, I will ask you once more. It is vital for you to answer. Your life…it is in the balance. Once again, are you a gentle person?"

She answered, whipping Flores viciously across his face. With his old duster, Flores wiped away his blood, offering Annabella one last opportunity.

"If you are to be judged by your actions, the answer to my question would be…you are not a gentle person. Therefore, as I did with Josefina Espinoza, I must assume the worst. Senora, I am sure, from your early catechism, you are familiar with beautiful Psalm 37. I pray your heart, like mine, embraces the prophecy. Starting with Verse 27:

"'Turn from evil and do good; then you will dwell in the land forever, for the Lord loves the just and will not forsake his faithful ones. Lovers of evil will be completely destroyed; the offspring of the wicked will perish. The righteous will inherit the land and dwell in it forever.'"

He then raised high over his head the cross of Christ crucified.

"Senora de Leon, if you are just and faithful, forgiven by the blood of Jesus Christ, do you embrace the Lord and renounce the devil?"

Her answer came quickly…another lash to his cheek.

"I am saddened, senora. The demon possessing your body and spirit forbids you to repent of your sins as you did as a little child. Now, your life, for the world to see, mocks Our Lord. You are guilty of cursing His forgiveness and blaspheming the Holy Ghost.

"If anyone sins deliberately by rejecting the Savior, after knowing the truth of forgiveness, this sin is not covered by Christ's death; there is no way to get rid of it. There will be nothing to look forward to but terrible punishment of God's awful anger, which consumes all his enemies. Hebrews Verse ten, lines twenty-six and twenty-seven.

"Hardness of your heart, senora, nails Him to the cross again." He slowly lowered the cross, turning his back to Annabella.

———

LAUGHING AT HIS SANCTIMONIOUS ATTEMPT, ANNAbella watched the little man walk away. But the army of ravens flying off the picket fence flocking above her stopped her laughter. Running toward the skittish stallion, for the first time in her life, Annabella was afraid. But from his mistress and the burgeoning cloud of black birds, Rojo Grande bolted away.

Anxious to repeat the execution inflicted on Josefina Espinoza, the ravens circling over Annabella readied for an attack. Forming up into V-shaped units, on their leader's command, wave after wave, they attacked Annabella in perfect precision, over and over again.

At last, devastation absolute, enter now the Grand Raven to mete out final vindication for the just and faithful. Clawing through what remained of her hair, standing on her skinless skull, assured his visage would be her last, taking time, he plucked out both of Annabella's eyes, first the left, then the right.

Curses repaid, vanity vanquished, bones bloodied, flesh shredded, and sockets emptied, the remnants of the once beautiful Annabella, mistress of Piedra Blanca, lay scattered.

The Grand Raven led his army of righteousness into the sky. Diffusing the light, sifting opaque clouds, the massive convention darken the firmament.

Now enter the donkeys, cows, and horrible pigs, come to devour her flesh and bone, eating their fill, every part, eliminating Annabella's existence.

No hair, no blood, no skin, no bones, no clothes—nothing save the wedding locket.

Forever forfeiting any and all claims to the secret of the de Leon wedding locket, Annabella joined Josefina in Gehenna.

Sending Rojo Grande back to the stables, Flores salvaged the heirloom left conspicuously by itself on the ground.

With locket in hand but tasks undone, Flores de Flores, walked the fence line back toward the village of San Xavier.

CHAPTER 52

Detective Raymundo Muchado

<the search for Annabella continued. No one the police questioned remembered seeing her return from the fence-line ride taken three days ago. And a train ticket to Monterey left on her packed luggage furthered speculation but gave no answers.

A phone call to the Salinas police provided detectives with fanciful yet compelling information about her disappearance.

"Salinas Police Department, how may I help you?"

"Buenos dias…hello. Please, allow me a moment. It has been a trying day. Operator, are you there?"

"Yes, yes, this is the Salinas police. How may I help?"

"I have important information for the police."

"What is your name and address, please?"

"How good of you to ask. My mother and father named me Ricardo Cervantes Alberto Garcia Flores, but as life progressed, everyone just called me Flores de Flores. How may I call you?"

"Officer Ruby Sanchez. Mr. Flores, where do you live?"

"How nice to speak to you Officer Ruby. May I call you Ruby? Titles confuse me. That is like the people addressing me always as *Curandero* Flores, when plain old Flores would pass."

"Please sir, I need your residence address."

"My residence? Hmmm, my residence? But for my home, there is no address. It is not a town on the map.

"Traveling there is not possible. Making it your home? That is done by invitation only.

"You see, Ruby, I died years ago, and if I had my way, I would not be here now. On the orders of Melchizedek, the high priest, I am back to finish God's work."

"Excuse me, Mr. Flores. Would you repeat that...and very slowly?"

"Melchizedek, the king of Salem? Saint Justice? You remember him from your Bible study, do you not?"

She covered her mouthpiece and whispered to Mabel.

"Turn on the recording, call Muchado, and listen in. I got a lulu on the line. Says he died years ago and came back on orders from a Saint Mickey-something, to finish some work for God."

"Hello, Ruby, who is Mabel? Is Mabel your friend? Mabel, Mabel, are you there, Mabel? Can you hear me?"

"Yes sir, Mabel can hear you. In fact, she and Detective Muchado are listening in as well.

"That is good. Speaking to you and Mabel and the good Detective Muchado—anyone who finds the truth in what I say—it is good."

"Mr. Flores, this is Detective Muchado. Thank you for calling us today. I have a question for you. Is that all right?"

"Questions and doubts need answers and reassurances. Personally, I delight in sharing God's Truth."

"Thank you, sir. So that I can understand, please explain how you are dead, and yet I hear you speaking to me. As a police officer, trained to deal in facts, you must appreciate my difficulty believing I am actually speaking to a person long since gone to his reward."

"Senor, Detective Muchado, kind sir, I can see you are a sensible man, very much a servant, very much a believer too. Where you now cling to facts, if God has taught me anything, it is faith, not facts, that will come to rule your life.

"You are blessed and challenged at the same time to witness my return. When you search the records, you will find me, my life, the man who I was, and what I believed... even the date of my death.

"Faith is sufficient, and in this instance, your conversation with me, Flores de Flores, a living spirit, yet a man who is dead, must be based on faith alone, allowing you to believe what I reveal is the truth.

"Now, for the information....Three incidents that have occurred need accounting.

"Ruby, do you have a pencil? Please have Mabel write this down too. Detective Muchado, are you still there?"

"Yes."

"Very well...

"First, the matter of Annabella de Leon. Annabella is not missing. She is dead. Second, if you wish to reach her and her friend, Josefina Espinoza, who is likewise dead, they can be found suffering their lifetime of sins in Gehenna."

"Mr. Flores, how did you come to know Annabella de Leon and this Josefina Espinoza are dead?"

"Detective, I do not wish to shock you or the fine ladies, but I witnessed both of their deaths—Josefina's many years ago when I was still alive, and Annabella's, just the other day, long after my death.

"I am saddened to say they both rejected the Holy Order of Exorcism to release them from the devil's possession. Instead, they cursed the Holy Spirit and refused to repent of their sins or accept the Lord's forgiveness.

"That is when the Grand Raven and his army of blackbirds, aggrieved by such hatred and blasphemy, attacked the women, shredding their bodies, giving over what was left to be devoured by the donkeys, cows, and horrible pigs.

"I am obliged to tell you this because no evidence of their persons can be found. And my word is all you will have to corroborate their deaths."

"Mr. Flores, when did these deaths occur?"

"Josefina died a well-deserved death outside her new home near the ancient oak grove on a bright and sunny Friday. I believe it was June, the year, 1900.

"Then again, riding to the confluence of the creeks on the fence line in the narrows between the stone hedge and the picket fence, Annabella died on a very rainy September morning, in the year of the Lord, 1947.

"Both deaths took place on Rancho Piedra Blanca.

"Now, do not waste your valuable time searching for either of these dreadful women. No one will miss them. No one alive or dead had any hand in their deaths. Alive, they were Satan's assassins. Dead, they reap hell's eternity for all they sowed.

"Third, and finally, my accounting deals with the death of Emilio de Leon, the former patron of Piedra Blanca."

"Mr. Flores, you know how the Patron died?"

"Yes, yes, of course. He died the last victim of the curse Annabella and Josefina Espinoza many years ago, exacted on the de Leon family.

"The Patron's death substituted for Alejandro Gomez, the fine governor of New Mexico, the intended victim. He is the beloved child of Yolanda Gomez Prulette, Annabella's stepsister, another poor victim of the curse."

"Mr. Flores, please. What curse…and whose deaths?"

"My dear Detective Muchado, open the ledgers of Mission San Miguel to the year 1901 and read the history written in the hand of the good Padre Fray Tomas Sepulveda. It is all there. The deaths are documented, as is the sad tragedy of Pablo de Leon's life.

"The ambition and faithlessness of Annabella, the manipulative child bride…Pablo de Leon and his cuckold brother, Vincenti…Annabella's cursed alliance with Josefina Espinoza, the village *curandera*…the attempt and failure to reverse the curse and the consequential murders of the de Leons, Don Joaquin and Mama Dolores, the Montoyas, Martha and Rodrigo, and Yolanda Gomez Prulette, who was swept overboard returning home to Cuajimalpa de Morelos, Mexico, from Boston in 1906.

"Yolanda was the last of the cursed to die until the Patron died mysteriously in March."

"Mr. Flores, Sergeant Fontaine has joined us on the line."

"Mr. Flores, this is Fontaine. Can you come into Salinas headquarters to discuss these matters, person to person?"

"Sir, my means of transportation is limited, and I am far away from Salinas."

"Well, where are you? I can send a car to pick you up."

"Sergeant Fontaine, with no disrespect…please, may I speak to Detective Muchado in private? My trust is in God and he, thank you."

"He wants to talk to you…says he trusts you."

"Mr. Flores, this is Detective Muchado again. Hello, Mr. Flores, are you still there?"

"Yes, detective, I am here. After providing you with details of the patron's death, I will reveal my location…on one important condition."

"Fine, Mr. Flores, I am ready."

"Detective Muchado…Raymundo…please be sure no one else is listening to our conversation. What I must say is intended only for you."

"Fine, Mr. Flores. Give me a moment to be sure.

"OK, everyone but me has hung up. Ruby, Mabel, and Fontaine…they are no longer listening and no recordings are being made. It is just you and me, Mr. Flores."

"Very well…

"That wonderful day you married your Rosalie, you wrote her a love note on parchment and placed it in her bridal purse. In the heartfelt note, you expressed your love and happiness for accepting your proposal of marriage after almost three years of courtship.

"And on the back of the parchment, do you remember the drawing you made?"

At what he heard Flores de Flores saying to him, Muchado fell back into his chair, thunderstruck.

"Mr. Flores, how could you know?"

"Raymundo, the drawing of beautiful pink roses, painted in twelve parts, when unfolded, twelve tiny roses appeared shaped as your heart—do you remember?

"Most wonderful, Raymundo, you are such a romantic!

"Also, your five-year-old-son, Luis. He will be fine. It is only a ragweed allergy. His cough will be better tomorrow. And daughter Margarite, named for your mother, smart like her father…Little Margarite will skip grade three and be promoted to the fourth.

"One more thing…when you get home this evening, Rosalie has an announcement to make, but do not tell her I told you and spoil her surprise. You will be a father once again, another boy…and you will name him, hmmmmm…Flores!

"No obligation, of course.

"Now, detective, telephone your Rosalie, and ask if the plumber is still needed. She will say, 'Not anymore, but how did you know little Louie plugged the toilet?'

"Call now…I will wait."

He made the call, turning bright red when his wife repeated Flores's exact words.

Convinced, the detective returned to the line, ready to believe as fact any and all the dead *curandero* said.

"Practicing faith sharpens the sword of facts, Detective Muchado. Now, please allow me to tell you how the patron, Emilio de Leon, met his death."

CHAPTER 53

Faith Is Believing

⸗⸎⸗

"Now you know the facts. When your shift ends today, as you drive to the rancho, I pray you possess an ever-deepening faith, believing firmly you will see signs that direct you to me."

First, he called his wife to tell her he would be late. Then, as instructed, he left the police station at five p.m. sharp.

In a sing-song voice, Rosalie intimated: "Be careful dear. Tonight I have a special surprise for you."

He chuckled, knowing in advance his wife's special surprise.

Driving for about an hour, he reached the rancho's main gate. He never hesitated when he saw the bright red arrow fixed to the road sign, pointing the way to the village of San Xavier.

Faith, honed and perfected, Detective Muchado parked on the curb of Jose's Auto Repair Shop, across from Andeleto's and the occupied phone booth that stood in front of it.

A bright red arrow above the store sign pointed down to the entry door. At that moment, a boy vacated the phone booth and disappeared into the store.

Detective Muchado entered the store and saw the young boy from the phone booth sitting at the linoleum-covered counter with a "Happy Birthday" sign above his head. The boy laughed, digging into Andeleto's complimentary "Happy Birthday" sundae that overflowed with chocolate and vanilla ice cream.

With toppings dripping from his chin, the happy boy hailed the detective like a long-lost friend.

"Raymundo Muchado, how good of you to come. I trust your drive was pleasant?"

Staggered in disbelief, Raymundo Muchado stared into his own boyhood eyes! The ten-year-old-boy wearing his parent's birthday gift, polo shirt, shorts, socks, and gym shoes and holding a brand new Spalding basketball was, in fact, him, little Ray, on his tenth birthday!

In Flores's voice, the boy asked innocently, "Do you see someone you recognize, Raymundo Muchado?"

Speechless with drooping jaws, the grown-up version of the ten-year-old could only gawk in amazement.

"Please, sit next to me Raymundo, for today you and I once again celebrate your tenth birthday. But this time your presents are not an ice cream sundae, new gym clothes, and a basketball. Today my present to you is information, and this."

Retrieved from the pocket of his gym shorts, little Ray slid an antique locket fastened to a golden chain over the counter to his older self.

"Now, Detective Raymundo Muchado, look at the pictures and read the inscription. I believe this is the proof you require. This locket is the de Leon family heirloom. It was entrusted to Annabella, the last de Leon bride on the day she wed Vincenti de Leon.

"It is all that remains of her. You must return it to the rightful de Leon heir, Senor Pablo Cabrera Barrazo de Leon, the new patron of Rancho Piedra Blanca."

CHAPTER 54

Pablo's Reward Eternal

※

For the last time, far from celebration and celebrity, Pablo hiked the trail blazed years before as a younger man from the shepherd's hut to the ridge overlooking it.

Standing on the ridge, looking down at his modest domain, he thought about his life and the loved ones lost. A child of Alphonse and Lorena de Leon, his happiness and contentment came from knowing his place in the world and from the blessings bestowed on him by his friends.

Despite his compliance with Annabella's "little conditions," agony tormented Pablo still.

In the end, after all his efforts, only Alejandro had been saved.

Dangling the delicate chain from his finger, Pablo watched as the locket danced in the sun. He smiled, thanking God for the wisdom imparted to him yesterday when Detective Muchado came seeking him at the shepherd's hut.

"Senor Pablo, I am sure you will appreciate knowing that a ten-year-boy told me to do the right thing and return this beautiful locket to you, its rightful owner.

"This young boy, had I not known better, possessed discernment beyond his years. Truth be told, corroborating my newfound faith, this young boy was not a child at all.

"The wisdom that sprang forth from his lips…things I alone could know…be they events new or old, he claimed with such authority they could never be refuted.

"Senor Pablo, once again, Flores came back to serve you. For all to see, the truth is documented as fact. Long since dead, Flores still loved you so. Speaking truth and solving mysteries, Flores de Flores came to me, in the body and soul of a ten-year-old Raymundo Muchado.

"'By sharing his insight, Annabella's and Josefina's disappearances now are closed, and the Patron's death is ruled accidental.

"'In truth, iniquity took all three lives.

"'Senor Pablo, you know the truth. You witnessed Josefina's death long ago. Flores's eyewitness testimony confirmed Annabella suffered the same fate. On Rojo Grande, riding the narrows between the stone hedge and the picket fence, Annabella died a most unholy death, torn asunder by the black ravens and devoured every part by the donkeys, cows, and horrible pigs.

"'Flores, God's servant, came back to purge the legion of devils possessing these women. But in their pride and arrogance, they refused exorcism, declaring their guilt, rejecting unto death the Lord's grace and forgiveness. He witnessed both executions.

"'As for Emilio...no human hand caused his death.

"'After a long night of lust and depravity, death called to him as Rojo Grande carried him home sound asleep in the early morning hours.

"'At the confluence of the creeks, riding the narrows, a rattlesnake, like Eve's tempter, spooked the stallion, unseating his rider. The stallion reared to kill the snake but, instead, stomped the drunken Patron to death, hooves decimating his face, crushing his skull.

"Emilio's demise freed Alejandro, satisfying, the *curandera's* warning, a death for a death. Predicted by the old witch for daring to reverse the curses, in ironies of ironies, Gehenna demanded Annabella's death.

"That morning Alfredo came to the stables early to find Rojo Grande saddled and drinking at the trough. As happened in the past, Alfredo thought the Patron had left the stallion there after a morning ride.

"'Happy to care for the stallion without harassment from Montez, Alfredo removed the tack, feeding and watering the horse. He paid special care to the stallion's crimson-stained legs, bathing, brushing, and stabling the horse.

"'The police never questioned Alfredo.

"To you, Senor Pablo, Flores sends this message:

"'Congratulations Pablo Cabrera Barrazo de Leon, the new patron of Rancho Piedra Blanca...a reward for a noble life.'"

AT HIS AGE, FAME AND FORTUNE THAT CAME WITH THE title "patron" meant nothing to Pablo. Learning the secret of the locket...that meant everything.

In the eyes of the church as surviving husband of his dead bride, Pablo, the first de Leon to outlive his wife, earned entitlement to every locket revelation.

Speaking aloud, he debated his next move. It was unthinkable for the old shepherd to move to the rancho and make Hacienda de Leon his new home.

"All that loading and packing, that is a younger man's game, not mine. Without my well-intended friends, I would not know where to begin."

The hut did not compare with the comforts and conveniences of the hacienda, but the old man realized he would soon regret losing the anonymity and seclusion guaranteed to him on the crest of San Simeon in the shepherd's hut.

Now that the search for Annabella was suspended, as hard as he tried, he could think of no excuse that could rationalize his moving immediately into the hacienda.

His faithful listeners were not surprised when Pablo asked them to come to the hut that night to discuss what he should do next.

To relieve the old man's anxiety, they devised a simple plan to move him into the hacienda and limit his participation to three simple activities.

"First, decide which of any hut possessions to keep or discard. Second, determine the placement of those possessions in the hacienda. Third, just come along for the ride, nothing more."

His friends would do all the rest.

At the meeting's end, Pablo, who listened attentively to everyone's suggestions and even appearing interested from time to time, halted all conversation when he held up his hand and lit his pipe. Reaching up to the shelf above his bed, he took down seven wax-sealed envelopes, each bearing a beloved listener's name in bright red.

"God-given friends, understand," he said. "With the same instructions I give you now, I have already delivered envelopes like these to Alejandro and Helena.

"Do not unseal the envelope until told to do so.

"You must promise me this."

What was the old man was up to? Promising to follow his orders, they drove home, speculating what it all could mean.

———— ∞∞∞ ————

IN THE BRIGHT MORNING SUN, PABLO BEGAN HIS DAILY constitutional to the ridge when a terrible throbbing buckled him to his knees.

Praying the pain would ease, he bit his bottom lip, drawing blood. Time passed and so did the pain. Still shaken, he stood with the help of his staff. Never one to worry or complain about the relentless toll of aging, he smiled, laughing at his eighty-plus years and all the infirmities that came with them.

Brushing the dirt from his knees, he made light of this newest of many attacks, yet his chest continued to ache and breathing remained a burden.

Struggling, he reached the hut and sat in his favorite chair to rest. His chest relaxed at last, allowing him to drift.

A LIGHT RAPPING ON HIS DOOR WOKE HIM.

"Come in…the door is unlocked."

A timid and slight young boy entered, carrying a parchment. In beautiful hand, the names of hundreds of people were written.

"Senor Pablo, please excuse the interruption. Surely you remember me, Raymundo? Raymundo Muchado?

"We met when I was much older.

"Senor, today, September twentieth, is my tenth birthday. I believe today is your birthday too? Happy birthday to both of us, senor."

Not sure what the boy just said, Pablo pinched his arm, making sure he was wide awake.

"Young man, am I still dreaming? By my reckoning, September twentieth is ten days away, so I am afraid today it is neither yours nor my birthday!"

"But, senor, the Lord knows you have slept so long and so deep. You are now fully at rest. So please, Senor Pablo, stand and enjoy the birthday gift of renewed life."

Holding a mirror up to Pablo's face, the young boy waited.

Stretching muscles far too long asleep, Pablo stood up.

"Senor, please, to see the truth, look in the mirror and search the caverns of your eyes.

"The Pablo who stands before me today, senor, he is good and noble, a man loved by God.

"Keep looking deep, and you will see I am right."

"All right, all right. I will play along. Did Jose put you up to this?"

"Oh no, senor, one greater than Jose sent me!

"Please now, look and see for yourself. You are all new and ready for a life everlasting."

Pablo held up the mirror and saw a young glowing face, wrinkle-free, without blemish, cleanly shaved with ears free of hair, smiling back at him.

He dropped the mirror, falling back in his chair, and the mirror did not break.

"You see, senor, your life eternal has dawned. Come out and play with me, and let us, together, celebrate the day of your rebirth!

"This list I carry holds the names of those waiting for you, standing outside this door...people you know and who know you.

"Rejoice, come out. You and they will be together again, never to be separated.

"Your time is come. Forsake this worn-out hut to breathe heaven's air. Come!"

Eager to see old friends, Pablo opened the door to eternity.

In a twinkling, young Raymundo faded and Pablo's old friend, Flores de Flores, took his place.

"Senor Pablo, with my Elizabeth at my side, allow us to guide you to the vineyards of your dreams."

Flores and his Elizabeth reunited Pablo with those who passed before:

Alphonse and Lorena, Don Joaquin and Mama Dolores, Tomas and Humberto, Rodrigo and Martha, Juanita and Vincenti, and his beloved Yolanda.

Raising goblets brimming with glory's vintage, the happy family embraced Pablo, toasting God, thanking Him for Pablo's safe passage.

A Lasting Legacy

⸎

Hundreds of floral tributes—flowered hearts, wreaths, and sprays of every kind, large and small, from places all around the world—filled the Hacienda de Leon rotunda.

From foreign dignitaries to local villagers, condolences spilled into the courtyard, ringing the raised altar where Father Carmona said Pablo's funeral Mass.

Clutching Maria and Juanito throughout the service, regretting to her soul not being with Pablo when he needed her most, Rosa wept without ceasing.

Praying little Pablo, her week-old son, would be a comfort to the grieving women, Angelina, sitting between her mother and Rosa, wept openly. Thankful the babe was born a healthy boy, the "*nueva abuelita*," grandmother Conchita, held little Pablo over her broken heart like a soothing balm.

For a man she hardly knew but loved deeply for her husband's sake, Helena grieved for Pablo as she had when her parents died long ago.

Next to her sat her son, daughter, and their five children. Not one of them had ever met Pablo, but they came to honor the man who made their lives possible by saving the life of their father.

In somber attire, Alejandro, Manuel, Jose, Jaime, Francisco, and Alfredo the stable boy, attended as Pablo's pallbearers. While the others, in vain, tried not to cry, when the Mass ended, Alfredo sobbed loudly. Making a solemn way, the teary stalwarts shouldered the casket to the waiting hearse.

Mourners waiting somberly at the gate became a cortege silently following the four-horse carriage that carried Pablo's simple casket to the oak orchard cemetery beyond the courtyard and to the "Family de Leon" sepulcher.

Graveside acknowledgments ensued. While Alejandro's enduring story of Pablo's sacrificial love brought listeners to tears, his beloved tales, narrated by Manuel, Jose, and Jaime, in a moment of happy remembrance, warmed their saddened hearts.

Last to deliver eulogies were Governor Earl Warren and the executor, Mr. Merrell Small. They spoke admiringly of Pablo's selflessness, notifying his faithful listeners and the world, Pablo's journal would forever be preserved in the state's Historical Society library.

As the last mourners laid a rose on the coffin, Rose Fitzgerald Kennedy, with her husband, Joseph, prayed silently at the gravesite with others, saying their farewell. Hundreds more came to the reception to pay their respects.

As the evening faded and mourners departed, Mr. Small directed those invited to the library for the reading of Pablo's will.

Alejandro, Helena, and Pablo's seven faithful listeners welcomed Rose Fitzpatrick Kennedy, who, like the rest of the invitees, brought a wax-sealed envelope bearing her name.

Mr. Small nodded to his assistant that all the heirs were present.

"You have in your possession one part of Pablo's will, personal to you and you alone. The contents of all the envelopes together represent his complete last will and testament.

"I also hold this sealed envelope that contains a document witnessed by me, but according to Pablo's wishes, have not yet read.

"According to Pablo's instructions, I open it now, in your presence to learn its contents and any further instructions Pablo might have left."

Mr. Small broke the wax seal and silently read the document. When the long silence ended he lifted his eyes, cleared his throat, and read the contents aloud.

"'To all here present, let it be known, on September 1, 1947, I authored this document, that by his signature, Merrell Small witnessed, but is not privy to its content.

"'I, Pablo Cabrera Barrazo de Leon, of sound mind and functioning body, make my final wishes known, and do hereby apportion my estate as follows...'

"According to Pablo's instructions, when I call your name, please open your envelope. Then, when called on, please read aloud the contents of Pablo's personal letter to this audience and to me as a witness for the state of California.

"First, I call on Alejandro and Helena Gomez."

And so it went until the last name was read.

In addition to the estate paying off their mortgages, lifetime positions with increased incomes and pensions were bequeathed to each of his faithful listeners:

Manuel and Rosa and their Cambria cottage, Jose Ortiz and his business and home, Jaime's and Conchita's homes, respectively. And for Francisco, Angelina, and Alfredo, new homes to be built and paid for by the estate.

The cost of college education paid in full for Maria, Juanito, and little Pablo, and any other children born to the faithful.

To Rose Fitzgerald Kennedy, forever curious about the ways of the Wild West, when time and inclination allowed, an open invitation as a welcome guest to stay in the rancho's guest suite, for as long as desired.

"'To the Gomez Family, their children, and grandchildren, I bequeath the entire estate of Rancho Piedra Blanca.

"'When the last Gomez heir dies, the entire estate of Rancho Piedra Blanca is bequeathed in perpetuity to the citizens of California, to remain forever an historical monument.'"

THE GOVERNOR OF NEW MEXICO AND FIRST LADY WOULD spend their last days living there.

CPSIA information can be obtained
at www.ICGtesting.com
Printed in the USA
FSHW021716201221
87060FS